The Granite Key

N. S. WIKARSKI

The Granite Key
Book One of Seven – Arkana Archaeology Adventure Series

http://www.mythofhistory.com

ISBN: 1468115340
ISBN-13: 978-1468115345

EPIGRAPH

Until the lions have their own historians,
tales of the hunt shall always glorify the hunters.
--African Proverb

ACKNOWLEDGMENTS

The treasure hunt and cast of characters in this series are purely fictional, but the underlying historical assumptions are based on new theories about our distant past. I am indebted to the authors mentioned at the end of this book for having the courage to challenge cultural beliefs that we've accepted without question for far too many generations. I would encourage readers who want to delve more deeply into these topics to have a look at the works cited in the bibliography.

TABLE OF CONTENTS

1 – NIGHT VISION

Cassie felt herself sinking. She tried to jolt her sleeping body into action. "Wake up! It's just a dream. This can't be real, so move already!"

She was standing in the shadows against the wall in her sister's antique shop. The room was dimly lit by a green banker's lamp near the cash register. Sybil was frozen in position in front of the glass showcase—a phone suspended midway to her ear. Her eyes were fastened on a man who had just entered the store. He was wearing a Stetson hat, and he was pointing a gun at her.

"Where's the key, sugar?" He spoke with a Southern drawl—his tone lazy, almost casual.

"I… I don't know what you're talking about," Sybil stammered. She put the phone down and began inching her way along the showcase toward the rear storeroom.

The man shrugged. "Don't make no difference to me, but you don't want me tearin' up your neat little shop just to find it, now do you?"

"I told you, I don't know what you're talking about!" Sybil's denial sounded unconvincingly shrill.

Cassie wanted to rush forward to pull her sister out of danger. She tried to scream a warning, but all she felt was a rasp in her throat where the words should have been.

The man advanced down the center aisle. He was over six feet tall, in his late twenties or early thirties. Cassie knew this had to be a dream because of his strange outfit. Aside from the cowboy hat, he wore a short denim jacket, a string tie around his neck, jeans, and snakeskin cowboy boots.

The gun flicked slightly in his hand. "I tell you what. The service in this establishment ain't very friendly."

He flipped his hat aside, and it landed on an oak sideboard. His dark brown hair was combed back in a high wave.

"I guess if you don't want to help me, I'll have to roll up my sleeves and help myself." He moved toward the glass case.

Sybil darted past him and ran for the front door, but he was faster. He grabbed her by the arm.

"Now, that's no way to treat your customers, honey. Tryin' to run off and shirk your responsibilities like that." He twisted her arm behind her back.

Cassie could see Sybil wince with pain. Her sister looked around wildly for some other way out. The man tightened his grip with one hand and drove the gun against her temple with the other. Sybil struggled, but he only wrenched her arm harder behind her back until she stopped struggling.

"It seems to me like you can't hear what I'm sayin'." The man cocked his head slightly, considering the matter. "Maybe we should go someplace private where I can get through to you better."

As he shoved her toward the front exit, she twisted out of his grip and reversed direction. He lunged after her, tackling her. She fell head first against the showcase, sending shards of glass cascading across the room.

Cassie could feel a cry of despair welling up in her throat, but no sound emerged. She willed her feet to move. They twitched slightly but nothing more.

The man raised himself to a crouching position. A look of annoyance flitted across his face. He reached forward to check Sybil's pulse, and the look of annoyance deepened to a frown.

He let out a martyred sigh as he stood up, shaking bits of broken glass from his jacket. "Well, that ain't no help at all."

In a flash, the scene changed, and Cassie was back in her dorm room. She could feel the mattress beneath her. "Wake up, dammit!" she commanded herself. This time, as she clawed her way up to consciousness, her mind obeyed her. She sat up shakily, her skin clammy with cold sweat. Tossing off the covers, she sat forward.

On impulse, she grabbed her phone and started to call her sister. "It was just a nightmare, you idiot! What are you going to do? Wake her up in the middle of the night to tell her you had a bad dream?" She tossed the phone on the nightstand, disgusted by her own timidity.

Gradually her breathing slowed, and she lay back down. Curling herself into a fetal position, she drew the covers up to her chin. "It wasn't real. It was just a bad dream… Just a bad dream... Just a bad dream..." She chanted the words like a mantra for several minutes until she started to dose off.

Then the phone rang.

2 – A WAKE

At about three o'clock in the morning, far outside the city, four people were staring bleakly at one other across a kitchen table. It was an old-style oak table in an old-style country kitchen. The kind with tin ceiling tiles and tall glass cupboards above the sink. A single yellow nightlight glowed from the wall.

At one end of the table sat an elderly woman in a terrycloth robe and slippers. Despite the late hour, she had managed to roll her white hair into a neat little bun at the nape of her neck. She shook her head sadly. "This can't be true."

"It's true. Sybil's dead." The abrupt comment came from a blond man in his mid-twenties at the opposite end of the table. He slouched despondently in his chair, arms crossed. "When she called me around midnight, she sounded scared. She thought somebody was trying to break into the shop. Then the line went dead. I got there as fast as I could, but the cops beat me to it." He rubbed his eyes wearily. "It's my fault."

"How do you figure?" The question came from a middle-aged woman with bushy red hair sitting to his left. There were distinct frown lines around her mouth. She took a long drag on an unfiltered cigarette.

The blond man glanced up. "If I'd gotten there five minutes sooner, maybe we wouldn't be having this conversation. Maybe she'd still be alive."

"Did she give you a physical description of her attacker?" The question came from a young man in his early twenties seated to the right. He spoke with a British accent.

"Nope," said the blond man succinctly. "For the past week or so, she had the feeling somebody was following her, but she never knew who it was."

"I think we all know who was responsible." The elderly woman rose stiffly out of her chair. She walked over to sink, filled a kettle, and put it on the stove to boil.

The other three stared at her in shock. Anger flashed in the middle-aged woman's eyes. "Those bastards!"

"Take it easy, Maddie," soothed the blond man. "We don't know for sure it was them."

The woman called Maddie snapped back at him, "Then who else?" She ground out her cigarette and immediately lit a new one. "What the hell was she working on? Didn't she tell you anything about it, Griffin?" Her sharp eyes focused on the Brit.

"No, nothing," the young man whispered with regret. "Perhaps if she had, I might have helped her or persuaded her to stop."

The elderly woman shuffled toward the cupboard over the sink. "There's still the matter of her sister," she observed quietly. "Poor child, as if she hasn't lost enough already. This is too cruel."

"Does the kid know anything?" The blond man at the far end of the table asked.

The woman at the sink turned around to glance at him mildly. "Do you think you could find that out for us, Erik?"

Erik sat up straighter, alert now. "What do you want me to do, Faye?"

The kettle rumbled to a boil. The old woman rummaged around in the cupboard for cups and saucers. "I think you should follow her at a distance. Keep out of sight, but let us know immediately if anything unusual occurs."

She went over to the stove to switch off the heat. "Griffin, it might prove useful to know what Sybil's latest recovery was."

"Yes, of course," he agreed. "I'll look into it immediately."

Faye was now spooning loose tea into a porcelain pot. She paused to consider. "What could they possibly want of ours? What, to them, would be worth killing for?"

3 – PRAYER MEETING

In the silent hour just before dawn, Abraham Metcalf was standing in his study, scrutinizing the spine of a volume of sermons on his bookshelf. His study was the size of a public library and his home the size of a medieval castle. It needed to be. He was the head of a very large extended family. Despite the barest glimmer of light in the east, Metcalf was expecting a visitor. Fully dressed in a black suit, he cut an impressive figure. His mane of grey hair had been swept back from his forehead and trimmed just long enough to reach the top of his collar. His moustache and beard had been shaped into a precise goatee. Despite his seventy years, he possessed a muscular build and ramrod-straight posture. His eyes were a frosty shade of blue. They bore a fierce expression under bristling white eyebrows suggesting very little escaped his notice or gained his approval.

A timid young man tapped lightly on the door. "A visitor to see you, Father."

"Send him in."

A man wearing a Stetson hat advanced into the study.

Metcalf turned to face him. "Hats off indoors, Mr. Hunt," he instructed curtly.

His visitor smiled lazily and doffed his hat. "Thank you kindly for remindin' me. My momma, God rest her, would pitch a fit if she seen me forget my manners like that."

Metcalf sat down behind his massive oak desk. He did not invite his visitor to seat himself. He studied Hunt in silence for several seconds. The younger man did not flinch under his gaze but stood grinning, his stance relaxed.

"I don't see the key in your hands, Mr. Hunt."

"No need to stand on proper names now, is there? How about you call me Leroy, and I'll call you Abe?"

"You may call me Father Abraham if you wish," Metcalf offered stiffly.

"Sorry, boss, but you ain't my daddy. Don't rightly know who he was, come to think on it."

Metcalf's face remained impassive. "I don't see the key, Mr. Hunt."

Leroy Hunt shrugged off the implied rebuke. "That's cuz I encountered a bit of trouble in obtainin' said object."

Metcalf had picked up a letter opener and was examining it intently. "Define trouble," he commanded.

Hunt selected one of the chairs in front of Metcalf's desk and sat down. "Well, sir, it was like this. That gal you set me to followin' had herself an unfortunate accident. We got into a tussle. She fell and bumped her head, and now she's dead."

"Dead!" Metcalf echoed in disbelief.

"That's right, boss. Not to rise again till Judgment Day."

"Dead," Metcalf repeated somewhat less emphatically.

"Yup, dead," Leroy concurred, smoothing the wave in his hair.

The older man considered the problem in silence for several moments before he spoke again. "You did manage to search the shop at least?"

"That I did. I spent a half hour pokin' around before somebody called the cops. I had to high tail it when I heard them sirens, but I was through lookin' anyhow. That key you set such store by couldn't be found for love or money."

Metcalf stood up and towered over Hunt. "I'm most disappointed in your report, Mr. Hunt."

Leroy chuckled. "I guess if I was you and I wanted that key so bad, I'd be a bit down in the mouth too, boss."

"I hardly think this occasion calls for levity, Mr. Hunt." Metcalf's eyebrows bristled in disapproval.

Hunt looked up at him appraisingly. "Boss, I don't expect there's much in your life that you'd think would be a fit occasion for levity." Before Metcalf could supply a retort, he continued. "Now don't you go worryin' yerself to pieces over this. I still ain't done. Gal's got a sister, don't she? How's about I follow her for a bit? Maybe see what's what?"

Metcalf relaxed his scowl by a hairsbreadth. "Yes, that would seem to be the proper course of action to take at this juncture."

Leroy stood up and gave a mock salute. "You got it, boss." He retrieved his hat and turned toward the door.

"Before you go, Mr. Hunt, let us say a prayer together."

A flicker of anger crossed Leroy's face. "I ain't one of yours."

Metcalf was already on his knees behind his desk, hands folded. "Yes, I know. None of my flock is equal to the work that needs to be done. That's why I've enlisted your aid in this great undertaking. An undertaking which requires divine assistance to complete. You will pray with me now."

Wordlessly, Hunt returned to the opposite side of the desk. He knelt, folded his hands, and screwed his eyes shut as if in anticipation of a bad tasting medicine.

Metcalf addressed his remarks to the chandelier overhead. "Oh Lord, guide this man's hand that it may do your bidding. Let him smite down those who oppose your will. Let the wicked be put to shame that the Blessed Nephilim may inherit the earth. Amen!"

4 – SISTERS AND OTHER STRANGERS

Cassie was sitting cross-legged on the living room rug in her sister's apartment. There were stacks of paper piled around her. Boxes of magazines and scattered articles of clothing littered the couch. Tears were running down her cheeks, but she didn't bother to brush them away. She had been crying for days now. Maybe it had been a week. She couldn't remember. It started right after the phone call came. The police were at Sybil's shop. They needed her to identify a body, but she already knew who it would be. Her nightmare had been a 3-D technicolor preview of the real thing.

She felt as if she was still sleepwalking when she arrived at the antique store. The green banker's lamp was on. Her sister lay sprawled across the floor, face down exactly where Cassie had seen her fall. The only difference was that now there were photographers and police swarming like flies over her sister's remains.

Rhonda, her sister's business partner, was there too. White-faced and shaking, she came up to hug Cassie. The two clung to each other for several moments, too much in shock to speak.

The detective who questioned her sounded like he was standing in an echo chamber. His voice was distorted, coming at her from a distance. "What was Sybil doing in the shop alone at such a late hour? Was anything of value missing? Did she have any enemies?"

Cassie gave the same answer every time. "I don't know."

Even now she marveled at how little she knew about anything her sister was doing or why. "What were you involved in, Sybil?"

Cassie didn't know much about antiques, but she did know that a lucrative black-market trade existed. Had Sybil been doing something shady? Smuggling artifacts into the country illegally? Again, she didn't know.

The only things she did know for certain were that a man in a Stetson hat had killed her sister over a key, and she'd dreamed the whole thing while it was happening. She didn't think that was the sort of information the detective was looking for. He probably wouldn't believe her. Small wonder since she didn't believe it herself. She wasn't given to odd psychic experiences. In all her life, she'd never been accused of having so much as a hunch about anything. She was a rational person—more or less.

Her mind skipped forward to the task at hand. She was sorting through a box of old bills and papers. The easy stuff. She couldn't bring herself to sort through the clothes yet. She had tried earlier that day, but it had been a mistake. She'd realized that the minute she pulled open a drawer of sweaters. There was lavender sachet inside. Her sister had always smelled like lavender. It was a comforting, familiar scent. Someone once told her that people remember the way things smell long after they've forgotten how they look or taste or sound. The sense of smell is primal. Like blood, like family, like death. She shoved the drawer closed and left the bedroom in tears. She doubted she would ever smell lavender again without crying. It was safer to sort through the papers. They didn't smell like lavender. They didn't smell like much of anything at all.

She wiped her eyes and tossed the used tissue onto the pile that was accumulating on the floor. How many boxes had she gone through? Like the number of days she'd spent crying, she'd lost count of that too. It had all become a blur. Even the funeral. That mother of all ordeals. The service had been small and quiet because they hadn't been living in Chicago long. There was no other family. Aside from Rhonda, there was nobody who could be called a friend either. Sybil had been Cassie's only anchor to this place, and now the girl felt like a boat drifting with the current. When other people lost a sister, there was always somebody else to fill the void. Cassie doubted if anybody could understand what her particular brand of loneliness felt like. The word "orphan" didn't begin to cover it. She broke down and started to sob.

"Enough!" she commanded herself sternly. She looked up at the ceiling to blink back the tears. For a few minutes, she focused on nothing but breathing. Just breathe and don't think. Breathe in. Breathe out. Breathe in. Breathe out.

Finally, she calmed down enough to regain focus. She reached for another box of papers. It appeared to be a stack of old charge card receipts. Why Sybil had kept this junk was beyond her. She dumped the box upside down on the coffee table. As the pile of papers spewed out, something hard fell on top of it.

Cassie cocked her head sideways, examining the object. Strange-looking thing. It was shaped like a ruler. About a foot long and about two inches wide, only it had five sides. Solid in the middle but five-sided. What would you call a shape like that? A polygon? She looked at the surface of the ruler lengthwise. There were strange markings inscribed in the stone. Some looked like long hash marks, and some looked like pictograms. They resembled Egyptian hieroglyphics; only they weren't Egyptian. She'd seen enough of those in museums to recognize them. Along the sharp edge that divided the ruler into five sides were more hash marks and loops.

Cassie made no move to pick up the stone ruler. She dismissed it as something from the shop that Sybil had decided to keep. Her sister did that all the time. She'd come across another "treasure" that she just had to have for her own. The apartment was full of things she couldn't seem to part with. African masks on the walls. A rare Chinese vase in a niche by the door. Fragments of Greek friezes. It begged the question of where the money came from for Sybil's expensive private collection. Cassie frowned and regarded the stone ruler again for a few moments. Maybe she'd ask Rhonda about it when she saw her next.

Her eyes swept the room. The papers and the clothes and the antiques and the artwork. So much more to get through. Suddenly, she felt very tired and more than a bit overwhelmed. Nobody else to do it but her. She sighed.

Without bothering to clean up the tissues on the carpet, she got up, grabbed her purse, and left the apartment. She wanted to head back to her dorm room for a long, long nap. She could come back tomorrow. Everything would still be waiting for her. More memories to pop out of a drawer or jump off a shelf to remind her that she was alone in the world. It would keep. She'd cried enough for this day.

5 – CORVETTE AND MODEL T

A dozen hours after Cassie fell into a restless doze, dawn broke over a suburb on the far outskirts of the metro area. It was a hamlet that had once been rural and still retained a few of its American gothic homesteads. Daylight crept toward the oldest of these original structures—a two-story farmhouse standing on an acre of green land. It was surrounded by one hundred and twenty acres of tract housing but, so far, had managed to resist being engulfed by the neighborhood. A high wooden fence surrounded the backyard which encompassed both a flower and a vegetable garden. The front lawn was wide and deep enough to accommodate massive shade trees that had been old long before the first cornfield was plowed.

Light advanced across the lawn to the house itself which was concrete stucco painted a shade of cornflower blue. A cupola in the middle of the roof had attracted a flock of burbling pigeons who hoped to warm themselves in the early sun's rays. When an elderly woman emerged onto the Victorian gingerbread porch, the pigeons flapped off. Broom in hand, she immediately set about sweeping the front steps. An apple tree growing close to her porch was shedding its blossoms. It appeared as if her stairs were covered in bits of pinkish-white confetti. She swept briskly, if absentmindedly. It was clear that she was lost in thought. She didn't register that someone was coming up her front walk until he stood directly in front of her.

"Faye?" the young man asked tentatively.

"Oh, Erik, you gave me a start." Her hand flew involuntarily to her heart. Then she smiled and motioned him towards the house. "Please, do come in."

He preceded her through the door.

"Why don't we sit in here." She directed him to the front parlor. In anyone else's house, it would have been called the living room, but Faye was different. She radiated a sense of having skipped back in time. She was wearing a cotton housedress—the kind that was spattered with giant flowers in garish colors. It was topped with a green cardigan whose front pocket sagged from the weight of an oversized handkerchief. Her white hair was molded into a smooth bun at the back of her head. She might have been in her eighties, or she might have been one hundred and ten. It was hard to tell. Despite her ancient appearance, Faye's eyes sparkled with vitality. Like her house, they were cornflower blue, and they missed nothing.

The young man who visited her couldn't have provided a starker contrast. If people were automobiles, he would have been a Corvette to Faye's Model T. He had a lean, muscular frame. Not extremely tall but not short either. His dark blonde hair was shaggy and perpetually in need of a barber. Maybe it was an image that Erik wanted to project. He was so good-looking that he didn't have to worry about how his hair was cut. In his mid-twenties, with green eyes and a cleft in his chin, he was the stuff of which movie idols are made. Whether he was consciously vain was open to question. He liked to pretend he didn't notice how women reacted to him. He believed he had a mission in life.

Erik removed his suede jacket and tossed it on the couch. His car keys landed on top of the coat.

Faye gestured for him to sit down. "Can I get you a cup of tea, dear?"

She was about to shuffle off to the kitchen, but her guest stopped her. "No thanks, Faye, I'm fine."

The elderly woman settled herself into a plum armchair opposite him. It had a doily perched on the headrest. The kind that was once known as an antimacassar. The chair itself might have dated from the time when men still used macassar oil to dress their hair, and the doily kept them from soiling the furniture. Faye probably expected that patent leather hair would come back into vogue someday and was prepared for it.

"Well then, what can you tell me?"

Erik shrugged. "Not much. She lives in a dorm at school. Keeps to herself a lot. I've been following her around ever since…" He trailed off.

Faye sighed. "Yes, we all miss Sybil, dear. It was a terrible shock. A terrible loss."

Erik cleared his throat uncomfortably. "Anyway, ever since it happened, I've been following her. Went to the funeral, but I kept out of sight. I didn't see anybody odd. She drove to Sybil's apartment yesterday. I guess she was sorting through stuff. I stayed out in the hall for a while listening." He hesitated. "I heard a lot of crying."

"Poor child," Faye said quietly. She smoothed the folds of her housedress. "Poor lost child."

Erik hunched forward on the couch. "Do you think she knows anything about Sybil's recovery? About us?"

Faye shook her head. "No, Sybil was most emphatic. She told me that she didn't want her sister involved. She wanted to keep her safe. She believed the less Cassie knew, the better."

Erik looked skeptical. "I don't see how keeping somebody in the dark is going to keep them safe. They're more likely to do something stupid when they don't know what they're up against."

The young man stood up and began to pace. "It just seems wrong. Somebody ought to tell her."

Faye fixed her gaze on her visitor. Her expression was mild, almost curious. "Exactly how could we explain ourselves in a way that she would understand?"

Erik ran his fingers through his hair. "I don't know. We probably can't. But this whole thing is making me edgy. I don't like it. Just hanging around and listening to a kid cry." He threw himself back down on the couch, exasperated. "Can I quit yet?"

"I'd like you to keep watching her for a while longer."

Erik picked up his car keys and jingled them distractedly between his fingers. "What exactly do you think is gonna happen?"

"I expect that sooner or later the person who killed Sybil will reveal himself."

"He probably found what he wanted in the shop. He's probably long gone by now."

Faye stood and walked over to the picture window. She watched the morning breeze shake loose another batch of blossoms. "And if he didn't obtain what he was looking for, how long do you think it will take him to find Cassie?"

Erik stopped jingling the keys. He looked down at his hands. "I guess I wouldn't want that on my conscience."

"Nor would I, dear." Faye turned toward Erik. "Let's watch her a little while longer just to be sure."

6 – COMPOUND INTEREST

Despite her best intentions, it was after sunset the following evening before Cassie found her way back to Sybil's apartment. Time to put all this in the past, she told herself decisively as she got out of her car and crossed the street toward the Gold Coast high rise. Yeah right. She was so eager to put things behind her that she'd procrastinated until nightfall to avoid confronting the residue of her sister's life again. And she didn't even have the excuse of going to classes anymore. School was on hold indefinitely. There was still the tricky matter of deciding where to live. She would probably move out of the dorm and into Sybil's place. Right now, that thought made her shudder. Not quite ready to deal with it yet.

She got off the elevator on the fourth floor and headed toward Sybil's flat at the end of the hall. Her eyes were immediately drawn to the bottom of the door. There was light coming from inside. Had she forgotten to switch off the power the day before? Who knew? She shrugged and sorted through the keys on her ring. When she turned the lock, she thought she heard a click coming from inside. Cassie swung the door open wide. She stood on the threshold listening for a moment. The place was dark, completely still.

She walked across the room toward an end table to turn on the lamp. Something or someone slammed into her, shoving her sideways. She hit the wall, knocking the breath out of her lungs. As she scrambled to her feet, she caught a glimpse of a man fleeing through the open door. Cassie gasped. He was wearing a Stetson hat, and he was holding an object she remembered seeing the day before.

Before she could react, he was down the hall, through the fire exit door, and halfway to the ground floor.

"Hey, hey you! Stop!" She started to run toward the lighted hallway when she collided with another man. He shoved her back into the apartment. She didn't think she recognized this one, but the place was still dark, so she couldn't be sure.

"What happened?" he demanded.

"Who are you?" she countered. "Where did you come from? What are you doing here?"

"No time for that now!" His voice was urgent. "What happened?"

"A... a man. He must have broken in. He... he was wearing a cowboy hat," she stammered.

The stranger grabbed her by the arms and shook her to get her attention. "Now listen! This is important! Did he take anything?"

Cassie was having a hard time thinking clearly. She could hear the blood pounding in her ears. "Yeah, I think..."

"What?" the man shook her again. "What was it?"

"It was a stone ruler. Five-sided. About a foot long with weird markings all over it." She twisted away from his grasp. "That's all I could see. Now, who—" Before she could get the rest of the question out, the man vanished.

She heard him shout back at her from down the hallway, "Call the police!" Then she heard the fire exit door slam and the sound of feet clattering down the emergency stairs.

Cassie was shaking from delayed shock. She collapsed on the couch and switched on the table lamp. Trying to get her eyes to focus, she looked around at the contents of the room. Everything was just as she'd left it the day before except for one thing. The stone ruler was gone. It had been stolen by the man from her nightmare.

She got up weakly and crossed over to a bombé chest that held a telephone. When she picked up the receiver to dial 911, she noticed an envelope underneath the base of the phone. It had been hand-addressed. All she could see was the initial letter *C*. Putting the receiver down, she slid the packet out from its hiding place. In Sybil's script, the letters *C-A-S-S-I-E* were scrawled across the front. Her hands were trembling as she ripped the envelope open.

***

Erik could hear footsteps ahead of him at the bottom of the stairwell. He waited until the man had gotten to the ground floor before he moved forward. He didn't want Cowboy to know he was being followed.

Once the exit door slammed shut, he raced forward. Outside he saw Cowboy climbing into a red pickup parked across the street from the high rise. It tore away from the curb, heading north. Erik noted the license plate number. Shouldn't be too hard to follow. He jumped into his car and tailed the thief, careful to keep several vehicles between them. With all the early evening traffic on the roads, he didn't think he'd been spotted. Cowboy got on the northbound expressway. He drove past the looming shadows of downtown high rises, past the suburban bedroom communities, past the overcrowded shopping malls, past the point where any expressway lights remained to illuminate the road. It was almost an hour before the pickup took a westbound exit that led to nothing but farm land. Erik knew it would be harder to keep from being noticed out in the middle of nowhere. He got behind a semi-trailer that was going in the same direction. Cowboy drove on for another half hour through pitch black countryside then turned right onto a side road marked with a yellow Dead End sign. Erik couldn't follow him in there. It would be too obvious.

He pulled his car off to the shoulder and got out, hoping he wouldn't find one of those "Do Not Park Here" stickers plastered on his windshield when he got back. He started walking. Fortunately, lights appeared in the distance almost immediately. The road turned out to be a very, very long driveway. The building at the end of it couldn't be more than a quarter mile away. Erik kept to the shoulder, in the shadows.

The road ended in front of a pair of iron gates about ten feet high. Each of the gates was decorated with a capital letter *P* with an *X* through the middle of it. Erik didn't know anyone with that monogram. He noticed a guard shack with security cameras mounted on either side of the gates and quickly ducked farther into the shadows. A ten-foot chain link fence topped with razor wire surrounded the property. Company was clearly not welcome in this place.

He couldn't be sure how long the fence was, but he could guess it stretched around several acres. Beyond the gate at the far end of the gravel drive, Erik could see Cowboy's car. Somebody had been expecting his visit.

Erik headed for the trees that bordered the fence to the east where more of the layout was visible. He focused his attention on the house if you could call it that. The building was as big as a castle, or maybe "fortress" would be a better word. It looked as if it could withstand a siege. The design was squat and square with a flat roof, like a massive cinderblock. Towers flanked the front of the building on either end. Erik guessed there might be two on the back end as well. The fortress was studded with tall narrow windows recessed deep into the walls. Light glowed through drawn curtains making it impossible to tell how many people were inside. Floodlights bleached the limestone façade to a blinding whiteness.

Aside from the main building, Erik counted at least eight other structures around the perimeter—smaller replicas of the main house. Then he noticed an odd assortment of sheds, garages, and trailers that must have been used for storage. A compound. He smiled to himself. It had to be them. Nobody else would live like this. Now he knew for certain who had hired Cowboy to steal Sybil's find. The only thing he still couldn't figure out was why.

7 - KEY ISSUES

Leroy pressed the doorbell several times before the oak double doors swung open to reveal a clean-cut teenager in a suit.

The young man blinked once. He didn't ask Leroy's name. He simply motioned the visitor inside. "Come in, Mr. Hunt. Father has been expecting you for some time now."

The youth stepped aside to allow Leroy to enter the foyer. It was two stories high, with a single pendant light suspended from the ceiling. The only furniture the room contained was a pair of deacon's benches facing each other from opposite whitewashed plaster walls. The effect was simple and austere. Like a monastery.

Hunt followed his guide down a long, uncarpeted corridor. Doors on either side were shut. Other than the sound of their footsteps echoing on the stone floor, everything was silent. Eventually, the pair turned right at a hallway that intersected the corridor. It too contained row upon row of shut doors. The doors were plain slabs of dark wood with no carving of any kind. They stretched off into the distance with absolute uniformity. It was disorienting, like walking through a hall of mirrors.

"A feller could get lost easy in a place like this," Leroy observed to his guide.

The teenager smiled stiffly but made no comment.

Finally, they paused in front of another set of double doors. These opened to reveal a dining room whose dimensions were vast enough to rival a great hall in a medieval castle. Despite the grandiose size of the room, its furnishings were not designed to impress. They were ruthlessly functional.

The trestle table could have served forty guests easily. This evening a smaller party was dining there. At the far end sat Abraham Metcalf in a high-backed armchair. On either side of him were eight children, the boys on one side of the table and the girls across from them. Instead of chairs, the children were seated on rows of benches. The boys were all dressed alike in black pants, white dress shirts, and black ties. The girls wore shapeless grey smocks. Aside from the grouping by gender, they also appeared to be arranged in age order with the oldest girl and boy sitting closest to Metcalf while the younger ones took the places below. They ranged in age somewhere from early teen to toddler. On the girls' side of the table, in the place farthest from Abraham sat a woman. She might have been thirty. Her long hair was braided and coiled around her head like a beehive. She wore a simple gray cotton dress which was covered by a white apron. Though she wore no makeup, she was very pretty. At the moment, she was also very frightened.

Abraham was leaning forward over the table and glaring at one of the younger boys. Unaware that a visitor had entered the room, he continued to address the child. "Silas, I've warned you before about this behavior."

The boy squirmed in his chair, afraid to meet Abraham's gaze. He was about seven.

"Father, he didn't mean—" the woman pleaded.

"Silence!" Abraham commanded. "He knows his sin. Look at me, boy!"

The child stared down at the floor.

"I said look at me," the old man thundered and stood up. He rested his hands on either side of his dinner plate and leaned over the table. "Now, Silas!"

Quaking with fear, the boy complied.

"What is the greatest of all sins?"

"Disobedience," the boy squeaked.

"What did you say?"

"Disobedience, sir," this time the voice was louder.

"Disobedience is the greatest of all sins. The first of all sins." Abraham jabbed his index finger in the air for emphasis. "It is the reason that the human race lost paradise."

"Yes, sir," the boy whispered.

"Do you wish to burn in hell?"

"No, sir."

"You are risking your immortal soul, boy. Your immortal soul!"

The child gulped but said nothing.

"If I hear one more report of your bad behavior, just one more..." He paused for effect. "Then I will have no choice but to pronounce judgment."

The woman at the end of the table was twisting her napkin into knots. Her agonized gaze shifted back and forth from the boy to Abraham.

"Yes, sir," the boy said meekly. "I understand, sir."

Somewhat mollified by the child's abject submission, Abraham sat back down to resume his meal. The other children and the woman took their cue from him. They were about to do likewise when Leroy interjected himself into the scene.

"How y'all doin' this evening?" he asked pleasantly.

Metcalf looked up in surprise, aware for the first time that he had a visitor. "Mr. Hunt? Who let you in here?"

Leroy pointed behind him to the youth quaking in the open doorway. "That nice young feller over there."

"Y… y… you told us to let you know the m… m…minute Mr. Hunt arrived, sir. I… w…w… would never dream of interrupting your d… d… dinner otherwise."

Metcalf scowled at the teenager for a moment. "You might at least have announced your presence."

"S… sorry, sir. I didn't want to break into your ch… ch… chastisement."

"Enough!" Metcalf barked. "You may go."

The teenager fled, shutting the double doors behind him.

Leroy advanced into the room. He doffed his hat, his eyes fastened on the woman. "You must be the missus. Pleased to make your acquaintance, ma'am. My name's Leroy Hunt."

The woman nodded nervously, casting her eyes downward. She said nothing.

Hunt surveyed the other occupants of the table. "These all your young 'uns? What do I count here… five, six, seven, eight? My, my, you surely are a busy lady."

The woman now looked panic-stricken and turned toward Metcalf in mute appeal.

"Martha, take the children and go. I have business to discuss with this man."

Wordlessly, noiselessly, the woman and children slipped from the room like so many ghosts. They left their dinners uneaten.

Leroy dropped his hat on the table, walked up to the woman's plate, and helped himself to a chicken leg. He looked questioningly at Metcalf. "OK if I help myself? I've had me a long night, and it's a shame to see all these fine vittles go to waste."

Metcalf watched him eat, his face expressionless. Ignoring the question, he asked one of his own. "Do you have it?"

Leroy tossed the chicken bone back on the plate, fastidiously wiped his fingers on a napkin, and then advanced to the head of the table where Metcalf sat.

Reaching inside his coat pocket, he produced the stone ruler. "Yessir, I do." He laid it in front of the older man's plate.

In a rare show of pleasure, Metcalf smiled. "Excellent! This is the Lord's doing. Praise be!"

Hunt's expression was sour. "Beggin' to differ, boss, but it wasn't the Lord's doin'. It was mine. I don't recollect him bein' anywhere around when I nicked the thing."

Smoothly Metcalf replied, "You are the Lord's instrument, Mr. Hunt."

Leroy grimaced. "That bein' the case, your Lord must be mighty hard up for tools."

"The Lord works in mysterious ways…" Metcalf trailed off. He picked up the ruler, examining its intricate symbols with keen interest.

Leroy watched him for a few moments. "You call that doodad a key?"

Metcalf nodded.

"Strange shape for a key. What's it unlock if you don't mind me askin'?"

Metcalf was lost in contemplation of the object. "Someday you'll know. Someday the whole world will know."

"Guess I'll wait then."

The older man frowned as a thought struck him. "You didn't have any trouble this time, did you?"

"Nope." Hunt put his hands in his pockets and rocked back on his heels with satisfaction. "I got it before that little gal come in to straighten up her sister's place."

"Did she see you?" Metcalf transferred his attention from the ruler to Hunt.

"Not hardly. The place was dark, and I knocked her into a wall before she could get a bead on me. Lit out of there while she was still collectin' her breath to holler fer help."

Leroy noted that Metcalf's brow was furrowed in thought. "Something botherin' you, boss?" he asked casually.

"I wonder if she knows anything about this."

Leroy snorted. "Nope!"

"Why do you say that, Mr. Hunt?"

"Cuz if she did, she woulda done a better job of hidin' the damn thing stead of leavin' it settin' right on the coffee table like it was some kind of knickknack." Hunt sounded annoyed and a trifle disappointed. "Didn't hardly make it worth my while breakin' and enterin'. Didn't have to ransack nothin'. Just left it settin' out in the open, plain as day."

Hunt stopped speaking. A sly smile crossed his lips as a new idea occurred to him. "Course if you want I should go back and tidy up the situation for you, I aim to please."

Metcalf appraised Hunt with a look of thinly veiled disgust. "I think that leaving a suspicious trail of bodies behind can hardly be considered tidy."

Leroy shrugged. "Whatever you say. So long as I get paid, it don't make no never mind to me."

"You'll get your money." Metcalf stood up from the table, indicating that the interview was nearing an end. "I am satisfied that the antique dealer's sister is not involved in the matter. You no longer need to concern yourself with her."

He walked with Hunt toward the dining room door. "Once this key is translated, I will have more work for you."

"You know how to reach me, boss. Always happy to oblige." He retrieved his hat, tipped the brim to Metcalf, and left.

8 – DIGESTING THE INFORMATION

Much later that same evening, a familiar group of four people gathered together in Faye's kitchen. The mood was somewhat less grim than their last meeting as the old woman bustled about fixing them a midnight snack.

"Despite the lateness of the hour, I'm glad you were all able to join me to discuss Erik's latest findings," she said as she passed out platters of cold cuts and bread.

The security coordinator started building himself a three-decker club sandwich. He didn't need any further encouragement from Faye to launch into his report to the group. "You were right, Maddie, it was them."

"And you're surprised that they were behind it all along?" The red-haired woman blew a smoke ring into the air. She rose to help Faye bring a tray of cups and saucers to the table.

"At first, I wasn't sure. It didn't fit how they've operated in the past." Erik bit into his sandwich. "Besides, they aren't where we expected them to be."

"Don't talk with your mouth full, dear," Faye corrected gently as she poured coffee.

Griffin distributed the cups around the table. "Where we expected them to be? It isn't as though we encounter these people every day. When was the last time our path crossed theirs, Faye?"

"Long before you came to join us. About ten years ago, I think." Faye sat down and stirred cream into her coffee. "Much can change in a decade."

"Then I suppose it's to be expected." Griffin directed his next question to Erik. "Why shouldn't they have relocated their headquarters?"

Erik dutifully swallowed his bite of sandwich before speaking. "Because they don't exactly travel light, that's why. You should have seen this place. It looked like they've started building their own city."

Maddie scowled. "Bad news for our side."

Faye moved on to a more urgent topic. "What about this fellow who broke into Sybil's apartment? You said you don't think he's one of theirs."

"Not likely," Erik laughed. "He was wearing a cowboy hat."

"Did you get a good look at him?" asked Maddie.

"Not great. It was dark, and he was getting into his truck, but I saw enough to put together a sketch. And I got his license plate number."

"Well, that's a start." Maddie walked over to the counter for a bag of chocolate chip cookies. She brought them back to the table. "Did you have a chance to check out the plates before we got here?"

"Yeah," Erik hesitated. "It was a rental. I found out it was leased to a guy named Matt Dillon."

Maddie and Faye both laughed. "Our villain has a sense of humor," the old woman observed.

Griffin looked confused. "I'm sorry?"

"Never mind, old chap," Erik said in an exaggerated British accent. "I guess you lot didn't get Gunsmoke over the pond."

"Gunsmoke over the pond?" Now Griffin looked completely lost. "What on earth is he talking about?"

Maddie patted Griffin reassuringly on the back. "Nothing important. It's just an old TV series. What we Yanks would call a horse opera. You know, shoot 'em up stuff. Cowboys and Indians."

"How very extraordinary," Griffin remarked, helping himself to a cookie.

"And what about Cassie?" Faye asked.

Erik decided to skip the cookies and dipped into a bag of potato chips instead. "Today I trailed her from her dorm to Sybil's apartment. It was already dark when she got there. I waited for her to go up in the elevator before I followed. I was just getting off on the fourth floor when I saw this guy come tearing out of Sybil's place and head straight for the stairwell. He didn't see me. I ran inside the apartment to check that Cassie was OK. That he hadn't hurt her." Erik looked around the table at the others. Their faces were troubled. He continued. "But she was just shaken up. Lucky for us, she actually saw what he took."

At these words, they all stopped eating. A captive audience.

"Yes?" Griffin prompted.

"She said it was a five-sided ruler with markings on it."

"A what?" Maddie sounded suspicious.

Even Faye was taken aback. "Griffin, do you have any idea what she meant?"

"No, I've never heard of such a thing. Sybil never mentioned a find like that to me."

"We've been very careful to keep away from anything that they might consider interesting," Faye mused to herself. "Sybil knew that. She wouldn't deliberately go after a recovery if there was any chance they might want it too."

"If it's ours, then we get it back," Erik stated matter-of-factly, popping open a can of soda.

"No dear, we don't." Faye sighed. "If we lose a valuable find, then we lose a valuable find. It's far more important for us to protect our anonymity."

"So, we let them kill one of ours and take something that belongs to us?" Maddie's eyes were blazing with indignation. "Again?"

Faye glanced at her sadly. "Yes, I'm afraid we must. It seems like the last straw, but we can't retaliate. There's too much at stake here to risk exposure."

"I suppose." Maddie relented slightly. "What about the kid? Do we tell her anything?"

Faye folded her hands on the table, regarding her guests gravely. "Sybil died to protect our secret. We owe her a great debt. She always said she wanted to keep Cassie safe."

"By safe, you mean in the dark?" Erik asked, a slight edge of sarcasm in his voice.

"'If ignorance is bliss, 'twere folly to be wise,'" Faye observed softly. "I believe we have an obligation to respect Sybil's wishes."

The group was silent for a few moments, mulling over the old woman's decision. When the phone rang suddenly, they all jumped. It wasn't the phone on the wall, but a cell phone lying on the kitchen counter.

Griffin looked puzzled. "Who would be calling you at this hour and on that line?"

"Guess we're gonna find out." Erik reached over and handed the phone to Faye, so she wouldn't have to struggle to her feet.

She nodded her thanks to him. "Hello?"

There was a long pause.

"Why, yes. Of course, you may."

Another pause.

"Oh, I think it's much too late tonight. You'd never find your way here in the dark. How about tomorrow at noon?"

Faye then gave her address and detailed directions to her house.

"Fine, I'll see you then. We'll have much to talk about." She laid the phone down on the table. A look of bewilderment crossed her face.

The other three stared at her, waiting for an explanation.

Faye wordlessly got up and started to make another pot of coffee.

"Faye?" Maddie prompted. "Are you alright?"

"Hmmm?" Faye turned absently toward her guests. "Well, as I was saying, I believe we have an obligation to respect Sybil's wishes to keep Cassie away from this business."

"Yes..." Erik nudged her along.

She looked around at their baffled faces. "I just never expected her to change her mind—posthumously."

9 – LOST IN TRANSLATION

The morning after he acquired the key, Abraham was waiting for a visitor in his prayer closet. He called it a closet, but the dimensions were the size of an average living room. It was the space where he conversed directly with God. Heavy drapes barred the passage of sunlight through the room's two tall windows. Abraham liked cloaking the closet in shadow. It helped his concentration. There was an oak stand between the windows which supported a heavy leather-bound Bible. The wall to the right of the windows consisted of a series of built-in cabinets with locked doors. They contained sacred documents that were intended for his eyes only. A prie-dieu occupied the corner to the left of the windows. In a rare concession to comfort, the kneeler was padded. On another wall hung the portrait of an elderly man with a white beard. He bore a strong resemblance to Abraham, but the cut of his suit hadn't been in fashion for at least fifty years. His eyes stared down on the room. They were humorless and disapproving. A plaque embedded in the bottom of the picture frame announced that he was Josiah Metcalf—Diviner. Positioned directly below the picture was a small round table and two hard-bottomed chairs.

Abraham was leafing through some pages of the Bible when he heard a gentle knock on the door. He absently said, "Enter," without looking up from the page he was reading.

A man of about thirty came in. He was of medium height. Although his hair was cropped short, it insisted on asserting its curliness. No amount of combing could straighten it out completely. His eyes were dark brown behind horn-rimmed glasses, his complexion sallow. He wore the usual white dress shirt, black tie, and black trousers, but the clothes didn't seem to fit him properly. They seemed too big for his slight frame and rumpled even though they had been newly pressed. His shoulders sagged.

"Good morning, Father," he said tentatively. "You wanted to see me?"

Abraham turned toward his guest. "Yes, that's right. Sit down, Daniel." He indicated one of the two chairs.

The visitor glanced up briefly at the portrait before he slid into his chair. He sat forward anxiously, his hands grasping the seat.

Abraham remained standing near the windows. "Daniel, remind me again which of my sons you are."

The younger man didn't seem to consider the question odd. "I am your twentieth son, Father," he answered readily.

"And which of my wives is your mother?"

"My mother is Deborah, your fifth wife," Daniel looked down, "though she has passed from this life."

The older man's expression was vague. "Hmmm, yes, I do seem to recall now. She's been departed, what is it, nearly two years? Never mind, boy. She has gone to wait for me in the next world. We will be reunited there. How many wives do you have now?"

Daniel cleared his throat uncomfortably. "You have blessed me with three wives, Father."

Abraham looked pleased with himself. "That's a good start though some of your brothers at the same age have collected more." He paused to consider. "Still, it's a good start. And how many children?"

Daniel seemed to be fighting the urge to squirm in his chair. "Three so far."

"Three?" Abraham registered shock. "Are any of your wives barren?"

"N… no, I don't think so, Father." Daniel stared hard at the table.

Abraham took a pace or two forward. "And when did I give you your first wife?"

"When I was twenty," Daniel mumbled.

"Ten years," Abraham mused. "In ten years your wives have only produced three children. That's unheard of!"

Daniel shifted his position slightly. "I'm sorry, fa—"

The old man cut him off. "We are charged with the obligation to be fruitful and multiply—to extend His dominion over the earth. We must increase our numbers. You cannot hope to claim a place of glory in His kingdom otherwise. Surely, you don't wish to bring shame on your family."

Daniel shrunk back in his seat.

Abraham was standing above his son now. "Remember who is watching." He gestured toward the portrait. "Your grandfather is watching you even now from heaven. God, himself, is watching you." He paused for effect. "He is watching us all. He sees the secret sins of our innermost hearts, Daniel. He sees all, and he will punish all!"

Daniel gulped and nodded. "Yes, sir. I understand. I will pray for more issue."

"And instruct your wives to pray as well!" Abraham observed his son silently for a few moments. He seemed satisfied that he had made his point. "Good, that's settled then."

Metcalf walked to the wall cabinets. He took a brass key out of his pocket. "I am told you are quite the scholar. You have distinguished yourself above your brothers in the study of ancient languages."

Daniel seemed to puff up a bit at the encouragement. "Yes, it is the subject I love above all others. Translating the word of God."

"That shows a proper spirit," Metcalf nodded approvingly. "Come here. I have something to show you."

Daniel obediently walked over to join him.

Abraham unlocked one of the cabinets and withdrew the stone ruler. "What can you make of this?" the old man inquired, handing the object to his son.

Daniel held it up to the meager light coming through the windows. He examined the markings with great intensity. When he looked up again, his expression was one of dismay. "The script isn't Aramaic, or Hebrew, or Greek, or Latin. Not even Egyptian judging by the pictograms." Daniel now seemed a bit afraid of the ruler. He held it out toward his father as if he thought it was contaminated. "This is some heathen relic."

Abraham made no move to take the object back. He stood with his arms folded across his chest. "Yes, I know, Daniel. But the Lord has charged me with the task of finding out its secrets. And now I charge you with the task of translating these strange markings into some language that a Christian can understand."

The young man scrutinized the pictures and lines and loops again. "Do we know where it comes from?" he asked tentatively.

"Only that it was found somewhere in the east and that it is very ancient."

Daniel thought of something that caused a look of apprehension to cross his face.

"What is it, my son?"

"Well, it's just that we have nothing in our library that could explain this. Do I have your permission to go into the Fallen Lands? I will need to search in their libraries. Because it is pagan, they may have records that show what language it is."

Abraham sighed. "My heart is heavy at the thought of sending you into their world. So many temptations. So much you have never been prepared for. But it is God's will that this be so." Abraham's eyes bored into his son's face. "Daniel, you must find a way to translate this. Everything depends upon it. Do you understand?"

Daniel gulped. "Yes, Father, I will find a way."

10 – PHOTOGRAPHIC MEMORIES

The grandfather clock in the hall was chiming noon when Faye heard a gentle knock on her front door. She hobbled over to answer it as quickly as her aged feet would carry her. Standing on her porch was a girl in her late teens dressed in blue jeans, a pullover, and a light spring jacket. She was about Faye's height with the slender build of a gymnast. Her shortness and tiny frame gave her the air of a pixie.

The girl smiled hesitantly. "Are you Faye?" She tilted her head slightly to flip her hair out of the way. It was parted to the side and seemed to want to cover her face like a curtain. The color was a dark shade of brown. There was nothing remarkable about her features though they were uniformly pretty. Nothing remarkable but her eyes. They were large and grey, but not a clear grey. Opaque as sunlight struggling to burn through fog.

"Please, do come in," Faye offered.

"My name is Cassie." The girl held out her hand.

"I'm delighted to meet you, my dear." Faye shook her hand warmly. "It's such a lovely day for early spring, don't you think? Almost warm enough for me to remember what summer feels like. Why don't we go outside and talk in the garden?"

Cassie followed her toward the back of the house.

"Would you like some lemonade?" Faye asked over her shoulder as they passed through the kitchen.

"Yes, thank you. I would."

She helped the old woman carry a pitcher and two glasses through the screen door to the back yard.

Spanning a full acre, Faye's garden was a world of its own. Fruit trees, evergreens, and tall shrubs lined the eight-foot privacy fence, muffling sounds of traffic from the street. There were leafy rose bushes just starting to wake up to the season. Stepping stone paths skirted flower beds blooming with crocus and narcissus. At the far end against the fence was a newly cultivated plot of fresh dirt for summer vegetables.

"This is quite a yard you've got," Cassie said in amazement. "From the street, you can't even tell this is here."

"That's the idea." Faye smiled. "Shall we sit over there?" She led the way to a latticework pergola in the middle of the flower garden which contained a wrought iron bistro table and two chairs. The roof of the pergola was covered with wisteria vines. Clusters of purple flowers were just beginning to bloom. They hung down like a canopy over the two.

Cassie seemed ill at ease. Faye didn't press her, so they sat in silence, sipping lemonade.

Eventually, the girl set down her glass and reached into her jacket pocket. She pulled out a folded piece of paper. "I don't suppose there's any good way to talk about this. Here, read it for yourself." She pressed the paper into Faye's hands.

Faye looked questioningly at the girl, set down her own glass, and unfolded the paper. It was a letter. She began to read it out loud.

"My dear little sis,

I'm sitting here writing this and hoping that you never have to read it. The only reason you would come across this letter is if I'm gone. Maybe the danger will pass, and I can destroy this. Maybe not.

There are times when my work can be risky. This is one of those times. I've come across a find that has immense value to the people I work with, but it looks like somebody else wants this find too. Somebody who would be willing to kill for it. For the past week, I've gotten the feeling I'm being followed. It might be my imagination. In case it isn't, and in case something happens to me, I want you to call the number I wrote on the back of this sheet. Ask to speak to Faye. Give her the packet. She can explain everything.

There's so much I want to say, but there isn't enough time, and maybe it only comes down to this. I love you. Everything I did, even when you didn't understand it, was to keep you safe. No matter what you might have thought, I was always looking out for you.

Love,

Sybil"

Faye stopped reading. She glanced up to see Cassie wiping tears from her cheeks. "Oh, my dear, I am so sorry." She reached out to squeeze Cassie's hand lightly.

The girl stared off into the distance. She began to speak more to herself than to Faye. "It's funny the way she ended the letter. She must have thought that I hated her. I suppose I did a little. I blamed her for everything. All the moves. Every year, it was a new school in a new town. She never explained why. She just parked me with housekeepers most of the time while she was off doing whatever it was she did when she wasn't around. After we came to

Chicago, I told her that I was going to finish college at the same school where I started no matter what. She swore this would be the end of the line." Cassie laughed bitterly. "That was one promise she kept."

She impatiently brushed away another tear. "I resented her, but I loved her too. I wonder if she knew that. Maybe she didn't because we were always more like strangers than sisters. But I did love her. She was the only family I had after our parents died."

The girl shifted in her chair to stare directly at Faye. "Sybil said you could explain everything. Can you explain how somebody could walk into my world and wreck it without thinking twice?" Cassie's eyes welled up once again with tears. "Do you have any idea who killed my sister?"

Faye hesitated. She measured her words carefully. "We have a notion about who was responsible, and we're conducting our own investigation. We should have some information to share with you soon."

The girl nodded and straightened up. Reaching into her jacket pocket once more, she pulled out a thick envelope. She pushed it across the table toward the old woman. "My sister said to give you this packet."

Faye removed the contents: a series of photographs and a page of numbers.

Cassie leaned over to point at the first picture. "That's what he took. The man in my dream—" She stopped short.

"The man in your dream?" Faye enunciated the words distinctly. She gave Cassie a searching look.

The girl shied away. As she lowered her head, her hair swung down over her face. "No. That isn't what I meant. Bad choice of words. I mean the man who broke into Sybil's apartment. He took that ruler."

Faye returned her attention to the packet. "How extraordinary." She flipped through the snapshots.

"I think each one shows a side of the ruler. It had five sides," Cassie added helpfully.

"I see." Faye remained lost in thought as she studied the photos. Each side of the ruler contained one line of markings. The left half consisted of pictograms. The right half was a script in some language she couldn't identify. The bottom edge was etched with indecipherable hash marks and loops.

"And then, in the note with all the numbers, I think she's giving the measurements. The length and width of the thing. At least they seem to match the size I guessed it to be. Why do you suppose she would write all that down for you?"

Faye paused a moment to consider. "I believe she thought the people who wanted this item would try to steal it. If they were successful, the information you've provided would allow us to make a replica. But that puzzles me too."

"You mean you don't know why?" Cassie sounded concerned.

"All the artifacts Sybil recovered are originals. Their value lies in their antiquity. From that standpoint, a replica is worthless. Like paste jewels." She hesitated. "I'll need to discuss this with my associates."

"Your associates?" Cassie asked cautiously. "How many are there? And by the way, who are you people anyway?"

Faye smiled and sighed. "Where to begin…"

11 – BOWLED OVER

Cassie adjusted her chair to face Faye directly.

The old woman took a few minutes to gather her thoughts. "As you already know, your sister was in the antique business. Aside from her store, Sybil was part of an organization that collects rare objects. Objects that have a particular significance to our group."

Cassie pounced on the word. "Group? Does your group have a name?"

"Yes," Faye said gently but offered nothing further on that point. She continued. "We are involved in a large-scale recovery project. Its scope is immense. It reaches back far before recorded history and spans cultures across the entire globe."

"No wonder Sybil wasn't around much," muttered Cassie. "Sounds as if you kept her pretty busy."

"Not just her, dear," Faye took a sip of lemonade. "There are hundreds of people all over the world involved in this effort."

"What could be that big?"

"Nothing less than the true story of the human race," Faye replied cryptically. She stood up. "I think we need something to go with this lemonade. Don't you?"

Without waiting for a reply, she trundled into the house and emerged a few minutes later carrying a plate of oatmeal cookies. "Help yourself, dear." She set the plate on the table.

Cassie reached over to take one.

Picking up right where they'd left off, the girl asked, "What exactly do you mean by the true story of the human race?"

Faye laughed. "That's a big question to answer." She settled back in her chair and began to speak. "What if I told you that much of what you've been taught about the past is a lie?"

Cassie looked at her noncommittally.

"Have you ever taken an ancient history class?"

Cassie nodded.

"When do your history books say that civilization began?"

The girl considered the question. "I think it was Sumeria or Babylon. Where Iraq is now. The Tigris and Euphrates rivers were what they called the cradle of civilization. Sometime around 3000 BCE."

The old woman chuckled. "Yes, that is the prevailing theory. I'm sure they told you about the rise of the Egyptians, Sumerians, and later the Greeks and Romans. Great military conquests, empire building. All of it a straight march from barbarism to civilization."

"I suppose." Cassie poured more lemonade for the two of them.

"What if I told you that great civilizations thrived before that time? As much as four thousand years before that time. What if I told you that some of those civilizations were sophisticated enough to have written language, running water, and sewer systems and that warfare didn't exist."

Cassie stopped sipping her lemonade. She felt intrigued. "Really? Is this one of those ancient astronaut theories?"

Faye laughed. "Not at all, child. There were major civilizations scattered all over the world. We are in the process of proving that. In India, the Aegean, Africa. Everywhere really. Lost cities that you've never heard of and a way of life that you probably never dreamed existed."

"Then why isn't all that recorded in history books?" Cassie challenged.

"Because history is the conquerors' version of what happened. The defeated are written out of the story entirely."

Cassie impatiently shrugged her hair away from her face. "One country invades another country, and the winner gets to tell future generations how great they were. It's always been that way."

"Actually, it hasn't," Faye corrected gently. "Until about six thousand years ago, the human race didn't behave that way at all."

"That's kind of hard to swallow." Cassie appeared unconvinced.

"It's hard to swallow because recorded history wants us to believe that it's always been this way. That violence toward our own species is ingrained in our very being. Dog eat dog. Nature red in tooth and claw."

"So, your group has a theory that we used to be a kinder, gentler species than we are now." The girl's voice held a slightly mocking tone.

"Much more than a theory. We're building quite a compelling body of evidence to prove it."

"If that's true, something must have radically changed us. What?" Cassie sounded more intrigued than doubtful now.

"A number of factors: climate shift, agriculture, domesticated animals, settled communities, and global warming that makes our current dilemma look small by comparison. The combination of all these things was what you might call a perfect storm. It turned some of us into killers."

The girl raised a skeptical eyebrow. "Why only some of us?"

"Because others were lucky enough to settle in hospitable environments. Fertile farmland, a mild climate, and plentiful resources. And these fortunate people continued to worship the deity that all humans had worshipped from the very beginning of time. A benevolent mother goddess who readily supplied all the needs of her children."

Faye's face darkened. "But some were not so lucky. Hemmed in by mountains and trapped by floods during the last climate change. They suffered through prolonged droughts and famine. Their landscape became harsh and barren, and it yielded them nothing. They grew angry and turned their backs on the goddess. If she would not supply them, they would take what they needed from others by force and pray to a like-minded god. A thundering sky god with an appetite for gore.

"These outcasts became something the world had never seen before. Instead of killing animals for food, they slaughtered each other for possessions and dominance. Obsessed with warfare, they made raiding and pillaging a way of life. Raiding progressed to invading. As time went by, these invaders spread like a virus across the face of the earth, rewriting the story of every land they subjugated. The original nature deities of the vanquished were replaced with their own violent sky gods. Even the peaceful lands they attacked became warlike in self-defense. The cosmos was thrown out of balance when women were no longer honored. Aggression replaced cooperation as the supreme survival skill. And now we live in a world that has forgotten the time when humankind wasn't drowning in its own blood."

Despite the horror she was describing, Faye's voice remained matter-of-fact.

Cassie was silent, her expression grave.

Faye continued. "Our collective memory has been erased. I, your sister, and the rest of our group are trying to get it back. To remember our true nature."

"Remember, how?"

"We are digging up the buried past of the world. Site by site. Bone by bone. Artifact by artifact. We are putting the puzzle back together. We practice an alternative kind of archaeology—the kind that defies the fabrications of history. Which reminds me…" Faye stood up and walked over to a corner of the pergola. She picked up a shallow metal bowl that had been sitting on the ground.

Faye pulled her chair closer to Cassie. "Your sister was very good at authenticating our finds. I wonder if you would give it a try."

She held the bowl toward Cassie.

The girl made no move to take it. "I'm not a trained archaeologist."

Faye smiled. "I'm not asking for anything specific. Just hold it in your hands and tell me what you observe." She nudged the bowl closer.

Cassie reached out with both hands. The second she touched the rim something very strange happened.

She felt dizzy as if she were falling down a deep, black well. Eventually, she landed. She found herself in a cavern. An underground vaulted chamber of some sort. There was a woman perched on a high stool.

No, that was wrong. Cassie had become the woman perched on a high stool. At least that's where her consciousness was. She felt that she had somehow merged with this person.

She was dressed in a long white linen robe. In her left hand, she held a branch with leaves on it. In her right, she held a bowl. The same kind Faye had given her. Only now it contained a clear liquid. She was looking into it as if it were a crystal ball. In front of her stool, on the floor of the cavern, there was a crack in the ground. Strange-smelling vapors were drifting upward from that spot. The scent made Cassie feel light-headed.

There was also a man wrapped in a toga who was standing in the chamber in front of her. A large man with heavy muscles. He had a stern, almost cruel, expression on his face. He seemed to be hanging on every word she said. Cassie didn't know how she could understand the language much less speak it, but she felt herself telling the man he was about to win a decisive victory over his enemies.

The next thing Cassie knew she was back in the garden, sitting in a wrought-iron chair. Faye had lifted the bowl out of her hands.

"I think that's quite sufficient for one day." The old woman smiled. "Tell me what you saw."

Cassie was startled, disoriented. "What the freak was that!" she demanded.

"Just tell me what you saw," Faye prompted gently.

"It was bizarre. I fell into another place. Another time. I felt like I'd actually become someone else. I was a woman sitting in a cave telling the future to some king who wanted to win a major battle." Cassie's heart was hammering. She looked at her glass suspiciously. "You must have put something in my lemonade!"

"I did no such thing, my dear, and I think you know that. You've had unusual experiences like this before, haven't you." Faye sounded as if she was stating a fact, not asking a question.

Cassie shook her head violently. "No, never. Or… maybe… but only once. Only the night Sybil died. I dreamed it before it happened. Every detail. It was like I was right there. The man in the cowboy hat was there too. The one who stole the stone ruler. He wanted Sybil to tell him where the key was."

"You say he was looking for a key of some sort?" Faye sounded surprised.

"Yeah, a stupid key. And my sister is dead because of it. I watched it happen."

"Sometimes the gift first appears when there has been an emotional trauma. Your sister had her first experience right after your parents died."

"After… after my… What!" Cassie felt as if Faye had just punched her in the stomach.

The old woman reached across the table to touch the girl's arm. "Forgive me, my dear. It's a lot to take in at one time, but I had to be certain."

Cassie recoiled. "Be certain of what?"

"That you were meant to take your sister's place. It is your destiny to be our new pythia."

Jumping out of her chair, Cassie cried, "Destiny? I don't have a destiny! This is insane! I don't care what Sybil did for you, or why, but leave me out of it!" She backed away from Faye. "I have to go. Now!"

She ran from the garden and out of the house.

***

Off in the distance, Faye could hear her tires squeal as Cassie pulled out of the driveway and raced away.

The old woman smiled to herself. "We have found our new pythia," she murmured.

12 - POWER TOOLS

It was late afternoon when Abraham decided to allow himself the indulgence of half an hour in the treasury. It was a secret room concealed behind a panel in his office wall. Only a few trusted followers knew of its existence. The room's contents were too precious to become common knowledge.

He typed a code into the keypad next to the steel door. It swung open on noiseless hinges and then shut behind him. The design of the interior resembled a bank safe. A windowless space with rows of small metal doors lining the walls. Individual security keypads were mounted on each one. A fluorescent fixture glared down from the ceiling on a bare table standing in the center of the room.

Abraham walked up to one of the small metal doors and typed a code into its keypad. When the door swung open, he withdrew the most recent addition to his collection and placed the object on the table. It was a small round shield that a warrior would strap to his forearm. More properly, it would be called a buckler. This one was green. At its center were painted five small blue shields arranged in the shape of a cross. Each shield was decorated with five gold circles. The monetary worth of the buckler was negligible. It wasn't made of gold or adorned with precious gems, but its value lay in its miraculous history. In that regard it was priceless.

During the Middle Ages, Portugal was overrun by Moors who wished to convert the population to Islam at the point of a sword. Christians had fought against them for centuries in an effort to reclaim their country. In 1139, Don Afonso Henriquez was about to engage the heathen horde on the plains of Ourique. Shortly before the battle, he saw a vision in the eastern sky of Christ on a cross. He believed this to be a portent of victory. His troops went on to slaughter the Moorish army and, at the end of that day, Don Afonso was named the first king of Portugal. In commemoration of his vision, Afonso adorned his buckler with five shields forming the shape of a cross, each with five bezants representing the wounds of Christ. An invaluable treasure and clear proof of divine favor.

Abraham moved the buckler to the left side of the table and went to another compartment to retrieve a second item. It was much smaller than the shield. A jagged piece of iron. It was a fragment broken from the tip of a spear. Utterly worthless for the raw material from which it was made. But, once again, appearances could be deceiving. This bit of common metal was a piece of the Longinus Lance. The spear which had pierced the side of Christ when he died on the cross. It was called the Longinus Lance because it had belonged to a Roman centurion by that name, but the weapon had other names too. Most often it was called the Spear of Destiny. It was said that whoever possessed it could never be defeated in combat. Another portion of the spear tip had briefly belonged to Adolph Hitler during the Second World War. When he lost it to the enemy, his fortunes changed for the worse. That piece was now housed in the Vatican under the dome of St. Peter's Basilica.

The fragment which Abraham was holding had once belonged to Louis IX of France. The king had enshrined it, along with the crown of thorns from the crucifixion, in Saint Chapelle in Paris. Both objects disappeared from history after the French Revolution. One of them had now found its way into Abraham's private collection.

The old man moved the lance tip to the right side of the table. He went back to the metal doors again. This time he retrieved a helmet and carried it back to the table. Metcalf examined the object in detail. It was of Roman design, fabricated of copper and iron. It conformed closely to the shape of the head, covering the ears. A neck guard protruded from the back and cheek protectors jutted from each side. It was surmounted by a horsehair crest and a visor inlaid with precious gems. Unlike the other two relics, this object had great monetary value. Each stone in the visor was worth a fortune—unsurprising since this helmet had been worn by an emperor. Yet its most valuable feature was something the casual observer couldn't see. An iron spike embedded inside the helmet. A simple iron spike. Unremarkable in itself, but millions had died because they believed in what it represented—or didn't believe.

When Constantine the First was emperor of Rome, his mother Saint Helena converted to Christianity. She went to the Holy Land in order to find sacred relics. She was able to locate the true cross and the nails that were used in the crucifixion. She sent two of the nails back to Constantine. According to legend, she had one of them placed in her son's helmet and the other in his horse's bridle. It was believed that the relics would protect him from harm.

Metcalf was holding in his hands the helmet of the Emperor Constantine. He felt sure that the emperor's success as a military commander was due in large part to the sacred objects he carried with him into war.

There were many tales associated with Constantine. Like Don Afonso, the emperor had been blessed with a vision. Just before a decisive battle, he saw a flaming cross appear in the eastern sky. A cross shaped like a *P* with a letter *X* through it. In Greek, the letters *P* and *X* or *Chi* and *Ro* spelled the first two letters of Christ's name. Constantine took this as a sign that the Christian god favored him. At the same moment, the emperor heard a voice telling him, "*In hoc signo vinces.*" In this sign conquer. The warrior's cross led his troops to victory that day.

Abraham set the helmet down in the center of the table and regarded the prizes of his collection with satisfaction. A shield, a lance, and a helmet. All of them had brought triumph in battle to their possessors. Taken together, they should prove to be invincible. The French had a name for such relics. They called them *objets de puissance.* Objects of power.

Metcalf looked up from the items on the table to survey the locked compartments that lined the walls. He had spent a lifetime acquiring their contents. Each artifact carried the sanction of God. Metcalf would need all their powers if the prophecy was to be fulfilled.

He knew that the Blessed Nephilim had lost faith over the years. They had waited more than a century for the Second Coming, but Judgment Day was long overdue. Metcalf feared for his wavering flock. The influence of the Fallen Lands crept ever closer to his refuge and to all the far-flung communities under his care. A stray television broadcast, a radio transmission, the internet. Their messages raised troublesome questions in the minds of his followers. No matter how tightly he restricted their access to the outside world, he could feel them slipping away. God would hold him accountable for this. If he failed to control the Nephilim, his punishment would be eternal damnation. The humiliation of such a fate horrified him. God would cast him into the sulfurous pit along with the Fallen that he so despised. He could never allow that to happen.

The prophecy had shown him a way out of his dilemma. God had spoken directly to him through the foretelling of a long-dead diviner. It was not his lot to wait patiently for the day when the Fallen would be banished to hell. He was to bring the heavenly kingdom to earth by whatever means necessary. That was what the Lord's sacred warriors had always done.

God was watching him, and Abraham would not disappoint his master. He would distinguish himself more than any diviner before him. His reward would be greater. His celestial rank would be higher. His name would be praised before angels and men alike. This was not pride on his part. It was God's will.

The day was coming soon when the Blessed Nephilim would redeem the world from the Fallen who now overran it. Men had forgotten how to fear the Lord. It was Abraham's destiny to remind them. Metcalf carefully returned his treasures to their compartments. "*In hoc signo vinces*," he whispered, shutting the safe behind him.

13 - DESTINY'S CHILD

Ever since Cassie floored the gas pedal to get away from that crazy old woman, her world had been spinning out of control. Every solid fact that she thought she knew about Sybil had been overturned. She could dismiss it all by saying that Faye had lied to her. That Sybil was a fine, upstanding citizen who bought and sold antiques. That she lived an absolutely ordinary life and never engaged in anything remotely risky. It was impossible for Cassie to believe that now. Too much had happened in the past weeks that defied explanation.

Not just about Sybil but about Cassie herself. The nightmare that accurately predicted her sister's death. The stone ruler that was stolen right before her eyes. Sybil's last letter to her. Everything Faye had told her. If that weren't enough, there was her encounter with the woman in white and her magic bowl. Cassie didn't know what any of it meant. She needed time to put things in perspective. To let the dust settle and see where it landed. In an effort to distance herself from the problem, she decided to do something a normal person might do. Talk to a friend.

The bell above the shop door jingled discretely when she walked into the antique store. At first, the memories of her last two visits hit her like a wave. A man with a gun, her sister falling, glass shattering, police swarming.

She took a deep breath and put on a brave smile. "Hi Rhonda, how are you?"

"Oh, sweetie, come here." Her sister's business partner rushed forward to embrace her. She was a motherly sort. Full-figured, in her fifties, with cropped black hair streaked with grey. She had a gentle, sympathetic face. The kind that encouraged confidences. At the moment, the concerned expression on Rhonda's face made Cassie's eyes well up with tears. The girl sternly ordered herself to think about newspapers, postage stamps, anything mundane. No more feelings for now.

She stepped away from the older woman. "I'm OK, Rhonda. Don't worry about me."

The concerned look didn't go away. "Are you sure?" Rhonda peered at her closely. "You look like you haven't slept for a week."

Cassie grinned sheepishly. "That would be about right, but really I feel OK." She changed the topic. "How have you been?"

Rhonda's eyes swept the shop. "Coping. It took a while to clean up the mess the police left. I think they're done hovering and asking questions. They seem satisfied that it was attempted robbery and that Sybil's death was an accident. I've beefed up the security system, and that's about all I can do."

"Do you think they'll ever catch the guy?" Cassie asked bleakly.

Rhonda sighed. "They didn't have much to go on. No physical description. No eyewitnesses. I'm not too hopeful." She put her arm around Cassie's shoulders. "Come on over here and sit down." She led the girl to a spare chair behind the counter. "We haven't had a chance to talk since ..." she trailed off.

"I know," Cassie said quietly.

"Would you like a bottle of water or something?"

"A can of soda if you've got any."

"Sure thing." Rhonda bustled to the refrigerator in the back room.

Cassie looked around the shop. The glass case had been replaced. No sign of anything being shattered—anything other than her own psyche. Everything was exactly as it should be in this upscale antique shop located in this high-toned boutique shopping district.

Rhonda handed Cassie her soft drink and pulled up a chair beside her.

"How's business?" Cassie flipped the tab on the can. It made a hissing sound.

Rhonda laughed ruefully. "A little slow, as you can guess. None of the usual customers wanted to appear morbidly curious, so everybody stayed away for a while. Now things are getting back to normal." She focused her attention on the girl. "Seriously, Cass, what are you going to do now? I know your sister would want you to stay in school."

"I know she would too." Cassie sighed. "But it's not that easy. I feel like I've just been sucked down into a whirlpool. I can't get a grip on anything. I don't even know which end is up right now. I think I need some time to get my bearings."

Rhonda patted her knee. "Of course, of course. That makes sense." She paused as a thought occurred to her. "You know that you're my partner in the business now."

Cassie felt startled. She hadn't stopped to think about her sister's will. Everything had been left to her. Between stocks and bank accounts, it had turned out to be a considerable amount of money. Enough to let her skate awhile without having to get a job or make any major life decisions. She'd forgotten about the joint ownership of the store.

"Do I owe you any money?" she asked warily.

Rhonda laughed. "Hardly. Your sister paid cash to buy her share."

Cassie took a sip of cola, considering the matter. "I don't think I want to keep her interest in the store. Too many bad memories."

The older woman nodded. "I understand. If you want me to buy back your share, I can do it. But it will have to be on the installment plan."

"We can work out the details some other day when my brain is actually… you know… functioning." Cassie finished off the rest of her soda.

The doorbell jingled again when a customer walked in. Rhonda smiled a greeting. Returning her attention to her visitor, she asked, "Are you going to stay in your dorm for a while?"

Cassie put her soda on the counter and slumped back in her chair. "No, I actually made a decision about that. For now, I'm going to move into Sybil's place. Take a few months and then decide if I want to go back to school in the fall."

"I suppose you need a timeout." Rhonda's voice sounded worried, but she made no other comment.

Changing the topic abruptly, Cassie asked, "How did you know you wanted to be an antique dealer?"

"How did I what?" Rhonda wasn't prepared for the shift.

"I mean were you always sure about what you wanted to be?"

"Oh, I see." Rhonda smiled knowingly. "I guess you must be feeling a little lost about where you're headed."

"Something like that."

"Well, I suppose it was just destiny."

"What?" Cassie sat bolt upright in her chair. There was that word again.

Rhonda registered surprise at the girl's reaction. "Everybody has a destiny, Cass."

"I don't," the girl said dismissively. "I haven't even picked a major yet."

"Sure, you do. You just don't know what it is. The destiny, I mean."

"How did you know?" Cassie urged.

Rhonda turned away for a moment to see what her prospective customer was up to. The woman was circling a Chippendale armchair. The shopkeeper turned her attention back to the conversation. "I had a summer job all through college in an antique store. I discovered that I liked it. After I graduated, the owner asked me to stay on full time."

"Sounds to me as if you fell into the business by chance and just stayed," Cassie observed.

"It might seem that way, but the arrangement always suited me just fine. I suppose if I'd been unhappy I would have tried something else, but I never wanted to. That's why I said it was destiny."

Cassie furrowed her brow, not following.

"I think it's like paddling a canoe," Rhonda explained. "If you're traveling with the current, it all feels easy and fun, and that's what following your destiny is like. If you decide to fight your destiny, it's like trying to paddle upstream against the current which is going to make you miserable."

Cassie felt exasperated. Rhonda was no help at all. "You think God decided ahead of time that you were supposed to own a store, and you decided it was easier to go with the flow than to fight it? Is that what you're telling me?"

The older woman shook her head. "I never said God had anything to do with it. Destiny isn't something unappealing forced on you by somebody else. It isn't brussels sprouts. It's a combination of your own interest and aptitude. It just so happens that I love what I do, and I'm very, very good at it."

The girl persisted. "But how did you know when you first started out that you were headed in the right direction?"

The customer was walking toward the counter with a Spode teapot. Rhonda got out of her chair to assist her. "In a nutshell, it just felt right."

"Meaning you trusted your instincts," Cassie observed cautiously.

Rhonda nodded. "Yes, that's a good way to put it. I trusted my instincts." She went to the cash register to ring up the sale.

"Hmmm…" Cassie said to herself.

14 - LATTE QUESTIONS

Faye carefully backed her late model station wagon into a parallel parking space. She'd almost forgotten how to do that. It was a skill that wasn't needed much in the outlying area where she lived. This day, she had ventured into one of the northern suburbs of the city. It had been devoured so long ago by the metropolis that one couldn't tell them apart. The suburb had a different name than the city proper, but it looked the same—congested streets blanketed with a thick layer of air pollution.

The old woman stepped to the curb and fed the parking meter. She was dressed in her Sunday best today—a floral cotton frock with pearl buttons down the front. Since the weather was still mild, she topped the dress with a light pink cardigan. Faye believed that one should always wear a hat in public. She had chosen a straw brimmed cloche with a green silk band around the middle.

Toddling down the street for half a block, she arrived at her destination. A shop with the unusual name of Buzz 'n Books. It was a two-story vintage bookstore that served coffee. Unlike its chain store rivals, however, this one seemed to have a personality. The building in which it was housed was about a century old. The brick exterior was in need of tuckpointing. The front door was glass and painted wood, but the wood was so warped that the door stuck when one tried to pull the brass handle. To Faye, this was a sign that only serious readers should venture inside. She proceeded to do so.

The interior was dark and smelled of espresso and old paper. It was a good smell. One that was oddly comforting. The coffee bar was to her left as she entered. The back half of the shop consisted of floor to ceiling bookcases lined up in rows. At the front of the store, near the plate glass windows were several tables occupied by people with computers. They were probably "surfing the net" as the saying went.

She looked around. He wasn't here. Her eyes focused on an open stairway leading to a loft. Faye sighed. Oh well, she would get her exercise today. She hobbled up the stairs to the second floor. There were more bookcases on the back wall, more tables in the center of the room and a solitary figure seated at one of them. It was his day off, and she hated to interrupt his free time, but this couldn't wait. He was poring over a page in a volume big enough to be an encyclopedia. A man in his early twenties. He was dressed neatly in a V-neck grey sweater over a white dress shirt and striped tie. Despite the casual nature of the establishment, he wore trousers instead of jeans. His hair was light brown, and it curled around his temples. At the moment, he was running his fingers distractedly through it and mumbling to himself. "No, that can't be right. I shall have to cross-check this in Robinson's Compendium." He spoke with a British public-school accent.

"Griffin?" Faye approached cautiously. She was wary of disturbing him when he was researching. It tended to disorient him.

"What?" The young man looked up. His hazel eyes were blank as if he didn't recognize his visitor. When his mind returned to the present, he looked alarmed. "Oh, Faye, do forgive me!" He jumped out of his chair and came around the table to help her to a seat.

"May I get you something? A coffee perhaps?" He bent his six-foot frame nearly in half to hover attentively at her side.

"Yes, I could use a pick-me-up. It was quite a drive." Faye laid her purse on the table.

"Of course, absolutely." Griffin had flown halfway down the stairs before he whirled around and asked, "What kind?"

Faye looked puzzled. "I don't understand."

He trotted back up to the loft. "I mean what kind of coffee would you like? Columbian, Sumatran, Ethiopian? Would you like light or dark roast? And then there's the question of temperature. Hot or iced. And what about milk? Soy, rice, or cow's milk? And what size cup do you want?"

"Oh, my," she murmured. "So many choices. In my day we just said coffee, and everybody knew what we meant."

Griffin waited nervously.

"Why don't you surprise me?" Faye's smile was angelic.

A look of dread crossed the young man's face at the prospect of surprising her.

"Just do your best, dear. I'm sure whatever you choose will be fine."

Griffin nodded uncertainly and ran down the stairs to fetch her beverage.

Faye looked around the loft. Very quiet. Noise didn't seem to filter up from the lower floor, and all the other customers were seated below. She knew Griffin was a solitary creature which was the reason he chose to sequester himself in this aerie. Less chance of being disturbed. That suited her needs perfectly considering what they were about to discuss.

The young man returned in a few minutes bearing an oversized cup and saucer. "I didn't think you'd enjoy anything extreme, so I made a conservative choice." He set it down in front of her. "There you are. A hot cup of medium roast Brazilian with cow's cream."

He returned to his seat and watched in apprehensive silence as she took her first sip.

Faye nodded her approval. "This is really very good. Just the way I like it. Brazilian, you say?"

Griffin relaxed and flashed a smile. "Yes, the trick, you see, is in the roasting process. A medium roast will give just enough body without overpowering the palate."

"Heavens, it sounds as if you're discussing wine." She laughed.

"In a way, I suppose they're quite similar. Coffee drinking in this country is a very serious business."

She took another sip. "What do you drink when you go back to England for visits?"

"Instant coffee."

"Really?" Faye sounded shocked. "Can't you get anything better?"

"Oh, it's quite normal, I assure you. Europeans drink it all the time. And with no ill effects, I might add."

Faye gave a half smile. She wasn't convinced of his enthusiasm.

Griffin sighed guiltily. "All right. You've caught me out. I confess I prefer the marvelous variety one finds in American coffeehouses."

Faye made a mental note. Given his high-strung behavior, she wondered if he liked American-style coffee a bit too much for his own good. Of course, she was polite and didn't tell him that. Instead, she opened her purse to retrieve a thick envelope which she slid across the table. "What do you make of that?" she asked.

Griffin removed the envelope's contents. He scanned the photographs with growing excitement. "I say, is this what I think it is?"

Faye nodded gravely.

"But this is brilliant!" He shuffled through them again before placing them on the tabletop side by side. "Fascinating pictograms."

"Can you translate any of them?"

He shook his head, still intent on the pictures. "Sorry, but I haven't a clue what they mean."

"You will try though, won't you?" she urged.

Griffin looked up and stared at Faye, bringing his mind back into focus. "Oh, absolutely! This is quite exciting, isn't it? We had no idea what object Sybil was recovering, and here we sit with photographs of it." He scowled for a moment. "By the bye, how do you come to have these?"

"Cassie brought them with her when she visited me." Faye sounded troubled.

The young man took note. "Didn't your talk go well?"

"It went very well. During the course of the afternoon, I discovered that she is our new pythia."

"What!"

Griffin's exclamation was so loud that Faye winced. "Please, dear, keep your voice down. We do belong to a secret society, after all."

The young man overcompensated by lowering his voice to a whisper. "But this is incredible, Faye! This is beyond coincidence! If I believed in such things, I would call it a miracle."

Faye sighed. "It is certainly a stroke of good fortune for us, but Cassie is having some trouble coming to terms with it."

Griffin's face took on a look of owlish concern. "You mean she doesn't want to be the pythia?" He sounded as if he could barely comprehend such a possibility.

"I think she needs time to accept her new role. I do believe that she'll come around in the end."

"But what if she doesn't?" Griffin's tone was anxious. "What are we to do then?"

Faye remained serene. "I am quite confident she will reconsider. After all, we are the only people who can give her the answers she seeks about her sister's death. I expect her to realize that soon enough." She picked up the page with random numbers scribbled across it and pushed it toward him. "Cassie thinks these are the dimensions of the object in the photographs."

The young man took the page and puzzled over it for a few moments. "Dimensions, but why—"

Faye cut in. "I think Sybil wanted us to build a replica in case we no longer had the original."

"But why should we want a replica?" Griffin was mystified.

The old woman picked up one of the photos and contemplated it. "Cassie gave me a hint when she talked about our elusive cowboy. She had a dream in which she saw the encounter in the antique shop. She said he wanted Sybil to tell him where the key was. When he ransacked her apartment, he took only this stone ruler. I would assume it is some kind of key. In order for us to know what it unlocks, we would need an exact copy. Do you think you could make one using the measurements I've given you?"

The young man became pensive. "I can't do it myself, of course, but I think there are a few chaps at the vault who may have the necessary skills. I'll get in touch with them first thing tomorrow."

Faye took another sip of coffee. She chose her next words carefully. "I believe building this replica should be your top priority."

"Well, of course," Griffin readily agreed. "It's quite a fascinating puzzle, isn't it?"

"It's more than that," Faye countered in a low voice. "It may have something to do with the Sage Stone."

"What!" Griffin half rose out of his chair at the mention of those words.

This time a few curious people on the lower level glanced upward toward the loft.

Faye raised her eyebrows but said nothing.

"Very sorry." Griffin cleared his throat uncomfortably and resettled himself. He leaned in closer across the table. "How can you be sure this object is connected to…" he trailed off as if afraid to utter the words.

"I can't be sure. Simply an offhanded comment Sybil made several months ago. She said she was on the trail of 'the find of the century.' Since I hear that phrase from field operatives almost every week, I didn't pay much attention. Until now. I believe she may have been right. We need to be certain before I alarm anyone else, so you'll have to proceed with the utmost secrecy."

"You haven't even told Maddie?"

"No, and I won't until we know what we're dealing with." Faye sighed. "For the time being, I want a semblance of normality to prevail. Especially when it comes to Cassie. She shouldn't be pulled into this maelstrom unless it becomes absolutely necessary."

"But Faye," the young man protested. "I'm a terrible liar!"

"I'm not asking you to lie, my dear. I'm asking you to avoid the topic with your colleagues and refrain from mentioning it to the girl altogether. As an added precaution, I think it would be wise to accelerate the training of our new pythia if, and when, she agrees to join us. Poor child! She'll have only weeks to learn what it took Sybil years to master."

Griffin lowered his head in acquiescence.

Faye glanced down at the photo of the key resting next to her coffee cup. "One person has already died because of this object. If this key can somehow lead the Nephilim to the Sage Stone, then one death will be only the beginning."

15 – PARANORMAL ANTIQUITY

Two weeks after she fled the place in terror, Cassie found herself standing on Faye's front porch once again. Somehow, she had talked herself around to this spot despite her misgivings. She knocked on the door.

After a few moments, Faye appeared. She was wearing a kitchen apron. Her cheeks and forearms were streaked with flour. When she saw who her visitor was, a perceptive smile crossed her face. "Come in, my dear, come in. I've just popped a few loaves of bread into the oven. They won't be ready for a while, but I can fix you a sandwich if you're hungry."

The girl entered the house hesitantly. "No, thanks. I just want to talk. There's a lot I need to say."

"Why don't we go out into the garden then," Faye suggested.

Cassie nodded and followed the old woman to the yard. By now, leaves had formed around the wisteria blossoms, and tulips and daffodils were starting to join the ranks of early spring flowers. It was a little cooler and more overcast than their last visit but still warm enough to be pleasant.

The girl hesitated before seating herself. It was the same chair she'd sat in when her brain collapsed into somebody else's consciousness. It wasn't a happy association. She braced herself and sat down.

Faye took the opposite chair. She wasn't hiding any mystic bowls in the shrubs this time, Cassie noted with relief.

"I guess I ought to start," the girl began abruptly. "I'm sorry about the way I acted last time I was here."

Faye chuckled. "No harm done, my dear. Now, what is it you'd like to talk about?"

"This pythia business. I need to find out more about it."

"Then you don't know what a pythia is?" Faye didn't sound entirely surprised.

Cassie shook her head.

"Wait here, and I'll show you a picture." The old woman shuffled back inside the house. It was several minutes before she emerged with a book. She placed it on the table between them and flipped to a page that had been tabbed. "Look," she instructed.

Cassie leaned over and gasped. The page contained an illustration showing a cup decorated with two figures dressed in ancient Greek costume. The first was a woman in white seated on a high stool. She held a shallow bowl in one hand and a laurel branch in the other. The second figure was a man in a toga who stood facing her. "That's…that's…" Cassie stammered.

"Yes, dear. That's the woman you saw in your vision, isn't it?" Faye didn't seem to find Cassie's revelation startling.

"But how…" The girl was still at a loss.

"Let me explain." Faye settled back in her chair. "Around 3000 BCE, on the slopes of Mount Parnassus in what is now Greece, there was a place called Pytho. At this place stood a temple dedicated to the great mother goddess. The goddess was known by many names throughout the ancient world, but she was always worshipped by the people as their principal deity. They used the word Goddess with a capital G to describe her the way we use the word God. Up until quite recently, you see, most people thought that the creator of the universe was female.

"Beneath the temple at Pytho was an underground cave which the people of the region believed to be the center of the universe. This cave housed a round stone called the *omphalos*. The word '*omphalos*' means navel, and it was called that because the stone was considered to be the navel of the world. It was guarded by a great serpent named Python. Contrary to what you might expect, Python was female. She was the daughter of the great goddess, and she protected both the omphalos and the oracle who dwelt at her temple. This oracle was known far and wide because of the accuracy of her predictions. She was called the pythia.

"This state of affairs continued for many centuries, but around 2200 BCE the area began to change. Do you remember those outcast tribes I told you about last time you were here?"

Cassie gave her a quizzical look. "You mean the tribes who morphed into professional pillagers?"

"Yes, quite so," affirmed Faye. "Those tribes had figured out how to domesticate the horse and use it for warfare. They were able to expand their range of conquest, and many of them moved away from their harsh homeland. Some began migrating into Europe, down through the Balkans and on into Greece. The tribes that reached Greece were called Hellenes, and they displaced the original inhabitants who were known as Pelasgians. The transformation took a long time to accomplish. Over fifteen hundred years passed during which the Hellenes fought amongst themselves vying for more land. At some point during their perpetual power struggles, they invaded Pytho. They claimed the temple of the great goddess for themselves and rewrote the history of the place. Instead of a site to honor the goddess, the invaders said it was a site to honor their god Apollo."

"Isn't that the Greek sun god?" asked Cassie.

Faye nodded. "I see you know a little classical mythology. According to the Hellenes, the god Apollo fought a great battle and defeated the serpent Python. When Apollo killed Python, he threw her body into a chasm in the ground. The rotting corpse emitted fumes up through a crack in the earth. In fact, the word Python derives from the Greek verb *pythein* which means 'to rot.'"

Cassie felt keen interest at those words. "That was the smoke I saw coming up through the cave floor. It made me dizzy to breathe it."

"That's right," the old woman agreed. "Recent geological studies have shown that the crack in the earth at that spot may have emitted some kind of noxious gas. It might have been methane, or carbon dioxide, or even hydrogen sulfide which would have smelled like rotten eggs. At close quarters, the fumes would probably have been hallucinogenic, and these may be responsible for the strange visions the prophetess received. It was said that the air in the cavern shortened her lifespan. Once a pythia died another would rise to take her place."

"Just like Sybil and me," Cassie observed quietly.

Faye's face held a troubled expression. "No one expected it to be you, child."

"Go on. Tell me the rest of the story." The girl's voice was flat. "What happened after Apollo killed the serpent."

The old woman complied. "Although Apollo and the Hellenes could do away with Python, it was much harder to get rid of the pythia. Her fame was so great in the region that the Pelasgians would have rebelled if she disappeared. The invaders had no choice but to incorporate her into their new myth. She remained at the temple which was now dedicated to the worship of the sun god. The location was no longer called Pytho but Delphi which is derived from the Greek word for "womb." A distant reminder of the mother goddess whose home it had been before Apollo arrived. The pythia became known as the Oracle of Delphi."

"That's a name I've heard of." Cassie registered surprise. "She was supposed to be the most famous oracle in the ancient world. People would come from all around the Mediterranean to have her tell their fortunes. That is if you believe in that sort of thing. Nobody important made a move without consulting the oracle first."

"Yes, that's true," Faye agreed. "Her influence in classical Greece continued from about 700 BCE until 395 CE when the Roman emperor ordered her temple to be officially closed. It was no small achievement for a woman's words to have such power in the overlord cultures of the ancient world."

"Overlord cultures?" Cassie asked. She had never heard the expression before.

"It's our term for the rootless tribes who wandered the earth and grew powerful by waging wars of aggression. Their entire way of life depended on exploitation and tyranny, so we call them overlord cultures."

"What's this ancient pythia got to do with me?"

"Ah," Faye smiled. "We've come to the point at last."

At that moment a distant beeping sound could be heard from inside the house. "Oh my, that's the timer for my bread." Faye hastily struggled to her feet. "I think we should continue this discussion inside."

***

Cassie watched as Faye turned out the loaves onto cooling racks. The aroma was heavenly. She'd never seen a real homemade loaf of bread being baked before. Sybil and her hired housekeepers hadn't been much for cooking. The closest they ever came to homemade was dough from a can.

Because Faye had persuaded Cassie to eat something, the girl now sat at the table in front of an array of raw vegetables, dip, potato chips and a tall glass of iced tea. Faye was stirring around the kitchen and putting her baking supplies away.

"You were starting to talk about how the pythia legend applies to me?" Cassie prompted.

"Oh yes, quite right." Faye stowed a bag of flour in one of the overhead cabinets. "Just as the Pelasgians and the Hellenes relied on the counsel of their pythia, we rely on the advice of ours to help us authenticate our finds."

"Then what you call a pythia is sort of a psychic bloodhound?"

The old woman moved to the sink to wash out a mixing bowl. She chuckled. "I suppose that's one way of saying it."

"I don't believe in the paranormal," Cassie said dismissively.

Faye paused in her clean-up operation to study the girl's face for a few moments. "Then how do you explain your dream about Sybil? Your vision of the oracle?"

Cassie shrugged though she seemed unwilling to meet the old woman's eyes. "Everyone has bad dreams. Maybe I've got an overactive imagination. Maybe I'm just plain crazy."

Faye smiled briefly. "And it would be easier for you to question your own sanity rather than to believe in the unseen?"

The girl remained silent, so the old woman continued. "The human brain has many functions. Some logical, some intuitive. Unfortunately, the modern world has rejected one half of the brain's functions in favor of the other. We put our faith in science, and science puts its faith in logic. At least it did until Newtonian physics fell out of favor. We don't live in a clockwork universe after all."

"What?" Cassie looked up blankly.

Faye laughed. "I'm sorry, my dear. I didn't mean to travel so far afield, but I'm trying to explain that your dismissal of intuitive phenomena cuts you off from the untapped potential of your own mind. Why do you think so many ancient cultures relied on shamans, oracles, and faith healers? It wasn't quaint superstition. These practitioners of the paranormal arts possessed real power. They understood how the mind actually works and were able to maximize its potential for the benefit of their people. Modern science's contempt for the magical has created an unproductive skepticism in the mind of the average person. Quantum physics is now beginning to explain the connection between spirit and matter. Yesterday's magic is fast becoming tomorrow's science. I'm asking you to move past what you've been trained to believe and try to keep an open mind. Can you do that?"

Cassie relented slightly. "OK, I suppose I can try. But it seems like you're putting a lot of faith in what's going on in somebody else's head. What if your pythia is having a bad day, and the radio signal to the great beyond is scrambled? They might say something is ancient when it's not."

"The pythia is only our starting point." Faye finished rinsing the bowl and put it in the dish drainer. "We balance intuition with factual evidence. We don't rely solely on her impressions. We validate everything she tells us."

"You said 'she.' Is it always a she?" Cassie selected a carrot stick from the platter on the table. She bit into it with a loud crunch.

Faye began to wipe down the kitchen counter with a dish cloth. "Not necessarily, though in the past it has tended to be that way. Women's brains work a little differently than men's. With regard to the skills required of a pythia, it seems to be an advantage to be female."

"Interesting." Cassie moved on to an equally crunchy stick of celery. "Tell me how this works. Does the pythia find the relic herself or do you give her something you think is a relic and let her tell you what it is?"

Faye paused and tilted her head to consider the matter. "A little bit of both actually. Sometimes she'll feel a strong pull to investigate a site and will unearth the relic herself. More often than not, we acquire things through the private antiquities market and bring them to her for identification."

Cassie sipped her tea. "How can you be sure she's right?"

"Once she's told us some of the basic details of an object, we can validate its age, place of origin, probable context, and come to some conclusion about her accuracy."

"Is that what you did with me? Validate?" Cassie asked cautiously.

Faye removed her apron and shook the flour from it before hanging it on a wall hook. She caught a glimpse of her flour-streaked face in the hanging mirror and hastily wiped the smudges away before continuing. "Yes, I already knew what the bowl was before I asked you to touch it. When you described it accurately with no help from me, then I was certain."

Cassie changed the subject. "I pick up objects all day long. Why don't I go into a trance every time I touch something that belongs to somebody else?"

"We have no explanation for that." Faye reached across the table to test the temperature of the cooling bread. "It seems to be a function of our pythia that her gift applies only to ancient antiquities."

Cassie registered relief. "That's good to know. I don't think I could explain trances in a grocery store whenever the checkout clerk hands me my change. How many of these antiquities have you gotten so far?"

"Thousands, perhaps millions," Faye said offhandedly as she began to sweep the kitchen floor.

The girl felt stunned. "Millions?"

"Our organization has been in existence for centuries. My predecessors were very industrious."

"Then you must have a huge warehouse to store all of it." Cassie's voice grew eager. "Can I go there?"

Faye stopped sweeping. She seemed to be struggling to choose the right words. "Cassie, I have an obligation to protect our treasures. If their location became known to people who want to destroy us, it would be a disaster."

"You mean the cowboy who went after Sybil." The girl's tone was solemn.

The old woman sighed. "There are people in the world who find our knowledge threatening. It contradicts their basic beliefs about the way things have always been and the way they're meant to be." She stared directly at the girl. "So, you see, I can't reveal any more information unless I know you are willing to help our cause. Will you do that? Will you join us?"

Cassie hesitated, at a loss for words.

The old woman read her expression. "I'm sorry, child. I didn't mean to force you to decide this minute. There really isn't a blood oath or anything like that. I just need your promise that you will protect our identity and the location of our treasures."

The girl let out a huge sigh. She stared at the table instead of looking directly at Faye. Her hair fell forward over her face. "Here's the thing. I'm not sure I buy what you're doing or how important it is. I don't care about any of it very much. The only thing I did care about was my sister, and I care that some random guy in a cowboy hat took her away from me."

She paused. "You and your people worked with Sybil every day. You saw a side of her that I never knew existed. Probably understood her better than I ever did."

Cassie stood up abruptly. She felt tears welling up, so she went to stand by the sink, looking out the kitchen window. "What I'm trying to say is that by helping you, I might feel like I'm still connected to my family somehow. Still connected to the world because, honestly, now that Sybil is gone, I don't feel as if I belong anywhere." She turned back to face Faye and smiled self-consciously. "I guess there was a 'yes' buried somewhere in all that rambling. Yes, I'll help and maybe helping you will help me feel less alone."

Faye walked over and wrapped her arm around Cassie's shoulder. "You were never alone, child. We were always looking out for you. Even before you knew we existed." She squeezed the girl's shoulder gently. "We are called the Arkana. Welcome to our family."

16 – TROUBLESOME RELATIONS

Abraham had waited, albeit impatiently, for Daniel to provide some insight into the mysterious stone object that was his newest prize. His son was gone much of the time now, working ceaselessly in the libraries of the Fallen. Every few days, Metcalf would ask for a progress report, but nothing had come to light yet. He had prayed every day on his knees that God would grant his son the knowledge he required. Apparently, the Lord was testing his faith. His prayers went unanswered.

He thought it might be best to turn to other matters. He had a flock to manage — both in the compound and abroad. It was time he paid more attention to day-to-day affairs. Perhaps that was the Lord's intention in denying him.

Daniel's lack of progress in translation wasn't the only matter troubling Metcalf. His son's lack of progeny was distressing, even embarrassing, considering who his father was. A son of the diviner was expected to be foremost in advancing the angelic kingdom. More than that, the Lord had spoken to him in a dream. The Almighty had told Abraham that he was watching him and would hold him to strict account for his son's failure. Metcalf was determined to get to the bottom of this.

The old man marched decisively to the nursery where the wives with small children spent their time. There were a dozen women managing the business of toddlers who outnumbered them four to one. They were dressed alike in gray shifts and white aprons—the garb of married women. The wives all saw him at the same time and rose as one body.

"Good morning, Father Abraham," they said in unison.

He nodded in acknowledgement. "I wish to have a word with Annabeth."

His eyes focused on a timid blond woman of about twenty standing far back in the corner. She was holding a girl who was about a year old. Another woman rushed forward to take the child from her.

Annabeth swallowed hard and walked forward timidly. "Here I am, Father."

"Come with me." Without waiting for a sign of assent, he turned on his heel and left the room, expecting her to trail in his wake.

He swung around to face her outside the common room. "Where are your quarters?"

Awed by all this direct attention from the diviner, Annabeth had difficulty forming a coherent sentence. "Th… there. O… over that way. I mean… that is… in that direction, Father." She pointed down another corridor.

"Show me," Metcalf ordered. "We will talk there."

With a sidelong glance of dread, Annabeth led the way. She obviously feared she was in serious trouble if the diviner had sought her out and wanted to speak privately. When she reached her door, she hesitated, looking over her shoulder at him. Then she stood aside and allowed him to enter ahead of her.

Abraham assessed his surroundings. The room was simply furnished as were all the sleeping chambers in the compound. A double bed with bleached white sheets and a pine dresser. A plain wooden cross hung above the headboard. His eyes traveled to the opposite wall. There was no crib. All the older children slept in dormitories, but those under the age of two remained with their mothers. That meant the child Annabeth had been holding was not hers. Two chairs faced each other across a small square table, occupying the space where a crib should have been. Abraham noted approvingly that his son's picture hung on the wall above the table. That showed a fitting respect on Annabeth's part.

The young woman stood gawking at him, unsure of what he expected. "Sit down," he ordered. She scurried to comply, and he took the chair opposite her.

"Annabeth, when did I assign you to be my son's wife?"

She hesitated as if she were solving a difficult mathematical equation. "I think it was… no… let me see… umm… it would have been uh… f... five years ago, Father."

Metcalf leaned forward over the table. "And what is your rank among his wives?"

"We are all of equal rank since we've all borne an equal number of children. Each of us has had one."

Metcalf was nonplussed by her answer. A wife's rank was determined by the number of offspring she produced. It was also a good indication of which wife a man favored most. He had started his inquiry with Daniel's most recent wife since the newest tended to receive the most attention from their husbands. But he could tell nothing from this line of questioning. He still didn't know which wife was the weak link in Daniel's chain.

Abraham forced a smile. He wanted to put the woman at ease. "Perhaps you can help me understand this. You say each of you has had one child. One?" He let the word hang in the air between them.

Annabeth clasped and unclasped her hands. Apparently, she was fighting an urge to bite her nails. They were already bitten to the quick. "Yes, Father. We have prayed for more issue. All of us. Daniel has instructed us to do that, and we have. Every day. We have."

"Is your child the youngest of my son's offspring?"

Annabeth cleared her throat. "Yes, that's right. She is three years old."

"She." Metcalf allowed a note of disappointment to creep into his voice.

The woman looked down at the table, flustered. "All Daniel's children are girls, Father. All three of them. They are good girls, too. They never misbehave. They are pure in the eyes of the Lord."

Abraham folded his arms and sat back in his chair, considering the facts he'd just been given. Something was quite amiss here. "Annabeth, when was the last time you and my son had relations?"

Obviously, the woman had been dreading that he might ask this question. She looked at the floor, at the walls, at every spot in the room other than into Metcalf's eyes.

"It has been some t… time, Father," she faltered.

"How long, precisely?"

"Since before my daughter was born, sir."

Abraham was appalled. "But that would be years, woman!"

"Yes, sir" she nodded vigorously. "About f… four years."

Metcalf made an effort to control his temper. He wanted more information. Again, he forced himself to smile. "You are one of the Lord's chosen, Annabeth. A consecrated bride. Do you understand that?"

She seemed to relax a bit. "That is what our holy books say. We are not like the Fallen. We have been selected from among all the women of the earth to be God's chosen vessels. It is through my children and the children of my Consecrated sisters that the Blessed Nephilim will increase the angelic kingdom."

"Very true. Yet you are failing in your duty to increase the kingdom."

"But—"

"Let me continue." Metcalf held up his hand to silence her. "It is often the case with a young husband that one of his wives can be overbearing."

A look of panic crossed Annabeth's face. "I… oh no, Father. Never! I would never do that!"

"As I was saying, if a wife is of a headstrong nature, she may intimidate her husband, and he will not seek her company."

"But I—"

Metcalf cut her off. "Annabeth, do you know what a consecrated bride's principal duty is?"

"Of course, Father, of course. It is her principal duty in life to marry and bear her husband's angelic offspring." She recited the words as if by rote.

"And do you think you have fulfilled the duty of a consecrated bride?" he asked quietly.

"I have always—"

He broke in once more. "Perhaps you should search your conscience a little more. Perhaps you don't deserve to be counted among the consecrated." Abraham stood up and towered over her. "You must pray, Annabeth."

She looked up at him confusedly. "Father?"

"I want you to get on your knees now and ask the Lord to give you a more pliable disposition."

"Just as you wish, Father." She scrambled out of the chair and knelt beside the table.

"You must ask God to change your unruly temperament so that you may win back your husband's affections."

The woman bit her lip to keep it from quivering. Tears began to run down her cheeks.

Abraham turned his back and walked toward the door. "You must pray unceasingly, Annabeth. God is watching you. He is watching us all."

17 – OLD SCHOOL

Cassie was venturing into unknown territory. She had been driving for over an hour in a northwest direction. There was a map spread open on the passenger seat along with a page of hastily scrawled driving directions that Faye had given her over the phone. She was outside the metro area and off into farm country, only this didn't look like any part of Illinois that she'd seen before. Instead of flat cornfields, everything was hilly and wooded. "The place where the last glacier melted" was the way Faye had described it. The place where mountains of ice had carved hills and valleys and lakes and rivers into Illinois' otherwise dull topography.

She passed through villages that might have been thriving a hundred years earlier, then crossed railroad tracks and bridges over rivers. The scenery became more wooded the farther she traveled—the roads became narrower and the traffic sparser. Eventually, she was driving on roads with no center line, and then roads with no shoulder, and finally on a road that was unpaved. Trees arched overhead, blocking out the sun. The underbrush on either side scraped against the doors of her car. In a small clearing, the dirt road ended abruptly. Noon sun flooded the glade with light, and at its center stood a two-story white frame building. There was a bell tower over the front entrance.

Cassie didn't see a No Trespassing sign to keep intruders away, so she pulled her car over to one side of the clearing, got out, and walked toward the building. It looked like something out of a Norman Rockwell painting—an old-fashioned country schoolhouse. The structure was at least a century old though the age was hard to guess because it was so well-maintained. The exterior had been recently painted, and the grass was neatly trimmed. Hyacinth bloomed around the foundation. Cassie couldn't see any other cars. Nobody seemed to be around.

The girl began to feel troubled. She still wasn't entirely sure why she was going along with this or what she was going to see here. She felt defensive and on guard. "Proceed with caution," she instructed herself.

Cassie walked up the three stairs leading to double front doors. Just as she touched the handle, the doors swung open. A young man in his early twenties with curly brown hair poked his head around the side and came to stand in front of her.

"Come in, please, come in. We've been expecting you. My name is Griffin." He spoke with a British accent. "And you must be Cassie." He held out his hand and shook hers briefly. "Faye has told me all about you, and may I say how pleased I am to meet you at last!"

Even though his words were cordial, something about the reserved tone of his voice put Cassie a bit further on her guard. Maybe he was just being British, or maybe he felt uneasy in her presence for reasons she couldn't quite figure out.

There was an awkward pause while they sized up one another for a few seconds. Cassie thought he was kind of good looking if a person could get past his twitchiness. She saw that he was dressed more formally than she was. He wore navy blue trousers, a white shirt, V-neck sweater and a striped tie. She felt as if she ought to be wearing a dress and heels instead of jeans, a sweater, and hiking boots.

"Right then," Griffin forged ahead. "Please do come in. Maddie was taking an important phone call, or she would have come down to meet you herself. This way, if you will."

They walked through a small vestibule and on into the main room. The ceiling was about twelve feet high with globe chandeliers suspended from heavy chains. Tall stained-glass windows took up the top half of each side wall. They ought to have given the building a churchlike quality, but the scenes depicted in the windows all came from nature. Bright green forests, azure waterfalls, silver lilies, and golden birds cast prismatic light across the center of the room. Right below the windows were several tiers of what looked like box seats.

"I thought this was an old schoolhouse from the outside," Cassie said as she took stock of her surroundings.

Griffin bobbed his head in agreement. "Yes, you're quite right. This was a schoolhouse about a hundred and fifty years ago."

"Kind of big and oddly furnished for an out-of-the-way rural schoolhouse," the girl observed.

"It doubled as the town hall when there was a town out this way. That's all vanished now, of course. Railroads took the place of river transportation, and the towns around waterways disappeared. And we've done some remodeling as well. The stained glass is new."

Cassie's attention turned to the center of the room. She expected to see rows of student desks, but there weren't any. Instead, she was confronted with a polished round table big enough to seat thirty people. She counted the chairs just to be sure. There were thirty of them.

"You hold Renaissance fairs here?" she asked dryly.

"I beg your pardon?" Griffin looked confused.

"You know, King Arthur, knights of the round table, et cetera."

"Oh, I see." He laughed self-consciously. "No, not as such. Actually, Arthur and his knights were not Renaissance figures." He pronounced "Renaissance" like "ReNAYsonce."

"They were most probably sixth century, but there is no scholarly consensus on the exact date. In point of fact, King Arthur and the knights of the round table are more closely associated with the Middle Ages than with the Renaissance. Perhaps because Geoffrey of Monmouth's *Historia Regum Britanniae* was written in the twelfth century and popularized in the courts of Europe at that time. Of course, Welsh and Breton folktales about King Arthur do predate Mallory's book. And then you have Chretien de Troyes adding the legend of Lancelot and the Holy Grail. Well, as you can see…"

He trailed off when he noticed the glazed expression on Cassie's face. "Sorry, more information than you could possibly require. I have an unfortunate tendency to provide irrelevant detail. I do beg your pardon." He checked his verbal torrent and stood looking at her in mute embarrassment.

Cassie turned away to glance around the entire room. "This is it? This is the giant vault Fay was telling me about? An empty schoolhouse with fancy bleachers and a big table?"

"Hardly." Griffin gave her a thin smile. "Faye thought it best to introduce you to us in stages. Today you're here to learn about the organization, not the vault. Don't want to overwhelm you all at once. This way, please."

Their footsteps made the oak floorboards creak as they crossed the main room to a door at the opposite end. It led to a short corridor that ran widthwise across the back of the building. At either end were exit doors and stairways that led up to the second floor.

Cassie followed her guide upstairs to stand in a short hallway that mirrored the one below. To their left was a corridor that ran the length of the building. As they walked down the hall, Cassie glanced through the open doorways on either side. There were conference rooms and offices with desks, but they were all empty. Nobody else was about, and none of the rooms gave a hint of the kind of business that was conducted here.

Griffin continued walking to an unmarked door at the far end of the corridor. Cassie guessed it must be positioned right above the entry vestibule.

"Just a bit farther," he said reassuringly. "In here." He opened the door to reveal a spiral staircase. "We're going up to the bell tower."

They could hear a voice echoing down to them. It was a gravelly female voice, and it was raised in anger.

Griffin smiled nervously. "That's our operations director. Don't worry. Her bark is far worse than her bite. You have to take some of what she says with a grain of salt."

"And let the chips fall where they may?" Cassie asked wryly.

"What?" Griffin looked puzzled.

"I thought we were swapping clichés." She laughed.

"Oh, yes, of course. How stupid of me." He cleared his throat and looked at his shoes. "Very amusing."

"I'm sorry, I didn't mean to offend you." Cassie felt instantly guilty.

"No, certainly, you didn't." He rushed to reassure her. "It's me. I always…" He trailed off and then changed the subject. "Well, up we go." He tried to sound cheerful as they climbed to the top of the staircase.

18 – THE WORLD ACCORDING TO MADDIE

Cassie peeked above the final spiral stair. To her surprise, she found herself emerging in the middle of the bell tower. It was a bell tower in name only because the room had been remodeled, and there was no bell anywhere to be seen. The open-air tower had been fitted with glass picture windows. It was a bright, airy space, or it would have been if not for the smell of cigarette smoke. The atmosphere was thick with it. Cassie was about to make a comment, but Griffin anticipated her.

"She would resign if we didn't let her smoke somewhere in the building," he whispered. His tone was apologetic.

The room was comfortably furnished with chairs and couches and tables.

"Is this her office?" Cassie asked in disbelief.

"No, her office is downstairs. This is a lounge area."

"A smoker's lounge?"

"That wasn't our original intention, but you'll discover it's very hard to say no to Maddie."

They advanced into the room. There was a woman seated on a sofa near the front window. She was talking on the phone but gestured for them to draw closer. "Uh huh. Uh huh. Well, you can tell him from me that he'll get paid when he delivers. No, that's not negotiable. Just tell him, all right?" She slammed down the receiver, looking irritated.

Griffin stepped forward. "Cassie, allow me to introduce Maddie, our operations director."

Maddie rose to greet them. Her bangle bracelets clanked. She towered over Cassie and matched Griffin's height which was about six feet. She looked to be in her fifties with an olive brown complexion and bushy hair that had been dyed a burgundy shade of red. When they shook hands, it made Cassie wince. Maddie's grip was as powerful as her physique.

"My name's Madeleine, but everybody calls me Maddie." There was a piercing quality to her eyes. Sharp and dark like obsidian arrowheads. "Have a seat." She indicated a spot next to her on the couch.

Griffin remained standing. He looked at Maddie questioningly. "You'll show her out when you're done?"

She nodded.

"Right, I'll leave you to it then. Until next time, Cassie."

"Bye, Griffin."

Maddie was scrutinizing a piece of paper and apparently wasn't pleased with what she saw. She muttered something under her breath and tossed the page face down on the coffee table next to the phone.

"Like my work space?" She laughed ruefully. "My real office is downstairs, but I needed a cigarette break, so that's why we're meeting up here."

She reached for a lighter that was balanced upright on an end table. Cassie noticed her fingernails—long red talons.

"Sorry about the smoke. Nasty habit. I keep trying to quit. Been trying for about ten years. I keep thinking it'll be easier when the pace slows down around here." She lit a cigarette and blew a puff of smoke up toward the ceiling. "Except that it never slows down around here."

Cassie didn't know exactly what to say. She must have looked sheepish because Maddie tried to put her at ease.

"Lots to take in, isn't it? Your sister. Us."

The girl nodded uncertainly. "I suppose that's why Faye sent me here. To get some answers."

"Then you came to the right place, kiddo. I've got answers for everything. At least that's what my colleagues tell me. Sometimes they don't like my way of putting things. What do you want to know first?"

"That's easy. It's the thing I've been asking for weeks now. Who are you people?" The words were spoken before she could catch herself. Out loud, the question sounded abrupt and rude.

Maddie threw back her head and laughed. "You know, I ask them that all the time."

"Maybe I should rephrase that. What is the Arkana exactly?"

"You're not gonna start with something easy like what's my favorite color?" Maddie teased. "It's red in case you hadn't guessed. But never mind that. Faye told me to give you the big picture and to give it to you fast. You'll get down to the nitty-gritty soon enough."

The operations director settled herself back into the couch cushions. "How much has Faye told you about the name Arkana itself?"

"Nothing." The girl shrugged.

"'Arkana' comes from the Latin verb *arcere*. It means to 'shut something up,' so you can keep it safe. The noun is *arca* which means a 'chest' or 'strongbox.' In English, *arca* became 'ark' as in Noah's Ark, or the Ark of the Covenant."

"I'm guessing you call yourselves the Arkana because you've locked up all sorts of artifacts to keep them safe?"

Maddie paused a long moment, considering the question. "The artifacts aren't the real treasure. They're simply the physical proof that we haven't always been the way we are now."

The older woman glanced as Cassie. Noting the girl's perplexed expression, she elaborated. "You have to sift through layer after layer of myth to get to the real truth. Let me explain by telling you a little story about a goddess named Gaia. Do you know who she is?"

"Yeah, I've heard of her," Cassie answered readily. "She was some Greek earth goddess, right?"

"Some Greek earth goddess." Maddie snorted in disgust. "That's pretty funny. Here's your first lesson in mainstream mythology, kiddo. Nothing is ever what it seems. By the time the Hellenes started writing their origin myths, they'd already done some creative editing to the story that came before theirs. You see, once upon a time, there was a single creator goddess. She gave birth to everything. Life wasn't a straight line back then. It was a circle. What came from the goddess went back to the goddess.

"Being straight line thinkers, and trying to set up a new heavenly hierarchy with Zeus at the top, the Hellenes didn't like her very much. So, they started chipping away—splitting her into lots of different pieces as a way to weaken her power. The part of her that was love and beauty was called Aphrodite. The part of her that was wisdom became Athena. The protector of wild creatures and the hunt was Artemis. Hera became the guardian of motherhood. The part of the goddess that ruled the fertility of all living things was called Gaia.

"Now, even to the Hellenes, Gaia was the oldest of the old ones. They admitted she had created everything out of herself before their gods arrived. Her name translates to something like Grandmother Earth. But to the people who worshipped her before the Hellenes took over, she was a whole lot more than just a nature goddess. She was the creator of the universe, and she lived in and through every part of her creation. Olympian mythology tried to tame her and make her play nice with the new kids on the mountain. The Hellenes told stories of how she defied their gods and got trounced by them, but they were never able to get rid of her completely. She was in the hearts of the people who worked the land."

"Like the pythia," Cassie said softly.

Maddie stared at her in surprise. "Did Faye tell you that story?"

"She did, and that they couldn't write the pythia out of their mythology either."

"You're exactly right, kiddo," Maddie nodded approvingly. "Gaia remained a thorn in the side of Zeus and his cronies. They loosened her hold but couldn't uproot her. In the end, they had to tolerate her existence even though she's the exact opposite of everything they valued."

"What do you mean?"

The frown lines around Maddie's mouth deepened. "Gaia is nothing less than the principle of creation. The overlords valued destruction because that was how they acquired land, wealth, and power. All the people who came before them valued creation, and creation was originally viewed as female."

"Why is that?"

The older woman rolled her eyes impatiently. "It should be obvious. When you talk about building life, biologically speaking, we all know which sex does the heavy lifting. The ancients knew it too. That's why the earliest origin myths tell of a primordial goddess who gave birth to everything. There might even be some science behind the notion of parthenogenesis. At least a few researchers are convinced that the female sex evolved long before the male. After all, there are lots of species on this planet that are all female, but none that are all male."

"What?" Cassie was stunned.

Maddie blew a final puff of smoke and ground out her cigarette in the ashtray on the coffee table. "The basic template for the human body, for all mammal bodies, is female. Until they're seven weeks old, all embryos start out being proto-female. It doesn't take a huge change for a fetus to grow up to be a girl. That's what it does naturally. But with little boys, at seven weeks, the Y-chromosome kicks in and testosterone turns a "she" into a "he." How else can you explain nipples on a male body? I mean, for crying out loud, what's that about?"

Cassie was speechless. This theory had never been discussed in her Biology 101 class.

"And it isn't just physical creation that's associated with the female sex. It's the creation of the necessities of life. Things that have been around for so long that we take them for granted: clothing, houses, cooking, not to mention agriculture, domesticated animals, and, oh yes, art and writing. All invented by female humans."

"But… but…" Cassie stuttered. "Everybody assumes men invented all those things. Didn't they?"

Maddie noted her expression and grinned. "Nope. Shocking isn't it when you realize how much you've been brainwashed by overlord values. I make some of my associates cringe when I get on my soapbox, but they know I'm right."

She seemed to realize she had roamed far afield in her explanation. More softly she said, "It isn't simply artifacts that the Arkana is protecting. The people who crafted those artifacts had a different way of looking at life. A more constructive way. That's what we're really protecting until the day comes when the overlord system loses its shiny appeal." She smiled ruefully. "I guess I've beaten your first question to death. Now you know why we call ourselves the Arkana. What else do you want to know?"

Cassie was silent for several seconds, trying to wrap her brain around the boatload of radical ideas Maddie had just thrown at her. When she had time to recover she asked, "If this is an international organization, what made you pick Illinois of all places to set up your operation? There can't be many artifacts here."

"Good one," Maddie commented approvingly. "Actually, the Arkana started out centuries ago in England right after the witch hysteria that swept Europe in the 1600s. You've heard about that, right?"

"Are you saying that you're all a coven of witches?" Cassie asked warily.

Maddie let out an exasperated groan. "We don't have enough daylight hours left for me to set you straight on all the popular misconceptions about witches. The short answer is that we're not. The point I was trying to make is that a lot of valuable information was lost during the witch craze. Women and men who were the herbalists, midwives, and healers died at the stake, and their knowledge died with them. Once the last fire burned itself out, whoever managed to survive went underground. A small group of them banded together to preserve what they knew about healing, about the natural world, and about the old deities of the earth.

"Things stayed that way for a long time until England expanded its empire to India, Africa, and the rest of the world. And the Arkana expanded too. We reached out to include other cultures whose origin myths turned out to be a lot like our own."

She leaned back further and looked at the ceiling, deep in thought. "We kept our headquarters in Britain until things got a little dicey during the Second World War. When the Germans started bombing England, nobody thought Europe was a safe place to keep headquarters anymore. Even though America joined the war, it wasn't being invaded, so we moved the vault here during the 1940s."

"Why not New York or LA?"

"Because Illinois is right in the middle. Easy to fly to either coast if you have to, and it's not going to be the first target in an invasion. Remember who got hit on September 11th?"

"I see your point. You've got centuries' worth of valuables collected. But why are you hiding all of it and hiding yourselves? Isn't it about time you went public and set the record straight?"

Maddie seemed uncharacteristically silent. She looked down at the coffee table before replying. "That may be your best question yet, kiddo." She sighed. "Every generation or so we rehash the issue about whether the time is right." She made air quotes around the last four words. "Even though the world isn't changing fast enough to suit me, it is heading in the right direction. For now though, there are still loads of people out there who would be scared out of their wits by our version of history. And it's the kind of scared that leads to killing. They would try to eradicate us and destroy everything we've recovered." She shook her head. "No, it isn't quite time yet for us to take center stage and brag about our finds."

Both of them remained bleakly quiet for several moments, contemplating how traditional minds might react to the Arkana. Then a new thought occurred to Cassie. "I haven't seen much of it yet, but if this is a global operation, how do you afford it? I mean, who pays for everything?"

"I do," Maddie replied grimly. "I keep this merry little ship of fools afloat."

The girl looked at her blankly, and she relented. "Forget that part. That's just me feeling pinched when I have to sign checks. I hate letting go of money. That's why they put me in charge of it." She grinned. "Truth is, we have hefty cash reserves. Sometimes we come across artifacts that don't interest us but are worth a fortune to collectors. We sell them on the private market or to museums. It's enough to fund our operations and then some."

Maddie reached for her lighter again. "Sorry," she said, a cigarette dangling between her lips. "Can't help myself. If I didn't smoke, I'd be three hundred pounds by now."

Cassie's brain was beginning to feel overloaded with too many new facts. She didn't want to ask about anything else that required a major explanation, so she settled for something small. "One last thing. When I came in, I noticed a huge round table in the middle of the schoolroom downstairs. Griffin didn't really explain what it was for."

"That's for meetings of the Concordance."

"An answer that leads to another question," she thought to herself ruefully. "And what is a Concordance exactly?"

"It's the governing council for the whole global enchilada. Sort of like the United Nations except that we actually get stuff done."

"I counted thirty chairs. That's a lot of people. Isn't it a free-for-all if everybody starts talking at once?"

"Thirty is only a fraction of the people involved. The wall seating is for the rest. As for a free-for-all, Faye keeps things moving."

"What's her title?"

Maddie chuckled. "She's the glue that holds everything together. The lynchpin of the entire operation."

Cassie waited silently.

"Oh, all right. If you insist on being so serious, her official title is the Memory Guardian. We think of ourselves as a collective. We don't like the idea of somebody at the top barking orders, but if the Arkana had a leader, Faye would be that person."

"Who appointed her?"

"The memory guardian gets elected by the rest of the Concordance."

"And how long does she keep the job?"

Maddie shrugged. "Until she decides to retire or if she loses the confidence of the Concordance, and they vote her out. I really don't see that happening. Everybody loves her." She was about to elaborate when she noticed the look on Cassie's face. "Are you all right, kiddo?"

The girl rubbed her temples. "I'm starting to get a headache. If I tilt my head, I think some of this new info will leak out of my ears. Can we stop now?"

The older woman laughed. "You think this was bad, wait until Griffin gets started." She hesitated for a moment, weighing her next words. "Before you leave, I've got a question of my own to ask."

Maddie reached out for the paper on the coffee table and turned it over. A sketch of a man's face stared up at the two women. "Is this your guy? Faye said you saw what he looked like when you dreamed about Sybil's death."

Cassie felt the breath catch in her throat. It was the cowboy, or almost. "How did you figure out what he looked like?"

"Erik caught a glimpse of him when he followed him out of the apartment."

"Oh, so his name is Erik. He never exactly introduced himself."

"He's part of the security team here. You'll meet him another time." She picked up the page and handed it to Cassie. "Did we miss anything?"

Cassie recoiled for a second before taking the paper. She studied it briefly. "In my dream…" she began hesitantly. "When I saw him in my dream, his eyes were narrower. Light colored and kind of mean. He took his hat off, so I know his hair was dark brown, and he wore it combed back like somebody from the 1950s."

"You mean wavy and high, like a pompadour?" Maddie asked in surprise.

"I guess that's what you would call it. His lips are thinner than this, and his nose is a little bit longer." She exhaled a deep sigh. "Otherwise, that's him. That's the guy who figured a piece of rock was more valuable than my sister's life."

Maddie's expression was grim. "We'll find out who he is. Don't worry. He won't slip away from us. Just give us a little more time, OK?"

The girl nodded mutely, unconvinced. It could take years.

Sensing her visitor's skepticism, Maddie added, "A guy like this has made a career out of shoving people around to get what he wants. He's left a trail somewhere for us to follow. But I'd be willing to bet that in all his years as a professional bully he's never come up against a goddess before." She gave a harsh laugh. "I don't like his odds this time."

Cassie noted the sharp gleam in Maddie's eyes. Her doubts faded away.

19 – CONJUGAL WRONGS

Daniel let himself into his wife Annabeth's chamber unannounced. He caught her sitting at the small table waiting, her hands jammed into her apron pockets, no doubt to keep from biting her nails. At the sight of him, she sprang out of her chair and ran to the mirror above the dresser. She smoothed her hair and tried to pinch some color into her pale cheeks before nervously turning to face him.

He paused at the threshold, feeling confused. "What is it, Annabeth? Is everything all right? Is our daughter sick? I received a message that you needed to speak to me."

Tugging lightly at his sleeve, she drew him into the room and hastened to reassure him. "Everything is fine with the child, Daniel. Don't worry."

"Then what?" The young man asked, still puzzled.

Annabeth looked at him expectantly for a moment and then rushed toward him. Flinging her arms around his shoulders, she attempted to kiss him.

He recoiled as if bitten by a snake. "Annabeth!" he exclaimed in shock. "What are you doing?"

She hesitated for a moment and then tried to twine herself around him again.

He pushed her away. "Stop that. What's gotten into you?"

Annabeth looked as if she was about to burst into tears.

Daniel relented. "Come over here and sit down, and you can tell me what this is all about." He led her to a chair and winced as he caught a glimpse of his formal portrait hanging above the table. It reminded him of the portrait of his grandfather that hung in his father's prayer closet. He couldn't bear the comparison.

She sat on the edge of her chair and looked at him beseechingly. "I don't know what to do. You must help me, Daniel. I don't want to lose my place in the kingdom."

Daniel was growing ever more bewildered. "Lose your place? What are you talking about, Annabeth?"

She couldn't speak for several seconds. Her lips were quivering as she dabbed away the tears streaming from her eyes. "The thought of being separated for all eternity—from my baby, from my kin, from you, from everybody I ever loved." She shook her head emphatically. "No, no. I can't even think about something as terrible as that. I don't want to go to hell. I don't want to be damned."

"Who said anything about you being damned?"

She ignored his question. "Do you find me domineering? Am I a bad wife?"

"A bad wife," he echoed uncomprehendingly. "Where would you get such an idea?"

She didn't answer him immediately. Turning her head, she looked over her shoulder at the bed. "It's been a long time since you visited me—since we had relations. What have I done to displease you?"

Her words had the effect of an electric shock. He sprang out of his chair and began to pace around the center of the room. "Nothing, you've done nothing wrong."

"Then why?" Her voice was plaintive.

"I've had a lot on my mind. You can't understand the kind of pressure I'm under. Father has charged me with a grave responsibility, and I fear the thought of disappointing him."

"But it's been almost four years, Daniel," she said softly.

He stopped pacing as a new thought struck him. "Who have you been speaking to?"

She didn't want to meet his gaze.

"Annabeth, tell me who," he commanded.

She raised her watery eyes. "The diviner came to see me."

The sound of that name chilled him to the bone. He had hoped this moment would never come but had secretly expected it. Daniel knew it was inevitable ever since his father had remembered he was alive and singled him out for attention.

"He... he said he was concerned." She began twisting the hem of her apron into knots. "He said we should have more children by now. And he told me..." she struggled to go on. "He... he... told me," she started to sob. "That I was an overbearing wife and that maybe I don't deserve to be among the consecrated." The words tumbled out in a rush before she began sobbing in earnest.

Daniel knelt down next to her chair and shook her arms gently. "Listen to me, Annabeth. Listen." He shook her again until she stopped sobbing and sat limp and quiet. "You are a good wife. A very good wife."

She raised her eyes to meet his. "Then why?"

He avoided giving her a direct answer. "If my father asks about the matter again, you are to tell him that we are trying to conceive another child."

"You want me to lie to the diviner?" Her pasty face drained of color completely.

"It isn't a lie." He tilted her chin upward. "We will try again. That's what you want, isn't it? Another baby?"

She nodded, sniffling a bit. "Why else did God create woman? What else am I fit for? Without a husband and children, I have no place in the world. No place in the kingdom." Annabeth hesitated. "I… I don't want to lose my place in the kingdom, Daniel. If I don't have more children soon, then your father will cast me out."

He put his arms around her lightly, in part to hide his tense expression. "Don't worry. I'll come to visit you very soon to try to increase our family." He felt a flood of revulsion at the thought and instantly condemned himself for it. He released her and looked directly into her eyes. "For now, just remember what I told you to say if my father asks. You will remember, won't you?"

She nodded again and wiped her eyes on her apron.

"You're a good girl, Annabeth."

20 - UNDERGROUND INTELLIGENCE

Cassie gave herself a few days to let her head stop spinning from her dizzying conversation with Maddie. When she felt that her brain had absorbed all the new facts that had bombarded it, she drove back out to the schoolhouse. "A glutton for punishment," she thought to herself ruefully. She didn't understand why Faye was pushing her to learn the basics so quickly. Sybil had been given years to understand the Arkana and how the organization worked. Something else was going on here. Something to do with the cowboy and the key, but she didn't know what. All she knew for sure was that she was taking the crash course version of Pythia 101. She pulled into the clearing and walked up to the schoolhouse door. A familiar face peered around it just as she reached the top step.

Startled, Cassie asked, "Why is it that I never get a chance to knock before you pop out like some jack-in-the-box with a necktie?"

Griffin gave her a slight smile. "We have security cameras monitoring the grounds. I was alerted and came out to meet you." He opened the door wide. "Please, do come in. Are you ready for your grand tour of the vault today?"

"As ready as I'll ever be," she said guardedly, remembering Maddie's warning. "Wait until Griffin gets started."

He seemed a bit less ill at ease in her presence this time as they walked through the main schoolroom. It was just as quiet and empty as during her previous visit. When they entered the short corridor at the back of the building, Griffin stopped in front of what appeared to be a janitor's closet. He pulled the door open to reveal another door immediately behind it—a modern steel elevator door. When he swiped a key card into a slot next to the door, Cassie could hear the elevator ascending to meet them.

Reading her surprised expression, Griffin gave her a knowing look. "I would respectfully remind you of the adage about appearances and deception."

The elevator doors parted, and they walked inside. There were no buttons to push for the floor they wanted. Instead, Cassie saw a keypad on the inside of the door. Griffin punched in a code, and they began to descend.

Nothing could have prepared Cassie for the sight that greeted her when the elevator doors opened again. They were standing in an underground room that was the size of a school auditorium. It was filled with desks—row upon row of desks. They were staffed by people of every nationality, race, gender, and age. Over a hundred of them. Some people were working at computers. Some were consulting books. Others were on the phone engaged in heated discussions with unknown people on the other end of the line.

The ceiling was twenty-five feet above them, glowing with overhead light from some unseen source. Even though they were below ground, it felt like sunlight on Cassie's skin. She was about to ask Griffin, but he anticipated her question.

"You like our lighting system? It's quite clever actually. Full-spectrum illumination that mimics the progression and intensity of natural daylight."

She looked at him skeptically. "You mean you have a sunrise and sunset down here?"

He nodded. "The duration and angle of light is calculated to match the time of year outdoors. It's brighter on the east side of the room in the morning and on the west side in the evening. Once our artificial sun goes down, people can use their desk lamps, of course, but we also have an artificial moon rise that corresponds to the actual phases of the moon. While our daylight sky is opaque, our night sky is transparent, complete with constellations appropriate to this latitude and longitude at any given time of year. We want to preserve a natural environment as much as possible."

"Speaking of which…" Cassie pointed to a dog which was lying patiently next to the desk of a middle-aged woman in the front row. On another desk, a cat slept curled up in an out-box. A third desk held a birdcage with a cockatiel inside.

"People are encouraged to bring their pets to work. The more nature we can incorporate into the environment, the better."

"I guess," Cassie offered noncommittally as her eyes wandered around the space. There were potted trees in the corners; some nearly reached the ceiling. Waterfalls trickled and splashed beside them.

"Are we still under the school?" she asked.

"Yes, partly. We excavated additional space around it too."

"There are so many people down here. Why didn't I see any cars when I drove up?"

"There's an underground car park on the other side of the building. The ventilation system is state of the art." Griffin cast a glance toward the multitude of desks in the middle of the room and gave a sigh. "It's unfortunate our technological innovations haven't yet extended to the information we collect. You see, we're still in the throes of converting our paper records to computer format. Some of us are being dragged, kicking and screaming, into the information age. I confess that I, myself, am far more comfortable with the printed page."

Cassie registered surprise. Griffin had to be in his early twenties, but somehow he'd managed to miss the digital bus. When it came to books, he seemed as technophobic as some Luddite in his seventies.

Griffin clapped his hands loudly. "Everyone, may I please have your attention?"

Immediately the cacophony of sounds in the room quieted. People who had been speaking on the phone paused in their conversations and looked up inquiringly.

"It is my very great pleasure to introduce to you Sybil's sister, Cassie. Our new pythia."

Suddenly a wave of humanity was rushing toward her. Cassie braced herself for impact. Hands reached out to shake hers, to pat her on the shoulder. Voices told her how happy they were to meet her at last. How much they had liked her sister. Everyone was offering encouragement and assistance with anything she wanted to learn, any time, any place. They all seemed to understand why she was here. They all seemed to know what she was supposed to do better than she did herself. They all seemed pleased to see her. She felt as if she'd stumbled into a reunion with a long-lost family she never knew she had.

"Do you still think our vault is, as you put it, an empty schoolhouse with fancy bleachers and a big table?" Griffin asked with a mischievous gleam in his eye.

Cassie was too dazed by the enthusiastic reception to speak.

Griffin waited for the initial hubbub to die down, and then he shooed the throng of well-wishers away. "All right now, everyone. Back to work if you please. Give the young lady a chance to breathe. I fear you've quite overwhelmed her."

Cassie darted him a grateful look as he disengaged her from the crowd and led her around the perimeter of the main room.

On the wall to the right of all the desks were six doors spaced equally apart. The sign on the first one read "Africa," the second one read "Asia," the third one "Australia," the fourth one "Europe," the fifth one "North America," and the final one read "South America." Cassie noted that there was no door for Antarctica.

"Do you keep the relics behind those doors?"

Griffin shook his head. "No, those are archives for each continent. We keep the records of our relics there. Oh dear, I'm going about this backwards. A proper definition of terms is in order. The room in which we're standing is called the Central Catalog. Its function is to account for the relics we've retrieved. The relics themselves are stored in places we call troves."

Cassie looked up and down the main room. "Then where are the troves?"

"Not here obviously. It's a major undertaking to keep track of them all. New ones are forever cropping up in the most unlikely of spots. Each continent has many of them scattered about. Individual countries have their own as well. Wherever a cache of important artifacts has been discovered, we attempt to build a collection site around it."

The girl tried to hide her disappointment at not seeing any actual relics. "Who manages the troves?"

"The person who is charged with the responsibility for a particular group of treasures is called a trove keeper though she or he also has many assistants."

Cassie wrinkled her brow. "Let me repeat this to see if I have it straight. The Catalog is the records department, and it keeps track of all the items in the troves?"

Griffin nodded. "Yes, that's right. While each trove has its own version of a records department, there is only one Catalog. One place that contains records of the objects in all the troves: maps, photographs, finder's journals, and written descriptions of each item recovered. The purpose of this facility is to keep track, at a summary level, of what's in all the troves around the world. We call this the Central Catalog or simply the vault. The one and only."

"I don't get it," Cassie said abruptly.

"Excuse me?" Griffin seemed taken aback.

"I see a bunch of doors geographically covering the entire planet. Anthropologists and archaeologists have been crawling all over the globe for at least a hundred years now. They have museums full of artifacts. What's the difference between what you're doing and what they're doing?"

The young man gave a thin smile. "As much as anthropologists and archaeologists may protest to the contrary, their work is highly subjective. Their observations are tainted by whatever beliefs they carry with them into the field. That was especially true a century ago. Many if not all of them drew highly inaccurate conclusions about the objects they were collecting and the cultures they were observing. As the old saying goes, 'a fish cannot see water.'"

"What?"

"A human being living in a particular culture is very much like a fish swimming in the ocean. The fish is immersed in the ocean and therefore cannot see the environment that supports it. Until quite recently with the onset of mass communication, humans were so immersed in the values of a given culture that they couldn't see their fundamental assumptions at all. Anthropologists of the past century would have been raised with overlord values. They would have overemphasized conquest and domination and underemphasized the pivotal role that the female gender played in establishing human civilization. Therefore, when confronted with ancient cultures and values, the only context they had for explaining what they saw was European."

Cassie stared at him skeptically.

"Some errors of interpretation are minor. Some misperceptions are so fiercely protected that any attempt to correct the record would result in bloodshed. For instance, the meteorite enshrined at Mecca which Muslim pilgrims kiss so reverently was not originally sacred to the god Allah but to the goddess Al Uzza, the Mighty One. Muslim worshippers circle their shrine seven times without ever realizing they are mimicking the actions of Al Uzza's priestesses almost two millennia ago.

"Instead, Muslim lore tells that the meteorite landed at the feet of Adam and Eve in the Garden of Eden and was subsequently found by the biblical patriarch Abraham. Now if I were to tell a Muslim fundamentalist about Al Uzza and her prior claim to the stone, I'm sure he would consider me blasphemous and instantly declare a jihad against me."

"Somebody once warned me never to discuss politics or religion," Cassie observed ruefully. "I guess it's true."

"People cling stubbornly to their beliefs. We are attempting to set the record straight, but our efforts carry a certain degree of risk. The evidence we are collecting is threatening to those who dedicate themselves to maintaining the prevailing historical fiction."

"I get your point," Cassie conceded. "I can see why you're going to so much trouble to protect a stack of papers."

Griffin frowned slightly. "We aren't merely protecting a stack of papers. We are protecting the fragmented memory of the human race itself from those who would like nothing better than to erase everything that is inconsistent with overlord values."

By this time, they had walked around to the left wall of the vault which contained three doors. The closest one read "Operations Division," the middle one read "Scrivener's Office," and the farthest one "Security Division." Passing the door marked "Operations Division," Griffin stopped in front of the one that read "Scrivener's Office." He opened the door without knocking.

Cassie hung back. "Should you be going in there? I mean, what if the scrivener catches you?"

"I'm sure he won't mind." Griffin sounded unconcerned. "After all, he is me."

"You're the scrivener?" Cassie gasped. "What's a scrivener?"

Her companion chuckled. "It's an honorary title much like the term 'pythia.' It refers to the person who is in charge of all the scribes." Anticipating Cassie's next question, he added, "We call all the record-keepers in the vault 'scribes.' Obviously, these antiquated names go back to the earliest days of the Arkana."

"That means you're in charge of the whole operation?" the girl asked doubtfully.

Griffin nodded. "Of the cataloguing tasks anyway."

"But aren't you sort of young?"

"My colleagues didn't seem to think that mattered when they elected me to this post. Though I am quite new at it. Just over a year now. Please come in and take a seat."

The scrivener's office was furnished in simple elegance. Two leather wing chairs faced the Sheraton mahogany desk. The desk was flanked on either side by floor-to-ceiling book cases. Cassie sat down while Griffin began opening and closing drawers, evidently looking for something.

"The scrivener must have a ton of responsibility. Nothing personal, but why would they pick you?"

Griffin didn't seem offended by the question. He continued turning over the contents of his desk drawers as he spoke. "I think it may have to do with the peculiarities of the way my mind works. I seem to have the ability to recall nearly everything I've ever read. It's called 'eidetic memory.'"

"That skill must come in handy with everything you have to juggle. I mean, this place is about as big as the Library of Congress, and you're the head librarian."

"Scrivener," he corrected. "Head Scrivener." He resumed his search, muttering to himself until he finally found what he was searching for. With a triumphant, "Aha! I've found you at last," he dug the object out of the back of a desk drawer and came to sit in the chair next to Cassie. Holding up the article, he said, "Tell me what you think of this."

Cassie gasped. In his hands, he was holding the stone ruler.

"How did you get it back?"

Griffin smiled. "We didn't. It's just a replica that we built here, but I'd like your opinion. Does it look anything like the original?"

Cassie took the ruler from him and examined it for several seconds from every angle. When she looked up, she perceived Griffin with an entirely new level of respect. "You got it exactly right. This is just like the one that was stolen. Same size, same markings. Even the same color. Everything."

Griffin seemed pleased at her words. "I'm relieved to hear you say that. We want this to be accurate."

The girl was puzzled. "Why would it matter?"

"If you made a duplicate house key that was a fraction of an inch too big to fit the lock on your door, do you think it would work?"

"I get your point. But it sure doesn't look like it would unlock anything."

Griffin took the object back and considered it. "It may not unlock a physical location. It's far more likely that it unlocks information of some kind." He hesitated and looked away for a second. "I'm very sorry to have to ask you this, but could you describe to me the encounter Sybil had with her attacker? Precisely what did they say to each other?"

Cassie's face drained of color. "I don't want to think about that."

"But you must," Griffin's tone was urgent. "So much depends upon information only you can provide. I know how difficult this must be for you, but please try."

The girl gave a deep sigh and shut her eyes, reliving the scene. "They didn't say much. He kept asking her where the key was. She said she didn't know what he was talking about. They struggled, she fell, and then there was shattered glass everywhere. Sybil didn't get up." The girl blinked several times to wipe away the memory and a few fresh tears.

"He wasn't specific about the name of the key or the language of it?"

Cassie shook her head. "No, he just called it 'the key.' That's why I didn't make the connection that this stone ruler might be some kind of key when I first saw it." She sighed. "So, you don't recognize the language of any of those doodles?"

"Sorry, not yet. Some of the glyphs do appear vaguely familiar though. I know I've seen at least a few of these before. I'll keep searching our records. Something is bound to turn up."

Cassie felt a sense of foreboding. "I hope you figure it out before the cowboy does. If he didn't mind leaving a dead body behind to get it, it can't unlock anything good."

21 - DAMNATION MOTIVATION

Abraham found himself standing in the middle of a rope bridge. It swayed precariously over a flaming gorge. He could feel the heat from below, roaring upward to bake his skin through his clothing. He imagined he saw a face in the flames. A demon leering at him. A demon with his own features. At the opposite end of the bridge, he saw the Lord staring at him. His father was there too and behind him scores of past diviners. Abraham looked down and realized he held the stone key. He raised his hands in supplication. "Look, I have the key. See, it is here. I have done your will."

The Lord was unmoved by his cries. He raised his staff and stamped it on the ground. It sent a tremor through the ropes that held the bridge together.

In horror, Abraham watched the ropes fray. Then the wooden steps began to fly apart and disintegrate in the blaze. He ran forward toward the other diviners. Toward the Lord. They all frowned at him. None reached out a hand to help. He felt himself falling as the bridge dissolved in flame. He felt himself collapsing into the demon shape that came rushing up out of the fire to absorb him.

"Nooooo!" He sat bolt upright in bed, drenched in sweat. An ordinary person might have breathed a sigh of relief that it was just a bad dream. But he was the diviner. For him, a bad dream was never as simple as that.

***

The following morning, Abraham decided to pay a long overdue visit to his son Daniel. He wanted a progress report. The evil sending of the night before had convinced him that they were running out of time. Fortunately, this was one of the rare days when his son hadn't sequestered himself in the libraries of the Fallen. He found the young man alone in the compound study room.

Daniel was seated with his back to the door, poring over a stack of volumes he had brought with him from the city. He didn't turn around to see who had entered. Abraham noted the public library tags on the book spines as he drew up behind his son.

"Father!" Daniel exclaimed in surprise and alarm when he saw who was looking over his shoulder. "I… uh… that is… uh… I wasn't expecting to see you here."

"I daresay you weren't." The old man attempted to soften his fierce gaze. No sense in alarming the boy too much. Nothing could be gained by that. Abraham took a chair across the table. "I see you are hard at work," he observed pleasantly.

"Yes, yes I am." Daniel bobbed his head in agreement. "I spend most days at the library in the city until Brother Jeremiah comes in the van to bring me home."

"And what have you learned so far?" The old man kept his tone deliberately mild.

Daniel sighed deeply. "I have made very little progress. At first, I tried on my own, but it was too difficult navigating the Fallen library records, so I finally had to ask for help."

Abraham felt a shockwave travel down his spine. "You spoke to one of them? You know that our community is set apart. We are God's chosen ones. We cannot allow ourselves to be contaminated."

His son looked guilty. "Yes, Father, I know, but there was no other way. I had to ask a research librarian, and he was very kind. Not at all what I expected."

"Really?" The old man raised a skeptical eyebrow.

"He was dressed very neatly, and he wore a gold cross around his neck. He said he was a Christian." Daniel smiled at the memory. "To me, he looked like one of the seraphim. His hair was golden, and it curled around his collar. He must have been about thirty. My age."

"Remember, my son, that the devil often appears in a pleasing shape. He adopts the guise of the young and fair, the better to gain the trust of the unwary."

Daniel frowned slightly, unconvinced. "His name was David, and he seemed very knowledgeable. He had the most beautiful blue eyes—"

Abraham cut in. "And how did this knowledgeable young man help you?"

"He showed me something he called the internet. A wondrous device that can call up information instantly from anywhere in the world."

"Yes, I've heard of it," Abraham said darkly. "I feared you might be exposed to its evil influence."

"Evil?" His son looked puzzled. "How could it be evil? In the space of a day, I was able to learn more information than I had been able to accomplish on my own in a week."

Abraham felt a growing sense of uneasiness. "My son, I told you there would be unexpected dangers in the world of the Fallen. This device, this internet, is a gateway to all sorts of temptations. Only think what other pernicious information is also available to you at the touch of a button. Vile things that no Nephilim ought to know."

"But Father, I was very careful. I asked only about ancient languages, and David did all the typing. He knows how to command this internet machine. I really think it will help us find the answer."

Abraham's attention was caught by the title of the book sitting on top of a stack of other library volumes. "What is this?" His tone was deliberately sharp.

"Why, it's something David thought I might find interesting. A history of comparative religion."

"Religion is never comparative!" the old man thundered. "Your immortal soul is never comparative!"

His son was taken aback and stammered a protest. "F… Father, he m… meant no harm. I meant no harm by reading it. P… please, don't be angry. I had no idea there were so many other faiths in the world."

"The faith of the Fallen has nothing to do with us! We are not like them! We are a race set apart!" Abraham sprang out of his chair and pounded his fist on the table for emphasis. "My son, you are being seduced by their world. This is the way their evil influence begins. They convince you there is no harm in anything they say. They draw you in, and before you know it they have taken your soul. Do you understand what you are risking? You would be cut off from us for all eternity!"

Daniel's eyes grew wide. He said nothing but looked up at his father in shock.

Abraham could feel the shadow of the outer world inching closer to his flock. Already it was corrupting the mind of his own son. He feared that in his zeal to unlock the secrets of the stone key, he had unlocked a portal for the devil to creep into this bastion of purity. He leaned forward over the table and sighed heavily. "Daniel, nothing has prepared you for dealing with these people. They are not like us. Their ways are treacherous, and you must remain on your guard."

"Yes, of course, sir," Daniel hastened to agree.

"Remember the task I have set you," Abraham urged earnestly. "Ask only about ancient languages and nothing else, is that clear?"

"Absolutely. I am sorry, Father." The young man bowed his head in submission. "I wasn't thinking."

The diviner became unnerved as a new thought struck him. "You didn't tell this David why you wanted the information, did you?"

"Oh, no sir!" Daniel quickly reassured him. "I was very careful. I showed him photographs of the characters I wanted to translate. He didn't ask me anything about them."

The old man relaxed his stance. "Good. That's good. Have you been able to establish anything at all yet?"

Daniel grew thoughtful. "Well, we are certain of all the things it isn't. With David's help, I've been able to rule out every ancient language including Egyptian and Sumerian, but that's where the trouble begins. All the history books in his library say that the earliest written language is Sumerian cuneiform. These characters look nothing like that. They may, in fact, be older, and we've gone back as far as 3000 BCE."

Abraham attempted to conceal his dismay. "My son, I don't think I need to remind you how important it is that you solve this puzzle for me."

Daniel stared at the tabletop, afraid to meet his gaze. "No, Father. I know. I would hate to disappoint you."

Abraham gave a humorless laugh. "It isn't me you would be disappointing, Daniel. It's God. This has all been set down in prophecy for nearly a century now. You will find the answer I seek, or I fear the Lord will be mightily displeased with both of us."

***

Daniel listened to his father's footsteps retreat out of the library. He swallowed hard. He remembered Annabeth's terror of damnation. Suddenly, her dread didn't seem so ridiculous anymore.

22 – IN SECURITY

Cassie knew that *déjà vu* meant you had the feeling you'd already done something once before. She wondered if there was a French expression for something you'd already done twice before. *Deja deux*? She shrugged and knocked at the front door of the schoolhouse.

This time there was no Griffin popping out to greet her. The door opened slowly to reveal a young man in his mid-twenties with shaggy blond hair. Cassie decided that he was much too good-looking, and since he probably owned a mirror, he already knew that. She tried not to stare.

"Come on in," he said laconically. "I'm Erik."

"I'm C—"

He cut her off. "Yeah, I know. This way." He turned his back and started walking, assuming she would follow.

Cassie stood in the doorway, shocked by his rudeness. Who did he think he was? She wasn't sure whether to fall in line or turn around and go home. Finally, curiosity won out over resentment, and she hurried to catch up.

He was already at the hidden elevator door, swiping his key card.

She peered at his profile for a few seconds until recognition dawned. "You're the guy from my sister's apartment, aren't you?"

"Yeah, that was me."

The elevator doors opened, and they entered.

"Why were you there? Were you following me?"

Erik punched in his code, and the elevator descended to the vault level. "Faye wanted me to keep an eye on you. We weren't sure if the guy who went after Sybil would go after you next."

"What does that make you? My secret bodyguard?"

He shrugged. "I guess you could call me that."

Cassie had known Erik for less than five minutes, and she already disliked him intensely. His good looks were only exceeded by his bad manners. "Are you always this charming?" she asked pointedly.

He looked down at her impassively and then gave an infuriating grin. He had perfect teeth too. Dislike was rapidly turning to loathing.

The doors opened, and Cassie found herself once more in the Central Catalog. Several people looked up from their work as the pair entered. They waved at her cheerily.

Erik jerked his head to the left. "This way." He once again turned his back, expecting her to trail along.

She complied but made a mental note to complain to Faye about him the next time she saw her.

Erik walked through the door marked "Security Division." The interior was a large space carved up into office cubicles which were staffed by about twenty people. Some were staring at security monitors. Others were working at computers. Still others were reviewing paperwork. In contrast to the scribes outside, nobody looked up when they entered.

Her guide didn't bother to introduce Cassie to anyone. "Over here," he said offhandedly.

She followed him into one of the offices against the back wall. There was no lettering on the door. Inside was a desk, computer, phone, and printer. Stacks of paper were piled on filing cabinets and scattered around on the floor. Half a dozen paper coffee cups were parked haphazardly on top of the cabinets. A greasy paper plate with a stale, half-eaten piece of pizza sat on the desk. Because of the mess, Cassie immediately concluded this must be Erik's office.

"Nice digs," she observed sarcastically. "Do you do your own housekeeping?"

He shrugged. "Neat is for wusses." Picking up a stack of papers that had been parked on a chair, he dropped it unceremoniously on the floor. "Have a seat."

"Great filing system too," she added.

He threw himself into the swivel chair behind the desk. "I hate reports."

"I would never have guessed," Cassie mumbled to herself as she took the offered seat. "So, what am I supposed to learn from you?"

Without a word, he selected a sheet from a pile of papers and shoved it across the desk toward her.

It was a photograph of a face that Cassie knew only too well. "It's him!" she cried. "The cowboy. You found him!"

Erik remained unmoved by her enthusiasm. "Are you sure that's the guy you saw?"

"I could never forget that face. It's him, absolutely. Who is he?"

"His name is Leroy Hunt. He got a dishonorable military discharge after the Gulf War. Too bad nobody checked his psychiatric profile before giving him weapons training. He parlayed that into a career as a pricey hired gun. Somehow he's managed to stay out of prison because anybody who could place him at a crime scene conveniently disappeared."

Cassie became lost in the photo. She still couldn't believe her nightmare had been that accurate. The man she saw in her dream was staring right back at her, and he had a name. She looked up to find Erik studying her intently. "What is it?" she asked.

The young man kept silent for several seconds before asking, "Do you know what you're getting yourself into?"

The girl was taken aback. "I... uh... of course. That is... what do you mean?"

"This guy is bad news. He isn't somebody you should be messing with."

Cassie decided it was time to return his stare. His eyes were an odd shade of green. There was a hint of gold mixed in, like new spring grass. Brushing that thought aside, she shot back, "My sister is dead! You forget I caught the whole show in 3-D. Do you think I need a lecture from you about risk?"

His face was an unreadable mask. "I think maybe you do because so far nobody has pointed out how dangerous working for the Arkana can be."

"I made my choice," she said with more bravado than she felt. She was still deeply ambivalent about her involvement in the organization, but she wasn't going to let him see that.

"You only think you made a choice," he contradicted her. "A choice is only a choice if you can actually understand your options."

"And you're convinced I didn't do enough soul searching before I agreed? Gee, it must be nice to be a mind reader."

He refused to rise to the bait. His voice was dead calm. "I think you acted on impulse. You figured this might be fun because you're just drifting, and you didn't have anything better to do."

Cassie could feel her face flushing to the roots of her hair. He had hit a nerve. "That's it." She stood up. "This conversation is over!"

He sprang out of his chair and reached the door before she did. He wedged himself in front of her, blocking the exit. "Wait a minute. You can't just wander around the vault."

"What are you going to do? Handcuff me? Shoot me?" She glared at him. Her eyes challenged him to lay a hand on her. "I want to talk to your boss. No, on second thought, I want to talk to your boss's boss!"

Erik considered the demand. "That would be Maddie." He stepped away from the door to let her pass. "Maybe she can talk some sense into you."

"Maybe she can talk some sense into you instead," she muttered over her shoulder as he escorted her from the Security Division.

***

About ten minutes later, Cassie was seated in the operations director's office venting to Maddie about Erik's rude behavior. "He was impossible! I mean, what did I ever do to him?"

Maddie offered no comment during Cassie's tirade. Her voice was uncharacteristically soft when she finally spoke. "You need to cut him some slack, kiddo. He was closer to Sybil than any of us. It's his job to coordinate security for the pythia when she's in the field. He went with your sister on half a dozen recovery missions."

"That's just great. Did you ask him why he wasn't there when she actually needed security? The night she died."

He was there the night she died," Maddie corrected mildly. "He just got there five minutes too late. I think he's been beating himself up for that mistake ever since." She sighed. "There isn't anything that you could say that would make him feel any worse."

"But why attack me?" Cassie protested. "I'm her sister, for crying out loud."

Maddie paused to consider. "Maybe that's the reason. It's because you're her sister and our new pythia. He's afraid the same thing might happen to you, and he couldn't stand to have that on his conscience."

Cassie relented slightly. She wasn't any more well-disposed to like Erik, but at least she was ready to move on to a new topic. In a less angry tone, she asked, "Do you know what was I supposed to learn from him?"

"Did he show you the photo of Leroy Hunt?"

Cassie nodded. "Yeah, he said the guy had a reputation for eliminating anybody who could identify him."

Maddie gave a half-smile. "Then I guess you're safe until dreams are admissible in court."

Cassie grew thoughtful. "If this guy has a track record as a gun for hire, then that means he didn't want the key for himself. Do you have any idea who paid him to find it?"

"It was the Nephilim," the operations director said matter-of-factly, "though I never would have figured them to tag somebody like that to do their dirty work."

"The Nephilim? It sounds like a disease."

Maddie barked out a laugh. "Between you and me, kiddo, that's how I think of them. As a disease. The name 'Nephilim' is Hebrew and, depending on who you listen to, it either means 'fallen' as in cursed or 'wondrous' as in superhero. The cult plays it both ways. Since I've only got a nodding acquaintance with the Bible, my facts may be a little bit sketchy but here goes.

"Way back when in Genesis, the Hebrew god appointed some angels to watch over humankind. After a while, these particular angels got tired of watching and took a fancy to the local tootsies. They started to date them if you know what I mean. The result was a hybrid race of giants known as the

Nephilim. The Hebrew god was so mad at this abomination that he started Noah's flood just to wipe them out. Well, a few of them survived, and their god allowed them to live as demons to tempt humanity. That's the last time they're mentioned in the Big Book of Begats.

"Now this is where it gets interesting. Around 1800, a New Englander named Jedediah Proctor had a vision. Jesus came to tell him that, because of his death on the cross, he had redeemed not only the souls of all mankind but the souls of the Nephilim, too. The reason Jesus was giving this intel to Proctor was because Proctor, himself, was a descendant of the Nephilim. Although the Christian god decided to give the half-breeds a second chance, he attached a few caveats.

"Proctor was to go around and gather together the descendants of the Nephilim who by this time were scattered all over the world. They were to band together in communities and behave themselves until the Second Coming. If they were all good boys when the big day came the Christian god would restore them to the rank of angel first class in heaven. If they weren't so good, not only would they go to hell, but they would be transformed into demons and join the ranks of Lucifer's satanic minions for all eternity. So, no pressure there."

"You said boys," Cassie noted. "What about the girl angels?"

"No such animal," Maddie stated flatly. "The Nephilim is strictly a boys' club. They believe only males carry the angelic bloodline. The girls are descendants of their human mothers—breeding stock and nothing more. This creates a little bit of a problem for the cult. Hard to get a date when the girls don't get any special perks come Judgment Day. It's an even bigger problem because the Blessed Nephilim are expected to breed in a big way. Jedediah Proctor was told that the Christian god was so disappointed in humans that he wanted the Nephilim to multiply and build up an angelic kingdom on earth. That's one of the reasons they're polygamous. They have huge families. The women, aka brood mares, are called consecrated brides to distinguish them from you and me, aka Fallen women. They get a pat on the head for being the wives and mothers of angels, and that's how they get a guaranteed ticket to heaven. By building up the angelic kingdom. The more kids they crank out, especially males, the higher their status upstairs."

The girl raised dubious eyebrows. "And this Jedediah actually got people to believe him? To follow him?"

"In droves. For the past two hundred years, their numbers have been growing. They keep to themselves mostly and try to avoid contamination from the outside world while they wait for the Second Coming. When Jedediah Proctor died, he passed on his prophetic powers to his successor who is known as the 'Diviner.' The diviner claims to get direct revelation from their god about what they're supposed to do. He's like the pope and what he says goes. Weird, huh?"

Cassie nodded. "Weird doesn't begin to cover it."

Maddie continued. "I wouldn't care how weird their cult is if they minded their own business, but now they're messing with us. When Erik followed Leroy Hunt from Sybil's apartment on the night he broke in, he ended up at the Blessed Nephilim headquarters out in the sticks."

Cassie was mystified. "I don't understand. If the Arkana collects artifacts that are pre-biblical, what would this Nephilim cult want with the stone key?"

"Aha!" Maddie jabbed the air for emphasis with a sharp fingernail. "That's the $64,000- dollar question, and we still don't know the answer."

"Maybe it's what Griffin said. There are lots of overlord sects that would try to destroy the Arkana if they could."

"You mean one artifact at a time?" the older woman asked jokingly. "That's got to make for some pretty slow going. Besides, the Nephilim don't know we exist."

"They don't?" The girl was flabbergasted. "Then how did they track down Sybil? They had to know she was the pythia."

"I don't think they did. I'm guessing they just blundered across an artifact that they wanted at the same time Sybil was going after it. She was an antique dealer, so they wouldn't question why she might want it. Something like this has happened a few times before."

"With the Nephilim?"

Maddie leaned forward across her desk to retrieve her lighter and a pack of cigarettes. "I haven't had a cigarette all morning, and I'm dying for a smoke. Let's continue this discussion topside."

The pair walked to the elevator where Maddie swiped her keycard. Once they started their ascent, she picked up the thread of the conversation. "Now where did I leave off?"

"You said that the Nephilim had taken some Arkana artifacts before this," Cassie prompted.

"Right. These other episodes happened before I joined the Arkana, so I'm vague on the details. The first time was about twenty-five years ago in the Balkans. Somebody from the recovery team was murdered, and an artifact was intercepted. Then about ten years ago, something similar happened in the Middle East. A team of ours was after an Asherah artifact. She was the main goddess of the Canaanites before the Hebrews invaded the area. By the time we figured out what had happened, two of our operatives were missing, and the artifact was gone. We eventually traced that theft to the Nephilim too."

Cassie felt a vague sense of uneasiness at Maddie's words—a memory being jogged loose somewhere at the back of her consciousness. She dismissed it, for the time being, more intent on understanding the strange behavior of the Nephilim. The elevator doors opened on the second floor. They strolled down the long hallway with its vacant offices and meeting rooms.

When they reached the bell tower staircase and began to climb Cassie said, "It just doesn't make any sense. If the whole point of their existence is to sit around waiting for Judgment Day, then there's no reason why they should care about some goddess artifact much less kill to get it."

Maddie paused to catch her breath before saying, "I'm beginning to think it has something to do with their current diviner. His name is Abraham Metcalf. The Nephilim have been around for two hundred years and the Arkana a lot longer than that without our paths ever crossing until right around the time this Metcalf took charge of the organization. It might be he's got an agenda that we don't know about."

The second they cleared the top of the spiral staircase into the tower, the operations director walked directly to the couch, sat down, and lit up a cigarette. "You know I promised Griffin that if the stairs ever got to be too much for me, I would quit cold turkey. I might be a little winded, but I guess my habit is safe for today."

Cassie sat on the sofa slightly downwind of her companion. "So, the Nephilim are living here in the Midwest?" she asked.

Maddie laughed ruefully. "I wish they could be corralled that easily, but they've gone global. They have satellite communities everywhere, and their so-called apostles are out beating the bushes for missing Nephilim as far east as China."

The girl felt puzzled. "How do they know when they find one? Is there a DNA test? A secret handshake?"

"In the screwiest bit of circular logic ever, they believe that if a guy joins their cult, then that proves he has angel blood. He's doing what he was meant to."

"Unbelievable." Cassie shook her head. "But I still don't get why anybody would want to join up with them. I mean if their diviner expects them to act like a bunch of lemmings, what's the appeal?"

Maddie blew out a long puff of smoke, cocked her head to the side, and considered the question. "Try to imagine you're some poor schmuck with a boring life and low self-esteem. Somebody comes along and tells you you're descended from a line of angels. You're better than human. Who wouldn't like to believe that?

"Besides, I think some people get turned on by the idea of Armageddon. Things go wrong in their own lives, and they automatically believe the whole world needs an overhaul. And who better to make that happen than some overlord god hurling thunderbolts. They can fantasize about a big sky daddy who's going to kick the asses of everybody who's ever been mean to them. Then they figure their lives will get better. Of course, that assumes they think they're on his good side."

"Still, why would anybody blindly play follow-the-leader like that?"

Maddie waved her hand in the air to waft her growing smoke cloud away from Cassie. "Faith is a tricky thing. A real slippery slope. It has to be balanced with some kind of reality check which people who join these organizations tend to avoid. Hundreds drank the Kool-Aid at Jonestown. A dozen people from Heaven's Gate committed suicide to board a spaceship. Eighty more loonies let David Koresh blow them up at Waco. Cults are made up of people who let somebody else make their decisions because they don't trust themselves to know what to do."

Cassie grew somber as her mind drifted off to another topic. She thought about a man with wavy hair. "Now that you know about this Leroy Hunt character, what are you going to do to him?"

"For the time being, nothing. He's part of a bigger puzzle. We need to find out why the Nephilim wanted him to steal the key in the first place. Singling him out for retribution at this stage isn't going to help us get the answers we need."

The girl felt crestfallen. "In other words, you're telling me that this guy is never going to have to pay for what he did to Sybil."

"All in good time." Maddie gave a knowing smile. "I have a feeling we're going to cross paths with him again very soon."

"At the Nephilim headquarters?" Cassie asked hopefully.

"Nope. Somewhere in the vicinity of the lock that fits that stone key. Griffin tells me he should know where to find it any day now."

23 – THE OBJECT OF MY REJECTION

Five minutes after the operations director escorted Cassie from the building, she called Erik into her office. The young man wore a sullen expression. He appeared ready for battle.

"Have a seat," Maddie said tersely.

Erik slouched into a chair and folded his arms across his chest, defiantly propping his feet on the edge of Maddie's desk.

She looked at the worn heels of his loafers. "You need new shoes," she commented.

He gave a wry smile in spite of himself. "Am I busted, chief?"

Maddie shrugged. "I don't know. Why don't you tell me your side?"

"My side of what?" Erik asked defensively.

The operations director shot him a reproachful look. "I think this would go faster if you stopped tap dancing."

The young man let out an exasperated sigh. "What did she tell you?"

"She said you were rude to her."

"So Little Miss Tiny got her feelings hurt? Maybe I should send her flowers or something."

His comment was met by dead silence.

He apparently reconsidered his approach. "You know this whole situation is nuts!"

"You don't like her? She seems OK to me."

Erik rubbed the back of his neck. "She isn't one of us."

The operations director was taken aback. She remained silent for several seconds before countering, "Her family has been part of the organization for generations."

"Maybe her family has been, but she was raised as an outsider without a flipping clue what the rest of her relatives were doing."

Maddie sighed. "So, she came from the outside. Way back when the Arkana first got started, everybody came from the outside."

Erik laughed humorlessly. "You know this is different. All of us, everybody who's in the organization now was raised in it or married into it or recruited into it after being screened. From the time I was sixteen, I knew about the family business. I also knew I wanted to be part of it someday. I had years to get used to the idea. And there's a good reason why it should take years."

Maddie was about to offer an objection when Erik added softly, "Or do you need to be reminded about your ex?"

"Don't go there," the operations director's voice dropped to a low growl. She didn't want to have that fiasco thrown in her face. She had thought about bringing her then-husband into the Arkana, but she waited seven years before opening the discussion. Just about the time she was ready to bring him in, he decided to clean out her bank account and head south of the border with a newer model.

"It was a good thing you waited to tell him," Erik explained. "That's all I'm saying."

"Then you've said enough about it. Cassie isn't like that."

Erik sprang out of his chair and began to prowl around the office restlessly. "How do you know what she's like? How do any of us know? That's just my point. Because she's an outsider, she's a wild card."

Maddie tapped her long fingernails on the desk pad. "She seems pretty level-headed to me. I think she's stronger than even she knows, and you aren't giving her enough credit."

"That's where you're wrong." Erik swung around to face her. "You didn't spend days outside Sybil's apartment listening to her little sister come unglued. The kid was crying all the time. What I saw…what I heard… was just a lost little girl looking for somebody to cling to because she was scared of the dark."

"You think Faye made a mistake to trust her?" Maddie's question was pointed. She was daring Erik to utter the unthinkable.

He looked profoundly uncomfortable and jammed his hands into the pockets of his jeans. "I trust Faye's judgment. I always have. But this time I don't know. Maybe she let her feelings get in the way. She felt sorry for a stray puppy and wanted to adopt it."

"Sit down, you're giving me a neck ache," Maddie commanded irritably. "It's not as simple as you make it sound. She isn't just a stray puppy. She's also the new pythia."

Erik threw himself back into his chair and leaned forward. "Based on what? One psi episode? Maybe two?"

Maddie raised an eyebrow. "You think we should have a stricter testing protocol? Maybe tie her up, throw her in a lake, and see if she floats? I mean, what the hell, Erik? Can you even hear yourself?"

"She's just a kid," he insisted.

"A kid with special gifts. When Sybil started having visions, nobody asked whether she should be the pythia or not."

Erik looked down at the floor. "Sybil was different."

"How? How different could she be?" Maddie challenged. "She was Cassie's sister for Pete's sake!"

"She was one of us," the young man said quietly. "We knew where her loyalties were because it took years for her to go through training. And now, we're stuck with her baby sister who in two weeks goes from knowing zip about us to poking her nose into every corner of the operation."

Maddie leaned back in her chair and folded her hands across her middle. "I thought you were the one who said she should be told about what Sybil was doing. Oh, don't give me that look. I was sitting right next to you at Faye's kitchen table when you said it."

Erik began to kick his chair leg irritably. "Sure, she should have been told something, but I didn't mean everybody should line up and take a number to spill the beans to her. This is insane! What's the rush? Why is Faye pushing everybody to explain the Arkana to her in five minutes or less?"

The operations director broke eye contact for a moment. In a nearly inaudible voice, she admitted, "I don't know. There's something going on behind the scenes. I can feel it, but Faye isn't talking. For now, we have to trust that she has her reasons for giving Cassie unlimited access to the Arkana."

Erik snorted in disgust. "By the time you're all done giving her the grand tour, she'll know absolutely everything about the Arkana. And we don't have a clue what she's going to do with that information. It's like handing a loaded gun to a two-year-old. What if she starts blabbing stuff to people outside?"

Maddie stared at him as if he'd lost his mind. "And why would she do that?"

The young man shrugged, at a loss. "I don't know. Maybe something sets her off, and she sours on the organization. She wants out because it's harder than she thought it would be."

The operations director was rapidly losing her temper. "You're making an awful lot of assumptions about what she would or wouldn't do!"

"And so are all of you!" Erik was nearly shouting now. "And don't even get me started on what she'd be like out in the field. What a joke! I can just see her having a seizure the first time she picks up a tainted relic. And the one person who could have trained her on how to protect herself is dead."

Maddie stood up, towering over Erik. She was out of patience and about to terminate the discussion. "Let's just boil this down to what's really bugging you. What's the worst that can happen by letting Cassie in?"

The young man rose out of his chair and leaned over Maddie's desk, staring her straight in the eye. "Someday… I don't know when, but it won't be long… that kid is going to bring the whole operation crashing down around our ears. And when that day comes, don't expect me to say I told you so because there won't be anybody left to tell. Maybe that's what it will take for you to finally understand what I'm saying. She's going to get us all killed!"

24 - MOTION SICKNESS

Daniel knocked hesitantly on the door of his father's office. It was ten o'clock on Wednesday morning. This was the day and time the diviner had set for a weekly progress report. The ordeal was always embarrassing for Daniel—almost excruciating in the way it underscored his incompetence. Every week he could see the feverish anticipation in his father's eyes when he entered the room, and every week he could see that anticipation change to cold disapproval at his lack of progress. He hoped today would be different.

"Enter," a voice commanded from inside.

When Daniel let himself in, he saw that his father was in a meeting with two western community leaders. He felt a spiteful sense of pleasure at their crestfallen expressions. Misery loves company. Apparently, his father was no better pleased with these two than he was with his son. They scuttled from the room after murmuring a greeting in his direction. Their eyes were downcast, their shoulders hunched as if to ward off imaginary blows. The diviner had a way of exposing the hidden weaknesses of his flock. At least Daniel could see that there was nothing personal in his father's abuse. Castigation was as natural to him as breathing.

Abraham regarded his son grimly. Daniel wasn't even to be treated to that fleeting look of anticipation this week. "I expect you have nothing new to report," the diviner said sourly.

"Then you'd be wrong," the young man thought to himself though he didn't dare say the words out loud. Instead, he adopted a mild demeanor. "Actually, I do have some news, sir."

The old man's head snapped to attention. "Then sit down and tell me."

Daniel felt somewhat disinclined to slouch today. He strode purposefully across the room and sat in the visitor's chair in front of his father's massive desk. The chair was low. It did not allow level eye contact with the diviner. A person would be forced to gaze upward to carry on a conversation. The young man speculated that this was no accident. He sat up straight and tried to look directly into his father's face.

"I believe I've translated one of the lines on the key," he announced matter-of-factly.

There it was. That look of intense fascination. He was to receive his father's favor after all.

"Have you, indeed!" Abraham exclaimed. He sprang out of his chair and began to pace, his hands clasped behind his back. "Tell me everything."

"It's written in a language that hasn't been spoken for three thousand years."

"Excellent, excellent!" The old man could barely contain the jubilation in his voice. He stopped pacing and came to stand next to Daniel's chair. "I suspected that might be the case. What does the message say?"

Daniel was forced to tilt his head upward. So much for level eye contact. "The text is rather cryptic. I don't understand what it means. It reads: 'To find the Bones of the Mother.'"

At these words, Abraham unaccountably fell to his knees beside the desk. "Thank you, Lord! Thank you!" He clasped his hands and bowed his head.

Daniel could see his father's lips moving in a silent prayer of gratitude. He didn't know what to do—whether he should join him in prayer or look away and allow the old man a moment of privacy to commune with God. Before he could decide on a course of action, Metcalf sprang back to his feet.

"Observe, Daniel. We see the hand of God in this." He was pacing again, talking to himself more than to his son. "The righteous are meant to prevail. It is a sign. *In hoc signo vinces*! This is the Lord's doing."

Daniel turned around in his chair to follow the diviner's erratic movements. "Do you understand what the message means, Father?"

"Yes, yes I do." Abraham paused to glance at his son, a triumphant smile on his face. "Among other things, it means the antiquities dealer who put me on the trail of the artifact wasn't lying about it. He said it had to do with the Bones of the Mother."

"And what exactly are the Bones of the Mother, sir?"

"Something very important to the future of the Blessed Nephilim." The old man measured his words carefully. "That is all I will say for now."

Daniel was beginning to feel a sense of foreboding. "If the message says the key will lead to the Bones, then that means you will have to send someone in search of them."

Abraham nodded vigorously. "Quite right. Quite right!"

The young man's apprehension grew more intense. Given his father's volatile emotional state, he didn't want to upset him further. He tried to keep his voice subdued and calm. "Sir, the language of the key is from a time before the gospels. From a time even before the Old Testament was set down. It is a pagan language, and the key will surely lead to heathen relics."

The old man gave his son an odd look as if he couldn't fathom the objection. "Yes, they are heathen relics. What of it?"

Daniel swallowed hard. He didn't know how to make his next words sound inoffensive. "Father, are you sure that such a mission is part of God's plan for the angelic bloodline? From the days of Jedediah Proctor, our very first diviner, we were instructed to live blameless lives and wait for the Second Coming. We were to keep ourselves pure from the contamination of the Fallen Lands. For fear of pollution, no member of the Nephilim has ever dwelt among the Fallen. Yet you would be sending someone directly into their world for what could be an extended period of time."

"Who is the diviner here, you or I!" Abraham thundered. "The Lord speaks to me, not you, and He has told me what must be done. Are you questioning my authority?"

Daniel's eyes fell. "No, sir. Your direction must be followed in all things." Even as he said the words, he knew he was lying. For the first time in his life, he doubted the divine origin of his father's instruction. He even doubted Abraham's sanity. The thought was frightening. It made him almost dizzy with panic that the person in whom he placed absolute faith might be wrong. Concealing as best he could the turmoil that was churning inside of him, he asked quietly, "Who do you plan to send in search of these relics?"

Again, the old man gave him an incredulous look. "Why you, of course."

"I?" Daniel gasped. "Surely there must be someone else. I'm hardly qualified—"

"You are supremely qualified," the old man cut in. "You have learned how to read this ancient language."

The young man could barely contain his panic now. "But Father, I... I am a scholar. I understand books. I do not understand the world."

In an almost benevolent tone, the old man said, "Fear not, my boy. You won't be sent off into the Fallen Lands alone. There is a worldly man in my employ. He performs special tasks for me, and I will send him to protect you."

Daniel's concern was hardly alleviated by the thought of a stranger, and a worldly one at that, accompanying him on this mysterious search. "In all likelihood, these Bones are to be found in the place where this language was last spoken."

"Yes, yes." Abraham nodded in agreement. "That is very likely."

"B... but, that's halfway around the world!" Daniel blurted out.

The old man's voice held a hint of warning. "Daniel, what is the greatest of all sins?"

The young man sighed and looked down at the floor. "Disobedience, sir."

"I hope I'm not detecting a wicked obstinacy in you."

"No, sir."

Abraham came to stand next to his son's chair once more. "God has charged me with a great responsibility. I am the servant of the Lord just as you are my servant. We are all links in the great Chain of Being. It will be your task to find me these Bones, wherever they may be hidden."

Daniel said nothing. He was too appalled to speak. The grim irony of the situation didn't escape him. He had originally been keenly interested to go to the library in the city and learn about the internet from the handsome young librarian. It was an innocent little adventure not far from home, and he had relished it. At the time, it had been his father who was alarmed at his interest in the outer world. His father who had cautioned him about the dangers of the Fallen Lands. And now it was his father who was pushing him directly toward those dangers to seek out a pagan abomination. Whether his father was divinely inspired or simply gone mad was beyond his power to discern, but he feared that his own soul hung in the balance.

Abraham took his son's long silence as a sign of consent. He continued. "You will proceed to translate the other symbols on the key. Hopefully, they will give us more information regarding the location of the relics I seek. You will come to me again only when you have deciphered the rest of the code. Then we will prepare for your journey."

Daniel felt as if he had just received a death sentence. "Yes sir," he said meekly. "I will do as you command."

25 – PYTHIA PRACTICE

It had been a few weeks since Cassie last visited Faye's house. The old woman had instructed her to come by to round out her training, whatever that was supposed to mean. The girl reflected that it might have been a century since their last meeting considering how much her life had changed in less than a month. Faye looked ancient as ever when she opened the door. She was wearing what Cassie took to be her uniform—an overly bright floral house dress.

Since it was raining when the girl arrived, chatting in the garden was out of the question. Faye asked her to have a seat in the parlor while the old woman went toward the back of the house to retrieve something.

Cassie sat down on the sofa. Like everything else in Faye's house, it gave the impression of great age although the velvet fabric wasn't worn, and the camelback upholstery didn't sag. The girl looked at the coffee table in front of her. There were three objects sitting on it—a clay pot, a stone cat, and a little carved statue. She had just reached out a hand toward the statue when she heard Faye's voice emerging from the dining room. "Don't touch those just yet, dear. We'll go through them one by one."

The old woman reentered the parlor balancing a tray of tea and cookies. She placed it on the table in front of Cassie. "I thought you'd like a snack. After all, it's a long drive out here from the city."

The girl transferred her attention from the relics to the food. She sipped and nibbled for a few moments in silence while Faye settled into the purple armchair across from her and poured herself a cup of tea.

The old woman regarded her visitor with bright blue eyes. "How has your introduction to the Arkana been going?"

Cassie shrugged. "Even though I'm going into information overload, some of it has been great. During my last session with Griffin, he told me that women were responsible for a whole bunch of inventions that men like to take credit for. Things like clothing, agriculture, domesticated animals, weaving, pottery, calendars, and writing."

"He's absolutely right," Faye said. "We've amassed collections of artifacts that prove those assertions."

"Even though I ended up with a brain cramp at the end of that day, those facts were fun to learn." She hesitated. "My training with other people didn't go as well."

"Oh?" Faye seemed concerned.

"That Erik is a real piece of work."

"Erik?" the old woman echoed in surprise.

"He's a total jerk. He was so rude to me that I walked out of our training session. I went to Maddie instead."

"I see," Faye said. Those two little words suggested volumes about what she inferred and understood. "Don't let his behavior trouble you. I believe he'll work through his 'issues' as you young people would say."

Cassie put her cup down on the table. "Actually, what he said didn't bother me half as much as something Maddie said."

"Oh?"

"She was telling me about the Nephilim and how they've interfered with some of your expeditions before and..." She paused.

Faye continued to sip her tea without comment.

"I've had a few days to put the pieces together." The girl gazed intently at Faye. "They killed my parents, didn't they?"

The old woman reached across the coffee table to squeeze Cassie's hand. "I'm so sorry you had to find out that way, my dear. Maddie didn't join the Arkana until sometime after it happened. She never knew your parents and probably didn't realize what she was revealing."

"Why didn't you tell me yourself?"

Faye darted her a worried glance. "I thought you already had enough tragedy to deal with after Sybil's death. I was waiting for a more opportune time to explain the rest."

Cassie stared off into space. "It's funny, but I can hardly remember them at all. My mom had dark, shoulder length hair. And my dad's hair was thinning on top. When I was a kid, I used to have a bird collection. Little figurines. Some were carved wood, or blown glass, or porcelain. They would always bring me a new one whenever they came back from a trip."

"They were wonderful people, your parents," Faye commented in a low voice. "They loved life, and they had the enthusiasm of children whenever they were able to locate a unique artifact. I believe their last mission had something to do with Asherah, the Canaanite goddess. They made phone contact with the local trove keeper shortly after they landed in Israel. Then they disappeared into the desert and were never seen again."

Cassie cleared her throat uncomfortably. "Which means nobody knows what really happened to them."

Faye shook her head. "The artifact they were sent to find was later seen in the possession of a Nephilim operative, so we know who was responsible."

Cassie was quiet for a long while. "I guess that makes it simpler," she said at last. "A single spot to lay the blame. The Nephilim are the one and only reason that my entire family is gone."

"We're still here," Faye added quietly. "You aren't alone."

Cassie nodded, blinking back a few tears. "It helps to know that. It really does."

Faye asked cautiously, "Do you want to postpone these exercises for another time?"

Cassie shook her head. "No. I'm OK, really. I've had some time to sort this out and get used to the idea. I just needed to hear it from you. Now I'd rather think about something else. Anything else, in fact."

She poured herself another cup of tea, regarding the curious objects laid out on the coffee table before her. Changing the subject abruptly, she asked, "So what's this about? More validation to prove I'm the real deal?"

"Not exactly. We're all quite convinced you have the necessary talent to help us. You should consider this more of a training session to hone your skills."

Her appetite returning, Cassie reached for a cookie. "What's to hone? I pick something up, I have a psychotic episode, and then I tell you what I see."

Faye chuckled. "Surely you meant to say 'psychic' episode."

"Nope," Cassie replied. "I meant what I said. Psychotic. Picking up that bowl last time I was here made me feel I was losing my mind."

"Ah, I understand. In that case, you should find this training especially helpful. We're going to attempt to put you in control of your visions rather than being at their mercy."

"I'm all for that," the girl agreed readily. She dusted crumbs off her jeans. "Where do we start?"

"Why don't we begin by working left to right," Faye suggested. "Just pick up an object and tell me what you sense."

***

Twenty minutes later, Cassie had accurately identified two of the items. The first was a clay pot created by the pre-overlord inhabitants of Egypt. The second was a fake—a stone cat which usually sat in Faye's garden. It had been made in a factory in China.

"You tricked me." Cassie registered annoyance.

"Forgive me, my dear," Faye chuckled at the ruse. "I wanted to see how perceptive you would be if faced with a forgery."

"Did I pass?" the girl asked archly.

"With flying colors." Faye's face took on a serious expression as her smile faded. "I assure you the next one is not a fake."

Cassie looked down at the third object sitting on the coffee table. It was about three inches high. A carving made from a polished piece of dark stone. It was a small figure with arms outstretched at right angles to the body. The figure wore a skirt with slanted lines incised across it. There were no feet so that the lower half of the body had a tubular appearance. The outstretched arms were squared off with holes bored into the ends. The rounded breasts indicated that the figurine was female, but the face was not human. It was the head of a woman wearing a bird mask. The beak jutted out prominently from the place where a nose should be. The eyes were enormous and shaped like horizontal teardrops. It was odd and off-putting—the strangest relic Cassie had seen yet.

She picked it up hesitantly. "OK, here we go," she said.

There was no warning. She was running or rather he was running. His lungs were burning from the effort to pull in enough air. Something was bumping against his collarbone as he ran. Cassie knew it was the bird woman figurine hanging from a rawhide string around his neck. There were tall pine trees surrounding his village. Both the trees and the village were on fire. He wasn't merely choking from the effort to breathe fast enough. He was choking from the smoke boiling out of the doors of houses. People were running in every direction, trying to escape the blaze. The scene was chaos. He ran forward toward a little girl—a toddler. She was standing some distance away from him, crying. Barely breaking stride, he scooped her up in his arms. Then Cassie noticed sounds coming from behind them. First screams and then thunder that seemed to surge up from the ground. The man briefly stole a glance over his shoulder. There was a beast bearing down on him. Half human. He didn't know what it was. He'd never seen such a creature before. He didn't know, but Cassie recognized it—a horse running at full gallop and closing the gap between them. Its rider bent low over the animal's neck urging it forward. The man couldn't run very fast because of the child in his arms. She was wailing now, her small voice merging with the shrieks echoing from every direction. The rider swung his arm downward. His long knife slashed into the side of the man's neck. The runner crumpled over, and Cassie felt herself choking, clawing at her own throat before everything went black.

***

She didn't know how long she had been gone. Faye was shaking her gently by the shoulder.

"Cassie, Cassie, wake up! You're here with me. You're all right."

The girl tried to speak, but no sound emerged. For some reason she was lying on her back on what she assumed was Faye's couch. Her eyelids fluttered open. Faye's face was bent over hers. The old woman's features gradually came into focus.

Cassie's hand flew to her neck. There was no blood. She tried to speak again. "Wha… what…" She swallowed hard. Her mouth felt dry. Sitting up, she propped her head in her hands until the room stopped spinning.

Faye sat beside her, rubbing her shoulders. "Just sit still until you feel stronger." The old woman sighed heavily. "My dear, I am so sorry. There was no good way to prepare you for this. You've had your first experience with a tainted artifact."

"A… a… a what?" Cassie finally managed to ask.

"Some of our finds have unfortunate past associations. I'm guessing that you experienced something…unpleasant?"

"Unpleasant?" Cassie croaked out the word. "Try murder!" She was feeling stronger and also angrier. The anger steadied her. She glared at Faye. "Somebody got his throat cut, or maybe it was mine. I felt like I was being killed! You never told me that might happen."

Faye looked contrite but determined. "I'm sorry to put you through this, but I had to know how you would react to a contaminated relic. If you were to encounter an object like this on a field expedition and you weren't prepared…" She trailed off. "Well, it would be too late, wouldn't it? This bird goddess figurine was the last recovery Sybil brought to us before she died. It came from a Vinca settlement that had been destroyed sometime around 4200 BCE."

The old woman handed her a glass of water. "Here, drink this."

Cassie reached eagerly for the glass. Her mouth felt as if she had swallowed gravel. She gulped down the contents without pausing for breath. When she finished, she exhaled deeply and sat up straighter. "That's a little better," she reassured her hostess.

Faye returned to her chair and regarded Cassie with a troubled expression. "Are you sure?"

"I'm fine, really." Cassie rubbed her temples. "Guess this must be the nature of the job."

The old woman tilted her head and studied Cassie's face intently. "It isn't the nature of the job so much as the nature of the individual pythia."

"What?"

"I believe you're acutely sensitive even for someone with psychic abilities. You're a natural-born empath whether you know it or not."

"An empath?" Cassie echoed, uncomprehending.

"Yes, that's someone who has the ability to sense what other people are feeling. In fact, you are able to feel what the people around you feel as if it were happening to you."

Cassie shrugged offhandedly. "Sort of. I thought everyone did that."

Faye gave a humorless laugh. "I assure you, they do not. Maybe if they did, the world would be a better place. The principle of 'do unto others' would be implicitly understood. If an empath were to hurt someone deliberately, she would be able to feel the pain she was causing. Empathy can be a double-edged sword. On the one hand, it's a tremendous gift. On the other, a tremendous burden to be saddled with so much of other people's emotional baggage. I suspect that you absorb it like a sponge."

"I don't know how to turn it off," Cassie admitted. "Maybe that's why being alone can be a relief sometimes. Not so much toxic clutter in my head when I'm by myself."

"Perhaps I can help you with that. Wait here." Faye rose and slowly ascended the staircase to the second floor. Cassie could hear the floorboards creaking above and drawers being opened and shut as Faye searched for some unknown object.

When the old woman returned, she was smiling. "I found it at last." She held out a necklace toward Cassie. A black stone disc suspended from a silver chain.

After her most recent episode, the girl was wary of touching any strange object.

Faye laughed. "It's all right. This isn't an artifact. It's an obsidian pendant. Very good for protection and blocking negative energy. Take it."

"You think some New Age trinket is going to protect me?" she asked incredulously.

Faye returned to her chair. "Those people who believe in the vibrational properties of crystals would say that obsidian is a grounding stone. It will anchor the energy of the wearer. Keep your feet on the ground so to speak."

"I feel safer already," Cassie murmured ruefully as she fastened the clasp of the necklace.

"On the other hand," Faye continued, "from a purely practical standpoint, it also functions very well as a mnemonic device. If you focus a part of your mind on the pendant while reading an artifact, you should be able to keep your identity separate from the more unpleasant aspects of the telemetric experience."

"You're saying if I pay attention to the black disk, I can avoid feeling like my throat is being cut?" she asked bluntly.

"Exactly," the old woman confirmed. "In the beginning, it might even be helpful to keep one hand wrapped around the pendant while you perform a telemetric reading with the other hand. Over time, it should become second nature. You will only need to think of the pendant for it to split your focus."

"It's worth a shot."

"Then shall we try again?" Faye suggested calmly.

Cassie's heart skipped several beats. "You don't mean you want me to pick up that creepy little bird woman again, do you?"

"If you fall off a horse—"

"I don't care about falling off a horse. I care about the one in my vision that was about to trample me!" Cassie exclaimed.

"If you'd rather wait, we can do this another time."

Cassie remained motionless for a few moments, considering her options. She could feel Faye silently willing her to continue. Eventually, she gave in. "What the heck. I suppose I should get it over with now. It'll be worse for me if I wait. I know I'll have nightmares about it."

The old woman nodded approvingly. "Very good. Close your eyes and grip the obsidian disc in your left hand for a few moments. Just concentrate all your attention on it. Tug lightly on the chain and feel its connection to your neck. Now, reach out your other hand and pick up the figurine of the bird goddess."

***

It took six agonizing tries before Cassie finally caught her balance. The first time, she lost herself immediately and began drowning in the massacre. When she was thrown clear, she refocused her attention more intensely on the black stone disc. A second, a third, a fourth time. With every new attempt, she held onto a shred of herself a little longer before the atrocity consumed her. By the sixth try, she was able to split her awareness and watch the terrible scene unfolding as if she were watching a horror movie from the safe vantage point of the audience.

"It still leaves me feeling awful," she commented to Faye after her final successful try.

By this time Faye had brought in a fresh pot of tea and a plate of cucumber sandwiches. She served more refreshments for both of them. "That just means you have a conscience," the old woman observed. "No feeling person could witness the murder of an innocent without some sympathy for the unfortunate victim."

"What happened to those people?" the girl asked. "Why were they being massacred?"

"You forget you haven't told me the details of everything you observed."

"Oh, that's right!" Cassie exclaimed. She then proceeded to give Faye all the sickening particulars of the scene.

The old woman's face drained of color. "Well, it's done, and now we know. You've had your trial by fire."

Cassie took a bite of her sandwich. Unaccountably, she was feeling better. "The upside is that it can't get much worse, can it?"

"No, it certainly can't. And you've just proven your ability to overcome difficult situations." Faye studied the girl's face for a few moments. "You really are a most extraordinary young woman."

Cassie blushed. Nobody had ever called her extraordinary before. She had always been treated like somebody's appendage or maybe just their baggage. First, she was toted around by her parents and afterward by Sybil. She'd never been anything in her own right.

"Extraordinary?" she repeated. "What makes you say that?"

Faye smiled. "Given the recent shocks you've experienced in your life, I can't think of a single person of your age who would willingly relive a scene of such horror. Not once but six times. It was quite brave of you."

The girl shrugged offhandedly. "Maybe stubborn is a better word. I hate to quit. It comes from all the moving around I did as a kid. I never got to finish anything."

"In our line of work, tenacity is a virtue."

"Speaking of tenacity, a while ago I asked you why all those people were massacred. I still want to know."

"Ah, yes." Faye stirred sugar into her tea contemplatively. "You've just seen an overlord invasion in all its glory."

"'Glory' is a strange word to use for it," the girl observed grimly. "'Gory' might be better."

"Yet how often history books like to use 'glory' to describe acts of viciousness." Faye sighed expressively. "The Vinca were among the last inhabitants of old Europe before the Kurgan invasions."

"What do you mean by old Europe? To an American, everything in Europe seems old."

Faye laughed softly. "Then maybe I should call them the original inhabitants of Europe. You see, what we think of as European civilization was founded on the destruction of previous cultures. Some far more sophisticated than that of the barbarians who displaced them. The Vinca were one such culture. They lived in southeastern Europe. Many of their artifacts were found near Belgrade, Yugoslavia.

"The Vinca were peaceful agriculturists. They possessed domesticated cattle and lived in villages with laid-out streets and two-story houses. Superb craftspeople. Their pottery and sculpture are more advanced than anything produced by their successors. The arrangement of graves and the magnitude of goddess statues suggest that they, too, were matristic. As you might have guessed by now, the bird goddess was their principal deity. They may even have invented the first written script. Archaeologists have found tablets dating to 5000 BCE with pictograms and symbols that recur in later matristic cultures on Crete and Cypress. The Vinca flourished between 5000 BCE and 4300 BCE, at which time they were displaced by the first wave of Kurgans."

"Let me guess," Cassie said archly. "The Kurgans are overlord bad guys."

"Yes, certainly bad for the Vinca and everybody whose lands they invaded though there were reasons why their culture became as violent as it did. Over time, I expect you'll learn a great deal about the why and wherefore of their behavior. Much more than I can tell you now. Suffice it to say that a wave of Kurgan invaders left the Russian steppes and moved westward—driving out the inhabitants and taking their lands. They imposed a war-based male-dominated society on the folk who remained. The first evidence of violent death in southeastern Europe dates from the arrival of the Kurgans. The archaeological record shows over eight hundred villages burned around that time. Some people fled west into more inaccessible regions such as the Alps. Those who could not escape were either murdered or assimilated into the new Kurgan world order."

"Why are they called Kurgans?" Cassie nibbled a crustless sandwich while Faye spoke.

"The burial practices of the invaders were very different from that of the Vinca and other cultures of old Europe. *Kurgan* is a Russian word meaning barrow. A barrow is a manmade hill. These people buried their dead, especially their important male leaders, in raised mounds. Frequently the chief's wife was ritually murdered to accompany him into the afterlife—along with his favorite horse, of course."

Cassie darted a swift look at Faye to see if she was joking.

Reading her expression, the old woman said, "I assure you, it's all disturbingly true. Horse skulls and weapons were interred with the deceased."

"I'm glad they're not around anymore," Cassie commented.

"Oh, but they are, though they've learned some manners over the ages. In fact, anyone of European origin is either a descendent of theirs or of the people they victimized."

Cassie gulped down the remainder of her sandwich. It occurred to her that there were some things about her family tree that she'd rather not know.

26 – LINEAR THINKING

The morning after Faye's training session with Cassie, she received an unexpected phone call from Griffin. At first, he was babbling. It took several tries to calm him down enough to get any sort of useful information. As was typical of Griffin, he started at the tail end of the explanation, and Faye had to coax him back to the beginning. Eventually, he blurted out the essence of what he was trying to say: "I've done it. I've cracked the code!"

Uttering a silent prayer of thanks that the waiting was over at last, Faye got into her station wagon and drove out to the schoolhouse to get the full story. She entered the vault and knocked on the door to the scrivener's office. When he swung the door open, his eyes were ablaze with excitement.

Maddie was already seated in one of the wing chairs wearing an annoyed expression on her face, her chin propped up by her hand. Faye had instructed Griffin to include the operations director in the discussion. The scrivener bustled the old woman into the other wing chair and then dashed around the office collecting a volume from a bookcase on one side, another from the opposite end of the room, a third from the floor behind his desk. He slammed them all down on the desk and dropped into his own chair, looking at the two women expectantly.

"He's been like this all morning," Maddie commented to Faye. "Absolutely whacko, but he wouldn't tell me anything until you got here."

Faye smiled to herself. Griffin might consider himself a poor liar, but he certainly knew how to keep a secret.

"It's the most extraordinary thing!" he exclaimed as if that explained everything.

"Yes dear, I'm sure it is," Faye said soothingly. "Now why don't you take a deep breath and calm yourself."

"No time for that," Griffin brushed off the remark. He had already dived into one of the retrieved volumes and was rapidly thumbing through the pages, muttering to himself all the while. "That's not it. Why on earth did I mark that text? Ah yes, I have it now!" He slid the volume toward the opposite end of the desk, so the two women could see it. "What do you make of that?" he asked triumphantly.

They both leaned forward in their chairs to study a full-page illustration. It was a table of mysterious symbols. They looked at one another blankly, at a loss for what he expected them to say.

Faye spoke first. "I can't make anything of it," she admitted. "Runes were never my area of expertise."

"Ah, that's just it, isn't it?" he asked in a significant tone.

"Is what?" She peered at him closely. Not for the first time, she had to remind herself that he was a bit eccentric. Geniuses often were. However, at the moment, he seemed to have crossed the line from mildly eccentric to bi-polar. "Griffin, you really must settle down. Now, what do you want to tell us about the runes, dear?"

He took a deep breath and steadied himself. "They aren't runes," he said abruptly. "That's it precisely. When I first started work on translating the key, I thought I recognized some of the markings as Scandinavian runes." He lowered his voice to a dramatic whisper. "But they're not."

Faye studied the page of symbols again. "They certainly look like runes to me. Are you quite sure?"

"Oh, absolutely," he affirmed. "That was the fatal flaw in my logic. I automatically assumed that since the characters appeared runic, the language would be one of the scripts associated with matristic cultures." He sighed deeply. "But I was wrong."

Maddie's voice asserted itself. "For those of us just tuning in who don't have a clue what you two are talking about, do you think you could maybe start with 'once upon a time'?"

"Oh yes, of course. Very sorry, Maddie." Her comment seemed to have a sobering effect on him. "How much do you know about the scripts of old Europe?"

"You mean the original written languages?" she asked. "Not much. Go ahead and assume I belong on the short bus."

"Very well then. I'll start at the beginning." He cleared his throat and gathered his thoughts. "It is quite likely that written language originated with the sacred symbols of old Europe. Signs that had spiritual significance were found inscribed on a variety of artifacts dated to around 5000 BCE. Their principal purpose was an invocation to the goddess, a prayer if you will. Though tablets found at a Vinca excavation site are the most well-known, the same symbols have been unearthed from a variety of other contemporaneous cultures in southeastern Europe. They have even been found on pottery and bone objects from as far away as southern Italy and western Europe. The ancient runes of Scandinavia also derive from the same source. It would not be an exaggeration to say that this script was a universal phenomenon of old European culture.

"The symbols consist of straight lines, dots, and curved lines in various combinations with each other. So far, two hundred and ten Vinca signs have been identified. About a third of them are symbols used in common throughout Europe at the time. These symbols all but disappeared during the first wave of Kurgan invasions around 4000 BCE. Writing of a different sort emerged in Sumeria at about 3000 BCE, but it was used for a very different purpose—in the service of law and bureaucracy. Devoid of spirituality, it counted property and promulgated edicts.

"Happily, the old script didn't die out completely. Because the Kurgan infiltration of Europe didn't extend into the middle of the Aegean Sea, the old script was carried forward to the island of Cypress where it evolved into the classical Cypriot syllabary. Likewise, it persisted in the hieroglyphics of Minoan Crete and in the Minoan Linear A script."

The scrivener reached into a desk drawer and retrieved the replica of the stone key. He slid it across the desk until it rested next to the open page of the book. "Compare the markings on the key to what you see in the book," he instructed.

The two women scrutinized both items carefully.

"It appears to me that one line of text on the key matches some of the characters in this book," Faye noted.

"Either way, it's all Greek to me." Maddie shrugged.

Griffin sprang out of his chair and leaned over the desk. Fixing Maddie with an intense stare, he said, "You are more right than you can possibly imagine!"

He flipped over to the next page in the book.

Faye read the caption aloud. "Mycenean Linear B Syllabary." She looked up at Griffin and smiled. "Oh, I see."

"Well, I don't. What's he talking about?" asked Maddie irritably.

Griffin sat back down, still glowing with exhilaration at his discovery. "Some of the characters on the granite key are Mycenaean. The Mycenaeans were early invaders of Greece and later Crete. They were descendants of the Kurgan steppe nomads, but we think of them as proto-Greek. So, when you said, 'It's all Greek to'—"

"Yeah, yeah," Maddie cut in. "Very funny. Get to the point."

Griffin dutifully complied. "You will note that each of the five sides of the granite key contains one line of script that corresponds to Linear B characters. Above each character is a symbol, a hieroglyph."

Faye picked up the key and turned it over in her hands. Maddie looked over her shoulder.

Griffin continued. "I believe the hieroglyphic symbols are meant to be translated into the corresponding Linear B syllables."

"So, it's like a substitution code?" the operations director asked. "A letter of the Greek alphabet for a hieroglyphic?"

"Not quite as simple as that," Griffin said. "Linear B is a syllabary, actually. Each character corresponds to a consonant and a vowel together or a vowel sound alone. The Mycenaeans got the idea from the Minoan Linear A syllabary, but they had to adapt it to their own language. The Greek language and all Indo-European languages are different from what came before. They cannot conveniently use alternating consonants and vowels, so the characters had to mean something different in Linear B than they did in Linear A or the Cypriot syllabary. We still have not been able to translate Linear A because the Minoan language has been lost. Linear B, however, is another matter. Fortunately for us, it has been translated into Greek."

"Then you can read what this line of script says?" Faye asked.

"I can read the syllables," Griffin admitted, "but that isn't the same as the message."

"OK, you lost me again," Maddie complained, rubbing her forehead tiredly.

"The key only shows which Linear B syllable corresponds to which hieroglyphic. The meaning of the message is in another location. I have a theory that the hieroglyphics are assembled in a particular order, and the key provides the Greek syllables to translate that message."

"But that could be anywhere," the operations director protested.

"On the contrary, it can only be one place in the world," Griffin replied proudly.

The two women looked at one another skeptically and then back at the scrivener.

"It's on the island of Crete," he said simply.

"On Crete," Maddie echoed, unconvinced. "How can you know that?"

"It's fairly straightforward, actually. There are a few reasons why I draw that conclusion. First, Linear B was used in only two places on the planet. One was in southern Greece, primarily the Peloponnese, and the other on Crete."

"OK, Mr. Wizard, that gives you two places to look, not one," the operations director contradicted. "The Peloponnesian peninsula is a pretty big place."

Griffin smiled angelically. "That's true, but there's one other bit of information that the granite key yielded which eliminated the Greek mainland from my search."

Without warning, the young man flew out of his chair and whisked yet another volume from off the bookshelf to his right. He placed it in the middle of his desk and, without explanation, sat down again. He continued, "There was one line of text on the key, just here, you see?" He pointed to one of the five sides which contained three lines of markings instead of two.

Faye handed the granite key to Maddie for her to examine.

The latter looked at it briefly then turned a questioning gaze to Griffin. "Do you know what the extra line says?" she asked.

"I do," he concurred. "The Linear B script roughly translates as the phrase 'To find the Bones of the Mother.'"

"And what is that supposed to mean?" Maddie asked, handing the granite key back to Faye.

Wordlessly, Griffin gave her the volume he had just taken from the bookshelf. "This is a field journal written by one of our operatives on Crete over a century ago. I would direct your attention to page twenty-seven."

Maddie found the page marked with a post-it note. She began to read aloud: "There is an ancient legend which tells of the time when misfortune befell the Minoans: earthquakes and tidal waves and barbarian invaders who forced new laws and new gods upon the people. After a time, the Minoans despaired. Thinking the goddess had abandoned them, they began to forget the old ways. A small number of those still faithful to the Lady struggled to uphold her rituals. They believed she would return to the land one day. To that end, they collected her most sacred relics which they called 'The Bones of the Mother' and hid them away."

Maddie paused and looked up at Griffin quizzically. "That's a pretty odd name for a collection of relics. 'Bones of the Mother.' You don't think they're actual human bones, do you?"

The scrivener shook his head. "Not human, no. In all likelihood, it's a reference to objects made of stone. The expression 'Bones of the Mother' has a precise mythological meaning. Most ancient cultures considered the earth itself to be the mother of all. Therefore, her bones could be defined as stone or that which could be mined from stone, such as ore, gems, or crystals."

Seemingly satisfied with the explanation, Maddie nodded. "Makes sense so far." She turned her attention back to the journal and continued reading. "It is said that the secret to finding the Bones of the Mother can be found at the high place of the goddess. A cipher in stone waiting to be unlocked by one who holds the key. It is also said that one of the objects in this collection of treasures is the Voice of Heaven itself."

"The Voice of Heaven is one of the many names given to the Sage Stone," Griffin explained.

"The Sage Stone," Faye echoed. 'Then my worst fears have been confirmed."

"What?" Maddie gasped. "That's impossible. The Sage Stone is a myth. It doesn't exist."

"Everyone thought Troy was a myth until the ruins at Hissarlik were excavated," countered the scrivener.

"You don't actually think there's something to this, do you?" Maddie asked cautiously.

"I do now," he replied in a solemn voice. "According to the field journal, a cache of Minoan sacred objects was hidden somewhere. I think the directions for finding them have been encrypted in code on Crete and that the granite key provides the means to unlock that code. The passage you just read explicitly states that one of those sacred objects is the Sage Stone which leads me to conclude that it does, in fact, exist."

Faye looked down at the granite key which she still held absently in her hands. "Now that we know all this, it seems even more incomprehensible that the Nephilim would pursue such artifacts. The Sage Stone is the quintessential matristic relic. Of what possible use could it be to a Christian fundamentalist cult? It's far more likely they would dismiss both the Bones of the Mother and the Sage Stone as heathen nonsense."

"So, what's our next move?" Maddie asked them both.

Griffin looked at Faye. A silent message seemed to be passing between them.

Faye sighed. "It was my original intention not to take any action to retrieve relics the Nephilim wanted. Better to let them have the artifacts than to risk exposing our organization. But under the circumstances, I believe that approach would be a mistake. The Sage Stone is too significant a find for us to sacrifice. More importantly, in the hands of the Nephilim, it could be put to a very bad use. I had hoped to avoid a confrontation, but I see no recourse. It's time to call a meeting of the Concordance."

27 – HUNT FOR THE BONES

Once Daniel had cracked the first line of code, it was an easy matter to sort out the rest of the markings on the key. In consequence, Abraham was finally able to set his plan in motion. As a first step, he made an uncharacteristic journey to the Fallen Lands. On a warm spring morning, Metcalf seated himself on a bench in Millennium Park in the heart of Chicago and waited. He felt distinctly out of place. This park was a monument to the worldly folly of the Fallen. It held a distracting array of fountains, pavilions, and modern art work which tourists came to gawk at. Metcalf thought briefly of John Bunyan's *Vanity Fair*. Little about Fallen nature had changed in four hundred years. He disliked the atmosphere, the noise, and the crowds, but it all suited his present purpose. The park gave him complete anonymity. He was orchestrating a delicate scheme, and he didn't want his flock scrutinizing his activities too closely at this juncture. Some matters couldn't be explained to them. Not just yet anyway. He looked at his wristwatch, noting that the hour for his rendezvous had arrived.

A shadow fell across Metcalf's body as he bent his head down to check the time. He looked up to see a man standing above him. The man was wearing a cowboy hat and chewing on a toothpick. He grinned affably.

"Mornin' boss. How y'all doin' this fine day?"

Abraham shielded his eyes from the eastern sun and treated his companion to a rare smile. "Good morning to you, Mr. Hunt. Please have a seat."

Hunt raised his eyebrows in surprise. He was apparently unprepared for such a cordial reception. Nevertheless, he sat down on the bench next to Metcalf and waited for an explanation.

"I have some more work for you," Abraham began.

Leroy removed the toothpick and placed it in his coat pocket. "Well, well. That's right kindly of you to keep me in mind for one of your little odd jobs." He chuckled at his own choice of words. "What can I do you for?"

"I need you to accompany my son on a journey to Europe," the old man said flatly.

Hunt appeared taken aback. "Sorry, boss, but babysittin' ain't in my line."

A scowl settled over Abraham's features. "It's hardly a babysitting task, Mr. Hunt. This is a matter of great importance. In fact, the utmost importance."

Leroy rubbed the back of his neck, pondering the matter. "Well, sir, you must set considerable store by the boy seein' as how you got a barn full of other young 'uns to swap in if he gets hisself misplaced."

"It isn't about Daniel," Metcalf snapped impatiently. "He is only a minor part of the plan. You recall the granite key I asked you to retrieve for me some while ago?"

Hunt smiled at the memory. "That I do, sir. Truth to tell, I had me some fun on that job."

Several pigeons had begun milling around the bench where the two men sat. A particularly brave bird pecked hopefully at the ground near Abraham's foot. The old man kicked at it in disgust, causing it to flap away. Metcalf continued. "Retrieving the key was only the first part of the project."

Leroy's eyes widened as comprehension dawned. "Oh ho. So that's how it is. You figured out what them squiggly lines mean."

"That is correct," Metcalf averred. "My son Daniel is a scholar of ancient languages. He was able to translate the markings."

"I guess you were right to set such store by him then. Boy's a keeper. No doubt about that."

Ignoring the comment, Abraham pressed on. "The markings speak of artifacts called the 'Bones of the Mother.'"

"Bones of the Mother, huh?" Leroy considered the phrase. "Who's momma was she?"

Abraham gave him a withering look. "That is irrelevant. I want you to accompany Daniel to retrieve the artifacts."

The two men were distracted by a female jogger in spandex running down the promenade past their bench.

"Mmm, mmm. Now that's fine," Hunt commented appreciatively.

Metcalf's scowl deepened at the sight of the woman's unseemly apparel. There was a reason he avoided visiting the Fallen Lands too often. The bold behavior of the Fallen females was particularly disturbing. They conducted themselves with appalling forwardness. The fires of the pit would burn away that impudence, no doubt. Nevertheless, the thought of their present freedom to do as they liked galled him. They were a dangerous temptation to the angel brotherhood—luring the righteous away from their own chaste and obedient wives. Fallen females, by their very existence, were a constant threat to the souls of the worthy. Shaking off the image of the jogger, he returned to the topic. "We were speaking of the Bones, Mr. Hunt," he reminded his companion.

"So, you want I should dig up some old gal's skeleton and bring it back here?" Leroy sounded less than enthusiastic.

"Of course not!" Metcalf was losing patience. "There is no skeleton. The Bones is simply a name that refers to a collection of artifacts which I want to acquire."

"These artifacts worth a lot of money, are they?" Hunt's face had taken on a calculating expression.

"No, they're not, Mr. Hunt. There is no monetary value associated with them. I want them for spiritual reasons."

"That so? You gonna send your boy halfway around the world to pick up some old thingamabobs that you got a hankerin' for?" Leroy shook his head and laughed. "Man, I tell you what. Meanin' no disrespect, but you're a weird duck, boss."

"Be that as it may," Abraham said stiffly, "I still require the objects to be found and brought back to me."

Hunt looked away for a moment. His eyes followed the motion of another female jogger as she darted around pedestrians on the promenade. "You got some idea exactly where we're supposed to look for this stuff?"

"Not precisely, no," Metcalf admitted. "Daniel has told me that some of the markings on the key are a sort of hieroglyphic code. The rest of the markings on the key are an ancient script that was found in two places in the world. Either in southern Greece or on the island of Crete. I would suggest you begin your search in Greece."

Hunt whistled. "That's an awful big haystack you want us to comb."

"Not as big as all that. Tablets of the ancient language of which I spoke have only been found in four cities on the Greek mainland. In each of those cities, you will have assistance. Communities of the Blessed Nephilim exist throughout the world. I will appoint some trusted brethren in that region to begin the search before you arrive."

Hunt repositioned himself on the bench to face Metcalf. He cocked his head to the side to study the old man for a few seconds. "Somethin' puzzles me about this, and that's a fact. You got all these other fellers runnin' around like Santa's elves to do your biddin', and you got your boy who knows how to read them markings. What y'all need me for?"

Metcalf gave his companion an appraising look. "Because you have a unique set of skills, Mr. Hunt. A set of skills that my flock does not possess."

"Boss?"

"Although I don't anticipate any difficulties, I want to ensure that this expedition proceeds smoothly. I don't want anything to stand in the way of my acquisition of these relics."

Leroy grinned appreciatively. "You think maybe I might get a chance to use some of my special skills?"

"Let us hope not. But should such a thing happen, you have my permission to use any means necessary to ensure a successful outcome."

Hunt chuckled and gave a mock salute. "Yes sir, boss. Don't you worry about a thing now, you hear? I always give satisfaction. I got a reputation for doin' quality work."

Metcalf gave a humorless smile. "I have the utmost confidence in your work ethic, Mr. Hunt."

28 – THE CONCORDANCE

The sun was just about to set as Cassie drove into the schoolhouse clearing. She was glad that she knew the way. It would have been impossible to find the place after dark if she hadn't made the trip before. To her surprise, she saw a few dozen other cars parked in the green space in front of the building. The tall stained-glass windows in the main hall, illuminated from within by a dozen chandeliers, cast watercolor shadows across the lawn.

A queue of visitors was slowly making its way up the stairs and into the schoolhouse. Cassie fell in behind several people who were chatting excitedly in a foreign language. When the pythia finally reached the vestibule, she felt a tap on the shoulder.

"Hello there. Nice to see you again."

It was Griffin. She gave him a relieved smile. "Hey, haven't seen you for a while. What's going on? Faye called and told me to be here by seven o'clock."

"Yes, she called me as well and asked me to be your escort. That's why I was waiting here for you."

"I need a date for this?" Cassie asked in surprise.

She noticed a slight blush suffuse Griffin's face. "A date? Good heavens, no. Faye just thought someone should explain what you're about to see, that's all."

"Don't tell me it's a human sacrifice!" Cassie exclaimed tongue-in-cheek. "It isn't, is it?"

"A human sacrifice?" Griffin echoed in disbelief. "Where did you hear such a rumor? Of course not. It's a special gathering of the Concordance, and we'd better get inside soon if you don't wish to stand through the whole meeting."

He hurried her into the main hall which, for the first time in Cassie's experience, was ablaze with light and life. More than two hundred people were milling around: some deep in conversation, a few greeting old friends, others climbing the risers to the tiered box seats that lined the walls.

Griffin motioned to two seats in a lower tier which they hastily claimed. Once they were settled, Cassie looked around curiously at all the new faces. Some she recognized from the vault downstairs, but most of them were strangers to her.

She noted that many people had adopted strange attire. Some wore business suits with sashes across the chest. Several were sporting unusual headgear—a turban, a fez, a burnoose. One woman was dressed in a silk kimono while another wore a feather cape over a black gown.

"If there's a dress code for this event, I can't figure out what it is," she confided to Griffin.

"For a ceremonial gathering such as this, some members like to show off their native costume. Unfortunately for the majority of them, the climate of the Midwest is a bit chillier than where they came from. Practicality dictates that they must dress for warmth, but they like to wear some scrap of indigenous clothing as a memento of their homelands."

"Good thing nobody's being judged on their fashion sense. It's a runway nightmare!" Cassie commented.

Griffin chuckled but offered no opinion.

As the pythia looked around the room, she noticed Erik. He was leaning against the opposite wall, his arms folded across his chest. While there were empty seats nearby, he chose to remain standing.

Her eyes narrowed. "What's he doing here?"

The scrivener followed her gaze. "Erik? He is an elected member of the Concordance, so he can attend if he chooses."

"Let's hope he doesn't open his mouth," Cassie murmured under her breath.

Griffin gave her an odd look. He was apparently unaware of the animosity between the two.

The pythia continued her inspection. Her attention settled on the round table. The thirty chairs were now occupied by people of various hues, nationalities, and odd styles of clothing.

"Why thirty?"

"Hmm?" Griffin asked absently. He had been looking in the opposite direction, waving at someone he knew across the room. He glanced back toward the center. "Oh, you mean the main table? Tradition. The original idea was to have five representatives from each continent, but that seemed unfair to the continents which had the majority of the troves. The current system provides proportional representation based on the number of troves. The allocation among continents changes from time to time as the number of troves changes."

"And who gets to decide who sits at the main table?"

"Each trove chooses a representative to the Concordance, and those representatives elect the people who sit at the round table which, by the way, is called the Circle. Circle members are the governing body of the organization. They are the ones who vote on matters of import affecting the Arkana. However, when a topic is up for debate any member of the Concordance may participate in the discussion."

"Will I be allowed to say something?" Cassie asked eagerly.

"Fortunately for you, the title of pythia carries with it automatic inclusion in the Concordance, so the answer is yes, you may." A worried look crossed Griffin's face. "What were you planning to say exactly?"

Cassie shrugged. "Not sure, but it's good to know I could speak up if I wanted to." She scanned the room once more. "I don't see Faye yet. Where does she sit?"

Griffin leaned over and pointed. "Look there."

Cassie followed Griffin's instruction and noticed two men carrying a chair forward to place it at the table. It was more of a throne than a chair with a high back and ornately carved arms. She seemed to remember seeing it parked against the back wall on her previous visits to the schoolhouse.

"That chair is only used if Faye, herself, is conducting the meeting," Griffin explained.

Cassie was surprised. "You mean sometimes the Concordance meets without her?"

"Yes, if it's an issue that doesn't require her involvement. But she called this session, so she will definitely be presiding."

Cassie shifted her full attention to Griffin. "Do you know what this meeting is about?"

He smiled cryptically. "Oh yes, and it should prove quite interesting to see how they take it."

"How who takes what?"

Cassie was about to badger him with several more questions when her attention was caught by a small white-haired woman making her way toward the center of the room. People stepped to either side respectfully to let her pass. The woman was wearing a white silk dress and long matching jacket. With a start, Cassie realized it was Faye. She had only seen the old woman in her flowery house dresses before. Tonight, her attire made her look more like the Queen of England with the regal bearing to match. Cassie smiled at the memory of the little old grannie who baked her own bread and tried to overfeed everyone who came to see her. This was a side of Faye that the pythia hadn't seen before.

All conversation in the room ceased the moment the memory guardian reached the table. Faye stood in front of her throne-like chair. She looked around the room and gave a pleasant smile. "Good evening everyone. Shall we get started?"

Those who hadn't yet found a seat scurried to get settled. Maddie rushed to capture a spot on the opposite side. She must have been outdoors finishing one last smoke.

The throne dwarfed Faye when she sat down in it but, despite her diminutive size, her voice carried through the hall. "To those of you who have come a great distance on very short notice, I give my thanks. This is an urgent matter that must be decided quickly. About a month ago, our pythia Sybil was able to acquire an artifact which we have since begun to call the granite key. We were unsure of its purpose because, as most of you know, Sybil died before she was able to tell anyone what the find represented."

Cassie could hear sad murmurings coming from various points around the room. It never occurred to her that so many other people besides herself had mourned her sister's death.

Faye continued. "Fortunately, due to the efforts of our scrivener, we were able to decipher the code inscribed on the stone key. I will let him explain the details to you."

Faye looked toward the tier seats. "Griffin, if you would."

Cassie stared in surprise at the young man sitting next to her. "You did it!" she exclaimed. "You figured it out!"

"I did indeed." Griffin gave her a quick smile. "Sorry I didn't get a chance to fill you in earlier." He stood to address the Concordance.

The pythia listened intently as Griffin talked about hieroglyphics, ancient written scripts, Linear A, and Linear B. He explained how the code worked and where the encrypted message was likely to be found. Once he finished his explanation, Griffin sat down and allowed Faye to take over.

"We are of the opinion that one of the artifacts collectively known as the Bones of the Mother is the Sage Stone," she said.

The last two words produced an excited buzz from all corners of the room. Cassie had never heard the term "Sage Stone" before, but she guessed it was important to the Arkana.

Faye raised her hand for silence. "I realize that the Sage Stone is generally regarded as a mythical object, but we have good reason to believe it exists and that we can acquire it by recovering the Bones of the Mother." She paused for a few moments to allow her audience to digest these new facts. A roar of incredulity shot around the hall.

Cassie noted the stunned reaction among the members of the Concordance. It meant that the secret Sybil had tried to protect was huge. "She didn't die for nothing," Cassie thought to herself.

She leaned over and whispered to Griffin, "Give me the details. What's this Sage Stone?"

"I'll explain later," he answered hastily as Faye raised her hand once more for silence.

The old woman continued. "My friends, we are being offered a singular opportunity to recover some of the most important artifacts of our buried past. The Bones of the Mother need to be retrieved and housed in our troves, so we can preserve them for future generations. I propose that the Arkana should send an expedition to Crete to recover them."

A rumble of approval rippled across the room as people eagerly discussed the implications of the find with their companions.

An Indian man wearing a sash and seated at the round table across from Faye spoke. "Such an expedition seems an obvious step to take. Why would you need the support of the Concordance to make this decision?"

Faye smiled grimly. "Because there is another factor to be considered. This expedition cannot be undertaken without grave risk to the Arkana. The Nephilim are involved."

A chorus of dismay broke from several quarters at once. Cassie was startled by the extreme reaction that the cult evoked.

Faye held up her hand again, and the babble instantly ceased. "You need to know all the facts before an informed decision can be made. We believe that Sybil was killed, either deliberately or accidentally, by an operative of the Nephilim. We also have reason to believe that the current diviner of the cult is actively seeking the Bones of the Mother, most probably to get to the Sage Stone. Once in his possession, that artifact could trigger untold disaster. Based on our previous experience with the Nephilim, we know they are prepared to kill anyone who gets in the way of what they want."

An African woman wearing large hoop earrings and a turban spoke next. "I don't think our biggest problem is that they're willing to kill for these relics." She looked around the room. "Going after this find means we risk letting the Nephilim know that the Arkana exists."

Several shouts of "Hear, hear!" affirmed her comment.

"But they must know about the Arkana already. Otherwise, why would they go after our pythia?" The question came from an elderly Hispanic man wearing a multi-colored woolen shawl over a business suit.

"We don't believe they know about the organization," Erik chimed in from the other side of the room. "They thought Sybil was an antique dealer who had something they wanted, that's all. The Nephilim aren't famous for religious tolerance. If they suspected the Arkana existed, they would have launched some kind of holy war to stamp us out." His eyes flicked briefly in Cassie's direction. "Starting with our new pythia. We'd know they were on to us because she'd be dead already."

All eyes traveled to Cassie. She glared at Erik, making no attempt to hide her dislike. "He wishes," she thought to herself.

"If our anonymity is still intact that's all the more reason to keep it that way," countered the African woman from the Circle. "We should stay as far away from those relics as possible."

Cassie could hear conflicting comments surging from different directions. "She's right," someone said. "We should go anyway," another disagreed.

Back and forth it went. The discussion continued for what seemed like an eternity. Just as the participants approached consensus, their opinion would be swayed in a contrary direction by a more eloquent opposing voice.

***

Cassie sighed and looked at her wristwatch. They'd been at it for almost two hours. She glanced quickly at Griffin. The glazed expression on his face suggested that even he was getting bored with the proceedings. She thought this might be a good opportunity to learn more about the Sage Stone.

She leaned toward him and whispered, "So what is it?"

"What's what?" the young man asked vaguely.

"Wake up, will you? I want the backstory on the Sage Stone."

Finally snapping to attention, Griffin turned to her. "Oh, that. It's a unicorn," he said soberly.

"You're kidding, right?"

He shrugged. "Well, it's like a unicorn. And King Arthur's Excalibur. And Santa Claus. The Sage Stone is a myth, a legend. Something that up until quite recently none of us believed existed."

"But what does it look like? What does it do?" the pythia urged.

"It's a baetyl."

"A beetle?"

"No, a baetyl," Griffin corrected. "A meteorite that fell to earth thousands of years ago."

Cassie gave him an incredulous look. "Like kryptonite?"

"Good grief, of course not." The scrivener sounded exasperated. "To the peoples of the ancient world, a flaming rock that crashed to earth was a sign from the deity. It was meant to be treated with reverence. Do you remember what I told you about the black stone at Mecca? The one Muslims kiss when they visit the shrine?"

Cassie nodded uncertainly.

"That is also a baetyl. Cultures around the world venerated these objects and attributed magical properties to them."

"So, I was right," the pythia persisted. "It is like kryptonite. I mean, they're both magic rocks that fell from the sky."

"Yes, but one of them fell from a comic book sky while the other—" The scrivener halted, noting the pythia's mischievous expression. "You're being deliberately outrageous, aren't you?"

Cassie smiled impishly. "What was your first clue?"

"Are you quite finished?"

"I'm done for now. Go on." She waved him along airily.

"As I was attempting to explain, the ancients took baetylae very seriously as objects of awe and worship. The Sage Stone was one of these. No one knows exactly what it looked like, but it was probably black. Most meteorites blacken after exposure to earth's atmosphere. It may have been cylindrical or oval in shape. Not very large. Perhaps the size of a human hand. In antiquity, it was called by various names but most typically the Speaking Stone, the Sage Stone, or the Voice of Heaven. The Minoans believed it was an oracular stone."

"A what?"

"To a perceptive ear, it was reputed to whisper messages which would then be used for the benefit of the people. The Minoans attributed the many achievements of their culture to messages received from the Sage Stone. Their advances in technology and the arts were all based on the promptings of the baetyl. Until the dark ages came."

Cassie frowned. "What dark ages?"

"The Minoans of Crete represented the final flowering of matristic culture in the Mediterranean region. Their civilization enjoyed two thousand years of uninterrupted peace and prosperity. However, beginning around 1400 BCE, things changed. Along with a series of natural disasters, the Minoans were subjected to a wave of overlord invasions that destroyed their way of life. They believed that the Sage Stone had abandoned them. Their seers could no longer hear the whispering in the rock."

"What happened to it?"

"Ah, that's where the legend begins," Griffin said mysteriously. "The Sage Stone disappeared from view. Lost in the swirling mists of time. No one knew what became of it, but there was a prediction. If the Sage Stone ever came to light again, it would presage the beginning of a new golden age."

"For the Minoans?" Cassie sounded incredulous. "They aren't around anymore, are they? I've never heard of them."

"Not for the Minoans. For the entire world. It would mean equality, prosperity, and, dare I say it, peace on earth. The end of overlord domination of the planet. In short, everything the Arkana has been working toward for centuries."

"That's some rock!" Cassie exclaimed, impressed.

Griffin shrugged. "Of course, no one actually believes in the prophecy nowadays. But the Sage Stone itself is a rare artifact. A mythical object that really exists. A matristic version of the Holy Grail. For that reason alone, we would want to protect it in our troves."

Cassie frowned as a new thought struck her. "Why would the Nephilim want something that ushers in the reverse of the kind of world they like to live in? Equality, peace on earth, and good will aren't really their thing. Do they just want to get their hands on it to destroy it?"

Griffin grew thoughtful at her words. "That assumes they actually believe the Minoan prophecy which is highly unlikely. The Nephilim only credit prophecies made by one of their own. To them, the Minoan prediction would be heathen gibberish. No, I think it's something else." He paused as a new thought struck him. "Aside from any putative mystical powers, the Sage Stone must have some symbolic meaning to the Nephilim, and that doesn't bode well. Fanatics tend to commit their greatest atrocities under the aegis of symbols, whether they be crosses, swastikas, or baetylae."

"Well, whatever they've got in mind for the Sage Stone, I think it's a good idea if the Arkana gets to it first," Cassie observed.

The scrivener nodded solemnly. "I quite agree."

The pythia checked her watch again. The Concordance discussion had now continued for two hours and fifteen minutes. "This is never gonna end," she whispered in Griffin's ear. "Why doesn't Faye just shut them all down?"

Griffin turned and whispered back, "Because this is a democracy, not a dictatorship. Faye is wise enough to know that everyone needs an opportunity to be heard. In the end, they may not agree with the vote, but they won't fight the decision. They'll have had a chance to express their views."

"You mean she's going to sit there and let them yammer on till doomsday?" the pythia asked irritably.

"A general discussion fulfills a very important psychological purpose. Wait and see. She'll choose her time, and when they've played themselves out, she'll nudge them in the direction she wants them to go."

At that moment, a young Arab man in the top tier of the box seats asked, "How do you know the Nephilim haven't gotten to the relics already? While we're sitting here debating, who's to say they haven't swept them up?"

Other voices joined his in asking the same question. The grumbling and objecting sounded like the buzz of angry hornets.

"I say they haven't," Faye observed quietly. Immediately the buzzing ceased as all eyes turned questioningly toward the memory guardian.

She gave a slight smile. "I would respectfully remind you that the Nephilim are a pseudo-Christian cult. They shun pagan lore because they consider it an abomination. It stands to reason that in order to decrypt the code on the key and find the exact location of the artifacts they would need experts in matristic culture to help them." She paused for effect and surveyed the faces looking back at her quizzically. "I don't wish to belabor the obvious, but I believe that all the experts who might be able to help them are sitting in this very room. Is there anyone here who would like to volunteer to assist the Nephilim? Please do raise your hands."

It took a second for her words to register, and then everyone started to laugh. The tension in the room immediately eased.

Faye continued. "While I think through trial and error they will eventually stumble across the information they need, we already have all the necessary resources at our fingertips. We have the skills, the training, and the knowledge to get there first. After all, we've been doing this for centuries."

Cassie listened to the comments being made within earshot. The voices of dissent were fewer now. Faye had timed her remarks to occur right at the point when everyone was getting tired of the topic and wanted to conclude the debate.

"You see!" Griffin exclaimed triumphantly. "I told you. I've seen her do this before. She's quite effective at turning the tide."

A tall dark-haired woman stood up. She had been seated in the bottom tier of box seats. "I am Xenia Katsouros, the keeper of the Minoan trove on the island of Crete. If anyone had been searching the area for the relics of which we are speaking, I would have heard about it. I am sure the memory guardian is right. The Nephilim have not come to Crete yet. I, for one, favor this expedition and will be happy to assist in the search should a team be assembled for this task."

When she sat down, several people applauded her words.

As Cassie's eyes travelled around the room, she could see from the expressions on various faces that the majority were now convinced it was a good idea.

"Is there any further discussion before we put the proposal to a vote?" Faye asked quietly. She paused for a full minute, waiting for the last sound of discord to die away.

When everyone was still, the Circle cast its vote. The decision was made by a simple show of hands. Four delegates were against the motion and twenty-seven, including Faye, were in favor of it. The motion was carried.

Cassie smiled to herself at Faye's ability to sway this fractious crowd. She had grossly underestimated the little old lady's tactical skills.

The meeting ended shortly afterward. Everyone was invited to a reception in the upstairs conference rooms. As Cassie and Griffin walked toward the back stairs to join the others, the pythia said, "I don't know exactly how she did it, but Faye got her way in the end. Who do you suppose she'll send?"

The scrivener shrugged. "Haven't a clue, but I expect it will be someone who knows what they're about. We don't need amateurs mucking this up. It's too important." He gave a sigh of relief. "It's times like these when I'm glad I work in a library."

"Vault," Cassie corrected with a laugh. "You work in a vault, remember?"

29 – TEAM QUIRKS

Cassie arrived at Faye's house at eleven o'clock the following morning. She'd been surprised when the memory guardian drew her aside at the reception the night before and asked her to stop by. Faye neglected to say what she wanted to see Cassie about.

"Sure, no problem," the pythia agreed, secretly wondering what hoops the old woman was going to make her jump through this time.

When she pulled into the driveway of the farmhouse, two other cars were already parked there. Cassie didn't recognize them and wondered what other company Faye might have.

The old woman greeted her at the door and ushered her into the kitchen at the back. Two people were seated at the table. Cassie smiled to see Griffin. And then to her horror, she noticed Erik sitting across from him.

"What's… sh…. he... doing… here!" Their voices clashed in mid-sentence.

Griffin looked in dismay from one to the other.

Faye chuckled. "Calm yourselves, my dears. Cassie, please sit down and help yourself to some banana nut bread. I just made a few loaves fresh this morning. There's tea if you like."

The thought of food was the last thing on Cassie's mind. She sat down at the end of the table, moving her chair slightly away from Erik's side and closer to Griffin's.

They continued to scowl at one another though neither spoke.

Faye drew up a chair for herself at the opposite end. "I believe you two got off on the wrong foot," she began. "That's unfortunate since you'll need to work closely together on your new recovery mission."

"What recovery mission?" Erik asked suspiciously, never taking his eyes off Cassie. "She hasn't come up with anything yet, has she?"

"Why don't you ask me yourself?" Cassie snapped. "I'm sitting right here."

"Well, did you?" the blond man demanded.

"No, as a matter of fact, I didn't. I'm still in training," the pythia said primly.

"That'll take a couple of years," Erik muttered under his breath.

"Am I missing something here?" Griffin interjected hesitantly.

"I think these two are going through a period of adjustment," Faye said mildly. "That's all."

Out of respect for Faye, neither one of them contradicted her. They just seethed in silence.

Ignoring the tension, Faye sliced a piece of nut loaf and handed it to Cassie, thereby redirecting the pythia's attention.

"I'm sure you're wondering why I called the three of you together," she began.

"I am now," Erik commented *sotto voce.*

"I should think it would be obvious, given the outcome of last night's meeting." The old woman glanced around the table.

The three visitors looked back at her blankly.

She smiled briefly. "Apparently not as obvious to you three as it is to me." She took a deep breath. "My dears, I have chosen you to be the team which will retrieve the Bones of the Mother."

They all sat thunderstruck. If she had just announced that she intended to take up a career as a professional wrestler, the trio couldn't have been more shocked.

"I beg your pardon," Griffin said, probably thinking he had misheard her.

"What?" Erik asked flatly.

"Huh?" was Cassie's eloquent contribution.

Faye seemed to be enjoying their consternation. She laughed. "Oh my, this isn't going to be easy, is it? Yes, you all heard me correctly. I don't see why any of you should be surprised. All of you have unique skills that will prove invaluable in recovering these artifacts."

The three of them started babbling at once, protesting their unfitness for the job. No single voice could be heard above the general rumble of discontent. Faye let them complain for a few minutes and then raised her hand for silence. "I think we might make better progress if each of you spoke in turn. Griffin, dear, why don't you start?"

It took the scrivener several seconds to catch his breath and assemble his thoughts. He sounded panic-stricken. "Faye, surely you can't be serious. I've never gone on a field mission in my entire life. My skills, as you call them, are of the bookish variety."

"Exactly," she concurred. "My dear, you carry an encyclopedia in your head. It's very impressive."

"At cocktail parties, possibly," he admitted. "But I hardly think it will be useful out in the middle of nowhere."

"Don't you?" she asked gently. "On the contrary, that's precisely where your knowledge would prove to be the most useful. This mission won't allow the luxury of a portable library or a reliable internet connection. Thinking quickly on one's feet is what will be required."

"But what about the central catalog? I am its director, after all."

"And you have a very capable staff who can fill in until you return," the old woman suggested helpfully.

He didn't appear convinced but was at a loss to come up with any further objections.

"And what about you, Cassie?" the old woman focused her attention on the pythia. "What is your principal concern about making the journey?"

"Me?" Cassie asked in astonishment. "I only signed on less than a month ago, and now you want to send me overseas? Even army recruits get more time in boot camp than that!"

"I never thought I'd say this," Erik admitted ruefully. "But the kid is right."

"I'm not a kid!" Cassie rounded on him.

"Yeah, you're a veteran." The blond man rolled his eyes and folded his arms across his chest.

Cassie turned her attention back to Faye. "Besides, I don't know what help I could be. You're expecting to find a code chiseled into stone somewhere, right? It doesn't take a pythia to decrypt that. Griffin should be able to crack the code with no problem. He's incredibly smart."

"Please stop helping me, I beg you," Griffin protested weakly.

"To tell the truth, we can't be sure what you'll encounter when you get to Crete," Faye countered. "It may very well be that the skills of a pythia are exactly what is needed."

"You really think she's up to it?" Erik looked at Faye curiously.

"I've seen her telemetric abilities firsthand. I can assure you; she's quite adept."

"Huh, go figure." Erik seemed genuinely amazed at Faye's glowing endorsement of Cassie.

"I hope the shock of knowing I'm competent doesn't kill you," Cassie commented acidly.

"It just might," the blond man said with an impudent smirk.

Cassie was about to go at him again, but Faye preempted her. "Erik, dear, what possible objection can you have for going on this expedition? After all, you love field work, and you've had plenty of experience."

Erik let out a long sigh. "It's not me I'm worried about. It's these two." He jerked his head in the direction of his companions. "I know what I'm doing, and I can handle whatever gets thrown at me. But I'd have to watch out for them every step of the way. It would be like letting toddlers loose in a mine field." He shrugged. "I know I'm only the security guy, and I can't actually find the artifacts. But I can think of five people in the Arkana right off the top of my head who could, and it isn't these two. You should listen to them, Faye. They're both telling you they're not up to it."

"Now just a minute, old man," Griffin protested. Apparently, it was one thing to downplay his own experience but to hear Erik's dismissive opinion was too much of an insult.

"You know what?" Cassie shot back at the blond man. "I'm suddenly feeling really up to it. If I don't do anything other than make your life miserable for a couple of weeks, then I'll die happy."

"'Die' being the operative word," Erik retorted.

Faye shook her head and laughed. "So much sound and fury signifying nothing. Please try to trust my judgment, my dears. I wish you could see yourselves as I do. I have very good reasons for choosing each one of you."

They glanced at one another dubiously, trying hard to imagine what shining qualities Faye could see.

She continued. "This mission is unlike anything the Arkana has attempted before. The circumstances are unique. We don't know the location of the message which the key unlocks, nor do we know what artifacts we're searching for. We don't even know how many of them there are. On top of that, we're very likely to run into dangerous competition for those relics. This is a highly unorthodox retrieval mission, and I believe it calls for an unorthodox team to bring it to a successful conclusion."

She peered at them all earnestly, willing them to understand the point she was trying to make. "This mission can't be conducted by the book. Seasoned experts often grow complacent, and complacency would be fatal in circumstances where you need to be especially on your guard. The project requires flexibility and ingenuity—a new perspective that comes from a fresh set of eyes."

Cassie and Griffin smiled at one another. Their shared naïveté created a bond. Neither one had ever considered lack of experience to be an advantage before. It was a comforting thought that there might be a strategic benefit to it after all.

"So, you're saying greenhorns are good?" Erik asked incredulously.

Faye tilted her head to the side, considering the question. "Yes, I suppose I am. For this particular mission anyway."

"Then why include me? I actually know what I'm doing. If you want a greenhorn to handle security, then bring in a blind German Shepherd."

The old woman remained unflustered. She smiled sweetly. "You have been chosen to provide balance. I think one field-tested veteran will round out the team nicely."

Erik's expression remained skeptical, but he held his peace.

The other two were still glowing at one another under the conviction that their shared weakness was really a strength. They offered no further objection to Faye's plan.

"Now, let's discuss strategy while I put on a pot of coffee," Faye suggested.

Cassie thought back to the previous evening when Faye had been able to sway an audience of two hundred to do what she wanted. This morning she had persuaded three antagonistic people to jump on a plane and retrieve lost relics for her. All that and she still had time to bake banana nut bread. "She's good," the pythia said to herself.

30 – HAPPY HOUR

It was a hot afternoon for mid-May. At least it would have been considered hot in Chicago, but this was Greece. A little seaside town in Greece called Pylos. Leroy Hunt was sitting alone at an outdoor café fanning himself with his Stetson hat. Three local boys strolled by and noticed his outfit.

"Cowboy. Bang! Bang!" they said cheerily in passing.

"Right back at ya, pardners," Leroy replied affably. He made a mock gesture with his thumb and index finger simulating firing a gun. The boys laughed and moved on.

Hunt briefly flashed on an image in his mind's eye. He saw their smiles congeal into expressions of terror when he pulled out the Sig Pro pistol that was actually concealed in his shoulder holster. The thought amused him. He chuckled. Too bad he was minding his manners this trip. He was ripe for a little dust up, but he had to keep a low profile.

He took another sip of liquor and considered his plight. A low profile was one thing, but he might as well be dead. He was bored out of his mind. No fun in trailing along behind Metcalf's hangdog kid watching him scratch around in the dirt.

Hunt rolled his eyes in disgust. So much for special skills. His talents were wasted on this trip. It was small comfort that he was getting paid handsomely to do nothing. He craved some action to get his adrenaline pumping, but it sure didn't look like he was going to get any. A glorified babysitter was all he'd turned out to be. The next time that crazy old preacher man came to him with some work, he'd tell him where to go.

In the meantime, his days were spent cooling his heels at every taverna between Thebes and Pylos while he waited for the kid to turn up something.

He'd learned a few useful words in Greek though: *Roditis*, *Retzina*. Man, those Greek wines really packed a wallop. Almost as good as the shine back home, but *ouzo* was his favorite. It must be something like 160-proof. They even named restaurants after the liquor—*ouzaria*. It was a place where you could sit all afternoon and sip the stuff while they brought you snacks to go with it. Too bad they didn't have any fried pork rinds. He couldn't bring himself to eat calamari. The dish reminded him of boiled rubberbands in glue. He sighed and drummed his fingers impatiently on the table and then looked at his watch. Four p.m. The kid said he'd meet him here at four, but the little runt was always late. He beckoned the waiter to order another drink.

This whole trip was screwy. When they flew into Athens, two of the Greek brethren showed up to whisk them off to a Nephilim compound out in the hills. Leroy took a pass and made them bring him back to a proper hotel. He wasn't going to sleep in a place that felt like a mausoleum for the living. Same as the compound in Chicago. All stone floors and squeaky-clean silence. Besides, he figured Junior would be safe in the hands of his freaky fan club. They practically kissed the ground he walked on. They kept calling him "the son of the diviner." You'd think he was Elvis the way they carried on. No, Leroy was sure Daniel was safe enough with them.

The next morning, he went out with the boy and his groupies to the first site. It was a heap of old ruins, and they started crawling over rock piles like a bunch of dung beetles looking for their dinner. The day was hot and dusty. After a few hours, Leroy decided he'd had enough of being sunburned and parched. He went to find the nearest taverna and did the same in every town they'd searched since.

So far nobody even remotely shady or suspicious had showed up to throw a monkey wrench into Junior's plans. Per the instructions of the old man, the local Nephilim had gotten Leroy his favorite type of hand gun, so he didn't have to try smuggling one into the country. Not likely he was going to get a chance to use it though. Hunt felt it was safe to relax his guard and doze away his time in Greece in an alcoholic stupor. He just told Daniel to check in with him every afternoon. That way he could expend the minimum amount of effort to be sure the little punk hadn't fallen down a rat hole or got himself killed some other way.

Hunt looked at his watch again. 4:10. At that moment, Daniel sloped around the corner of the building and slid into the other chair at Leroy's table.

"Well, son, glad to see you made it on time."

The young man glanced around nervously. He was clutching a black leather portfolio and still wearing that creepy Nephilim get-up even though it was ninety degrees in the shade. Hunt thought he looked like a demented Jehovah's Witness with a briefcase full of flyers to stick on people's windshields. Leroy flashed on another image involving his gun and a dead Bible thumper.

"Any luck today?" he asked pleasantly.

The boy appeared apprehensive. "No, Mr. Hunt. Nothing. I'm beginning to get very worried."

"Why's that now?" Leroy scratched his chin, doing his best to sound interested. The waiter returned with his *ouzo*.

Daniel glanced up at the man and lowered his voice. "We're running out of locations to check. Linear B tablets have only been found in four places in this part of the country. We've already combed Thebes, the ruins at Tyrins, and Mycenae. I've spent today at the local museum, but there's only one site left to check. I pray I find something at Nestor's palace or Father will be very displeased."

"Yep, I imagine your daddy won't be too happy if you come up empty-handed."

The young man's shoulders jerked tensely. "It isn't just that Father will be unhappy, Mr. Hunt. I would be failing God himself."

Leroy lifted his glass to his lips and sipped his *ouzo*. "Son, you spend way too many waking hours frettin' about perdition."

Daniel made no comment. Instead, he opened his portfolio and started reviewing the papers inside.

Leroy was just bored enough that he actually felt some curiosity about the boy's mission. "What you got there?"

Daniel slid one of the papers across the table toward Hunt. It was a magnified photograph of one side of the stone key.

It took a moment for Hunt to get his eyes in focus. Too much *ouzo* or maybe not enough.

"The hieroglyphic markings," the young man offered. "I expect to find them carved somewhere near the sites where Linear B tablets were excavated."

"So that's why you been crawlin' over them ruins and wanderin' around in museums?"

"Yes." The young man nodded. "The granite key possesses some markings in the Linear B language and some in hieroglyphic code. The only way to connect the two is to find the places where Linear B script has been found before."

"Uh huh," Hunt said knowledgeably. "And then what? What happens when you find them squiggly marks."

"They will lead us to the treasure."

Leroy's head snapped to attention at that last word. "What was that again?" he prompted.

"The reason we came to Greece," Daniel explained. "To find the heathen relics. The Bones of the Mother."

"You think maybe them Bones might be worth somethin' in cash money?" Even though Metcalf had told Leroy that the relics had no value, Hunt wanted a second opinion. The old man might have been lying. "Is that why your daddy wants you to find 'em so bad?"

Daniel looked puzzled. "I don't think so. I'm not sure why Father needs them, but I'm sure money isn't a motive. I'm sorry. It was a poor choice of words to refer to the artifacts as treasure."

Leroy immediately lost interest and lapsed back into his previous state of apathy. "Oh."

The young man shifted his attention from his papers to Leroy's hat. "Pardon my curiosity, but I've never encountered one of the Fallen who dresses or speaks the way you do, Mr. Hunt."

"What can I tell you, son? My heroes have always been cowboys."

"Were you ever a cowboy?"

"Nope, I just watched 'em on the silver screen. I'd see John Wayne or Gary Cooper or, hell, even Montgomery Clift ridin' off into the sunset. Man, that was a sweet way to live. Simple too. Wasn't a single problem them fellers couldn't solve with a gun."

Daniel looked perplexed. "What silver screen are you talking about? Were those men you mentioned all professional cowboys?"

Leroy regarded him sourly. "I gotta say, your daddy left some big holes in your education, boy."

At that moment, the waiter came back to the table and asked Daniel in broken English if he wanted to order something.

The young man recoiled in panic. "No, nothing, thank you!"

Hunt observed his reaction with amusement. "It ain't poison, son."

"I never partake of food or drink outside of the sanctuary."

"Too bad. For a travelin' man that just ain't practical. Now, what if you was to find yourself on a desert island someday, and that there waiter asked if you wanted somethin'. What would you do then?"

Daniel squinted at Hunt, trying to make sense of the question. "Why would a waiter be on a desert island?"

Leroy waved his hand airily. "Never you mind why. Just answer the question. What would you do?"

"I don't imagine I would ever have any reason to be on a desert island," Daniel replied seriously.

Leroy reached into his coat pocket but stopped himself short of gripping the handle of his gun. He could dream, couldn't he? A change of topic seemed to be in order. He wanted to get this interview over with, so he could concentrate on some serious drinking.

"Well, what you got in mind to do tomorrow then?"

The anxious look returned to Daniel's face. "My brethren and I are going to spend the day at the palace ruins outside of town. If nothing turns up there, I'll have to call father and let him know."

"Bet that'll be a hoot," Leroy observed mordantly. "Then what?"

Hunt could see the reaction his question provoked. The boy's pasty complexion lost what little color it had. Leroy wondered how a body could spend all day outdoors in the Greek sun and still look as pale as a fish's belly.

"We're running out of options. There are only two other known locations where Linear B tablets have been found. Those would be the palaces at Chania and Knossos."

"They anyplace hereabouts?"

"No, they're on the island of Crete," Daniel explained.

"Crete, huh. They got *ouzarias* there?"

"*Ouzarias*?" the young man repeated blankly.

"Never mind, boy. Never mind." Hunt waved him away. "See you tomorrow around four."

"Until tomorrow then. Good day, Mr. Hunt." Daniel tensely gathered up his papers and left.

The amount of alcohol in Hunt's bloodstream rendered him briefly philosophical. He hadn't spent much of his life contemplating the fiery inferno. In fact, he didn't believe in it. But now that he was working for a cult that was obsessed with it, the nether realm featured prominently in his musings. This trip to Greece had convinced him that hell was real and that he had managed to land smack in the middle of Satan's back forty.

31 - KNOSSOS

Cassie and Griffin wearily staggered off the plane at the Heraklion airport on the island of Crete. The pythia's head was spinning and not merely from jet lag. Everything was happening so fast. It had only been three short days since Faye had revealed her plan, and already they were in Greece.

At the last minute, Erik had been called away to handle an important relic shipment which meant he would travel separately and arrive later. Cassie was relieved. The thought of being trapped on a transatlantic flight with the security coordinator was unnerving. Ever since Faye's pep talk he had maintained a sullen silence around her. While she considered this a good thing, it was tempting fate to assume he could behave himself all the way from Chicago to Crete.

Once Griffin and Cassie had cleared customs and picked up their luggage, they took a cab to the hotel where their Minoan contact was supposed to meet them. Cassie saw her immediately when the pair entered the lobby since the woman's leopard print dress was hard to miss. It was the tall dark-haired trove keeper from the Concordance meeting. Her name was Xenia Katsouris. At close range, she appeared to be an attractive fortysomething with shoulder length hair, prominent eyebrows, and hawk-like features. Not the sort of person you'd want to cross even though she was smiling at the moment.

"Ah, I see you have arrived safely. Welcome to Crete!" She stepped forward to shake hands with them.

They walked together to the reception desk to check in, despite the fact that it was only 9 o'clock in the morning. They had agreed that sleep was a luxury they couldn't afford, and it would only make the jet lag worse. The trove keeper waited patiently while they went to freshen up and stow their gear in their rooms. Half an hour later they were all seated together in the hotel restaurant drinking coffee and struggling to shake off their fatigue.

Xenia smiled sympathetically. "It is a long trip, is it not? I just returned myself two days ago."

"How do you do it?" Cassie asked in amazement. "I feel like I've just been run over by a truck."

"I am a very good actress," Xenia joked. "I only appear to be awake."

"Have the Nephilim been seen on the island yet?" Griffin asked worriedly.

The trove keeper hastened to reassure him. "Do not concern yourself. I have sent several members of my team to monitor Minoan archaeological sites. They tell me that no tourists are engaging in any unusual search activity. I believe we are still ahead of them."

The scrivener relaxed his troubled expression.

While Cassie ordered another cup of coffee, Griffin passed out sheets of paper to his companions. "These are enlarged photographs of the markings from the granite key. Study the line of hieroglyphics on each page. Those characters are what we're trying to find."

Xenia perused the sheets. "Where do you propose to start the search?"

Griffin hesitated a moment. "I brought along the field journal of the operative who first mentioned the Bones of the Mother. According to legend, the secret of finding the relics was kept at the high place of the goddess. It seems to me the most likely location would be Knossos."

The trove keeper nodded her agreement. "Yes, that would make sense."

"What's Knossos?" Cassie looked around for the waitress with the coffee pot.

"The ruins of a Minoan palace. The largest Minoan palace on the island," Griffin explained. "Though palace is an inaccurate definition. The site fulfilled many functions, one of which was to act as a shrine to the Minoan great goddess. It might have been considered her high temple, so the reference in the journal to a high place of the goddess may well refer to Knossos. Aside from that, Knossos is also strongly connected to the Linear B language. The largest cache of Linear B tablets found on the island came from the palace."

"And you think we're going to find these symbols carved into a rock at Knossos?" Cassie squinted at the photographs.

Griffin sighed. "It's a stab in the dark really. We have so little information to go on, but we have to start somewhere."

While the other two were speaking, Xenia had been studying the pages carefully. When she spoke, her voice held a note of concern. "So much of the palace has collapsed. Fire and earthquake have taken a great toll. Not to mention the reconstruction of the early archaeologists. What you seek may still be buried under piles of rubble."

"I think it very likely that an inscription of this importance would have been placed in one of the ceremonial areas. Not in the underground storage rooms or the artisan's workshops. We won't have to cover the entire complex—just the central court, the corridors, and the main chambers."

"But do you not think that strange markings such as these would have been catalogued already if they had been found?" Xenia persisted.

Griffin smiled knowingly. "Ah, but you see that's the genius of the code. Look closely at these hieroglyphics. They are all common Minoan artistic motifs. The hourglass, spirals, meanders, dots, flowers, birds, fish, and so on. An archaeologist who viewed them would consider them nothing more than decoration. It's the arrangement of images that provides the meaning." The scrivener quickly sketched several symbols in succession. "For example, if I draw these symbols in this particular order, I've just spelled the word *potnia*."

"And that means?" Cassie prompted.

"*Potnia* is a Greek word which means 'lady' or 'mistress,'" Xenia explained. "In this context, it would mean 'the goddess' much as Catholics would use the expression 'Our Lady' to speak of the Virgin Mary."

The pythia studied the composite image Griffin had created. "So, we need to start by looking for this combination of symbols?"

"Actually, you should look for this symbol first." Griffin drew a picture of a flower. "It's a lily and the sacred flower of the Minoan goddess. Look at the photograph with three lines of code displayed on it. The top line is written in Linear B and says, 'To find the Bones of the Mother.' If you look at either end of the inscription, you will see a lily. I would assume that the lily is the symbol we should associate with that message. It acts like a directional arrow to get our attention. 'Look here' is what it seems to say. 'Pay attention. The symbols that follow will be about the Bones of the Mother.'"

"Got it," Cassie said. "Find the lily."

Griffin looked around the table to see if there were any other questions. Tentatively he asked, "Shall we get started?"

The trove keeper stood up, retrieving her keys from her purse. "Come, we will take my car."

***

Xenia maneuvered her small Citroen through the narrow city streets and out into the countryside. Apparently, Griffin's ordeal of being seated in a confined space wasn't over. As if being crumpled in coach wasn't bad enough, he insisted on folding himself in half so that Cassie could sit in the front seat of the car. It took nearly an hour to reach the site. As they motored down into a valley surrounded by green rolling hills, they were confronted with a sprawling multi-level hodgepodge of exposed stairways, two-story chambers, heaped stones, and reconstructed pillars. After parking the car, they walked up a winding path toward the entrance. The palace had collapsed in many places exposing underground vaults and massive storage urns to the sky.

"This place is enormous!" Cassie exclaimed in dismay.

"Yes, it is," Griffin agreed, "but not to worry. We aren't going to search all of it. The palace complex takes up approximately six acres of land and consists of over one thousand interlocking chambers. Parts of the original structure were five stories high. Calling it a palace is really a misnomer since it had a very different function than housing royalty. There are artisans' workshops and food processing areas that contain grain mills and wine presses. It served as a central storage facility for the region and was very likely the religious and administrative center as well. At its height, Knossos and its surrounding countryside had a population of several thousand people."

"You know a great deal about the history of this place," Xenia noted approvingly.

"It's what he does," Cassie confided. "He knows everything about everything."

"Hardly," Griffin protested. "I'm sure to get at least a few of the details wrong. I've only been here once before as a child."

"I think you are doing a good job. Please continue," the Greek woman said.

"As you wish," he conceded. "For Cassie's benefit, we'll have a short history lesson first. The site was originally excavated by Sir Arthur Evans in 1900. Like Heinrich Schliemann who was convinced that Troy really existed, Sir Arthur believed the fantastic stories of classical writers. They said that a great civilization had once flourished on the island of Crete. He set about proving it and unearthed the treasures of a culture which was unlike anything else in the ancient world. Even though Greece and Rome owe most of their cultural advancement to what came before in Minoa, it's still quite distinct."

"What makes it so different?" Cassie challenged.

"A great many things," Xenia said. "You will see as we walk along."

"Let's talk about where Knossos is situated for a start," suggested Griffin.

Cassie studied her surroundings in surprise. "It doesn't look all that different from pictures I've seen of other ancient ruins."

"Location, location, location," Griffin hinted.

Cassie raised an eyebrow. "It seems like a great location to me. Rolling hills, lots of greenery. A photographer would love this place."

They were standing in the middle of an area that was called the central court.

"Let's pause here for a moment," Griffin suggested. "Try to look at the location from an overlord perspective. Tactically speaking, this location is terrible if you're trying to fend off an invading army. It's in a middle of a valley, exposed on all sides. There are no battlements, no fortifications, no moat. Nothing."

"Then why build here?" Cassie asked perplexed.

"Because the Minoans were not a people in love with war," Xenia said softly. "They were in love with life. When this location was first chosen, the people who lived here had nothing to fear from invaders. They lived in a peaceful land, and this place was built as a tribute to the goddess they worshipped. Look here."

She drew Cassie over to a large stone sculpture that looked like the goalposts in a football stadium. "These are called the horns of consecration, and they are one of the most common symbols in Minoan culture though they did not originate on Crete. Horns of consecration first appeared in the artifacts of old Europe eight thousand years ago. In the ruins on the island, you will see them everywhere. Much like the crucifix is seen everywhere in the Christian religion. Come stand behind the horns and look through them. What do you see?"

Cassie complied. "First, there's a round hill, and then back in the distance, a mountain top."

"Yes, that is Mount Jouctas which was sacred to the goddess in ancient times. There is a reason why the palace was built exactly here, and it was not for military defense. It was an act of worship."

Griffin picked up the thread. "All four palaces on the island take advantage of the same topographical features. First, there is an enclosed valley where the palace is set, then a mounded hill on axis with the palace and beyond that, a mountain peak, also on axis with the palace. The landscape becomes part of the shrine."

"You have heard of the monoliths at Stonehenge and Avebury, have you not?" Xenia asked.

"I've heard of Stonehenge," Cassie admitted.

"All such structures had a cosmic significance to the people who built them. The monoliths connect the sky with the earth through their sophisticated calendar measurements," Xenia said.

"Nineteenth-century archaeologists posited that the monoliths in Britain had been built by some war chief and had a military function," Griffin added. "But, of course, they were wrong. Just as wrong as it would be to assume Knossos was built for defense."

Cassie remained standing behind the horns of consecration and considered the landscape from that perspective. "When Faye first started my training, she told me about ancient civilizations that didn't go to war."

"And this was the last of them," Xenia murmured.

"The last of them?"

"The palace was damaged and rebuilt many times because of natural disasters, but it was finally destroyed by fire around 1350 BCE," the trove keeper said.

"That's still over three thousand years ago," Cassie insisted. "How can this be the last of those peaceful civilizations?"

Griffin nodded. "I'm afraid she's right, Cassie. Cultures nearly as sophisticated and equally peaceful go back ten thousand years."

The pythia shook her head in disbelief.

"Perhaps we should begin our search now," the trove keeper suggested.

They paced through the central court, their eyes sweeping every stone for the lily symbol that matched the one on the granite key. As they moved farther afield, their search led them through a confusing array of short passageways, interlocking rooms, light shafts, and stairways.

Cassie found herself becoming disoriented. "Wait, stop for a minute. I think I'm getting dizzy. Where are we?"

Her two companions paused and exchanged a look. "That's probably how the invading Hellenes felt when they first came to this place," Griffin commented. "That's why they invented the myth of the labyrinth and the minotaur."

"The what now?" Cassie asked blankly. "Classical mythology always rated high on my list of trivia I could live without."

"Surely, you know the legend." Xenia sounded surprised. "That is the story that gives the civilization its name."

"It's safe to assume that Cassie's knowledge of antiquity is sketchy at best," Griffin confided to the trove keeper.

"But she is the pythia," Xenia protested.

"I'm afraid she came late to her calling," the scrivener explained.

"Would somebody please tell me about this—"

"Labyrinth and minotaur," Griffin cut in. Turning to Xenia, he asked, "Would you like to do the honors?"

"If you wish." She nodded and launched into the tale.

32 - ART AND FACTS

"The ancient Hellenes said that this island was once ruled by an evil king named Minos. He was evil because each year he demanded that the Athenians send him a tribute of maidens and youths who would be sacrificed to the minotaur. The minotaur was a mythical beast with the head of a bull and the body of a man. He lived in a maze that was called a labyrinth. It was so confusing that anyone who entered the labyrinth could never find their way out again before being devoured by the monster. A Hellenic hero called Theseus was able to navigate the passages of the labyrinth with the help of King Minos' daughter. He slew the minotaur so that no more Hellene youth would be sacrificed to the bull-man ever again."

Cassie listened skeptically to the account. When Xenia was finished, she commented, "Given what I've learned lately about Hellenic legends, I'm not sure I believe their version of anything."

"You are wise to doubt the tale. Overlord mythology is often propaganda to explain why the conquerors should be in charge of society. The Hellenes wished to create a story that would favor their heroes and discredit the civilization that came before."

"Was there ever a real King Minos?"

"No one knows." Griffin shrugged. "But Sir Arthur Evans was familiar with the legend, and that's the reason he called this civilization Minoan in honor of the fabled King Minos. You see, the language of the original inhabitants has been lost, so we don't know what these people called themselves. With respect to the minotaur, the bull was a sacrificial animal to the Minoans. As a result, it would have been easy for the Hellenes to fuse the notion of man and bull and give it a negative connotation. In fact, they said the beast was conceived by King Minos' wife after she mated with a bull. As for the labyrinth, the word roughly translates as 'place of the double axes.' Given the profusion of that particular symbol around the palace and the confusing architectural design, I think the Hellenes got the idea for their mythical labyrinth from Knossos itself."

They had been continuing their search the whole time Griffin and Xenia were unfolding the story. By the time the tale was finished, the trio found themselves in a room with paintings covering the walls. Cassie thought they were paintings until Xenia explained that they were frescoes—pictures painted over wet plaster. The images displayed at the palace were reproductions. All the original images had been moved to the museum at Heraklion in order to protect and preserve them.

"Sir Arthur Evans went to great pains to reconstruct the frescoes, and often he didn't have much to work with. He had to guess what the originals might have looked like," Griffin said.

"These are amazing!" Cassie exclaimed as she went from one image to another. The Minoans obviously loved nature. It was evident in the birds, flowers, monkeys, and dolphins. All in brightly colored motion.

"This doesn't look like any classical art I've ever seen," the pythia commented. The men in many of the frescoes were depicted wearing loincloths while the women wore dresses with open bodices, exposing their breasts. "These Minoans weren't shy, were they?"

Xenia laughed. "That is true. They had a very frank attitude about the human body and did not consider it a source of shame."

"It isn't merely the mode of dress that distinguishes them from other ancient societies," Griffin observed. "When one thinks of Babylonian, Egyptian, or even Greek art, the style is angular, geometric, static. Here the style is fluid and graceful. Almost alive." He paused to contemplate a picture of a blue bird at rest amidst flowers. "The difference in style is also reflected in a difference in subject matter."

He stood next to Cassie. "Look carefully and tell me what you don't see in these images. I'll give you a hint. Think about the typical Greek pottery that you would find in museums. What scenes do they depict?"

Cassie paused to consider. "Usually some warrior stabbing another warrior with a sword." She recalled Griffin's earlier comment about the non-defensive location of the palace. The answer came to her more quickly this time. "I'll go out on a limb and say that Minoan art doesn't show a lot of violence?"

"No warfare, no struggle, no weapons of any kind," the scrivener affirmed. "All of the images you see at Knossos speak of the benevolence of nature and of human beings living in harmony with that benevolence."

"Well, what about this one?" Cassie walked over to a fresco of what looked like a bull fight. "Here's a man gripping a bull by the horns, while another man is jumping over the bull's back, and a third man is standing behind. Isn't that violent?"

Both Xenia and Griffin started laughing simultaneously.

"The man, as you call him, who is gripping the bull's horns is actually a woman," the young man said.

"How can you know that? Her chest looks pretty flat."

"Based on the color of the skin," Griffin explained. "Like the Egyptians, the Minoans distinguished between the sexes in their artwork by depicting women with white skins and men with reddish brown. We also know that bull-leaping was a sport in which both sexes participated."

"Then why is she gripping the horns?" Cassie was still mystified. "Is she trying to break the bull's neck? Did the man who's positioned over the bull's back get tossed?"

"Your assumptions show how much you have been influenced by overlord values," Xenia remarked, still smiling. "The people in the picture are demonstrating their acrobatic skills. When the woman grasps the bull's horns, he will instinctively lower his head and try to toss her. She will use the momentum to spring over the animal's back and land behind him. The man depicted above the bull is doing a somersault, and he will alight where the second woman is standing. She may be in position to catch him."

Cassie was impressed. "Not even an Olympic gymnast would have the nerve to try a stunt like that. It looks incredibly dangerous."

"No doubt it was," agreed Griffin. "Bull-leaping was practiced in ancient Anatolia and India long before the Minoans settled here. To this day a variation of it is still performed in the Basque region of France. In terms of a test of courage, it seems much more sporting than bullfighting."

"That is a hideous blood sport begun in Spain by the Romans." Xenia's voice was filled with disgust. "A small army of men on horseback torturing an animal for hours by stabbing him repeatedly until he is weak enough to be dispatched by a matador with a sword. You see the difference in the world view. Bull-leaping shows the unity of human and nature. Bullfighting shows the overlord desire to subdue and destroy nature."

Griffin tactfully tried to soothe her. "Perhaps it's a sign of the times that bullfighting is rapidly falling out of favor with the public. It's even been formally outlawed in many places."

"The sooner, the better," Xenia growled. "Come, let us move on. We have more areas to search."

The trove keeper marched out of the fresco room.

It had just been an impression when she'd first met her, but now Cassie was sure that she didn't want to be on Xenia's bad side. It was a good thing no bullfighters were likely to cross her path today. Griffin suggested they give the trove keeper a few minutes head start to allow her to cool down.

After waiting a discrete interval, they caught up with her in a chamber that was called the throne room. When she saw them wander in, Xenia calmly moved on to a new topic. "This is quite incorrectly called the king's throne room because of that chair." She pointed to a carved alabaster seat fitted into the wall.

"Sir Arthur based his assumptions on the fact that the chair is centrally located ergo it must be a throne," Griffin added. "And where you have a throne—"

"You automatically must have a king," Cassie completed the thought. "If you were raised with overlord values." She laughed. "Am I catching on?" She turned to Xenia. "What do you think this room was actually used for?"

"It is very likely a room where the high priestess would have conducted rituals. You see the basin there." She pointed to a huge stone bowl on the floor. "That would be for libation offerings. Things like wine or oil."

Xenia shifted her attention to the wall behind the throne. She gave Griffin an amused look. "I should think this fresco would be your favorite."

The scrivener laughed.

Cassie looked from one to the other, puzzled by their secret joke.

"Do you know what these creatures are?" Xenia asked the pythia.

Cassie studied the figures. They were crouching or rather resting on all fours. They had animal bodies and the heads of birds. Like all the other frescoes of animals in the palace, they seemed light and joyful. The lines of their bodies were curved, not angular. Their heads were turned upward, the expression on their faces was soft and expectant.

The pythia shrugged. "Not a clue. What are they?"

"They are griffins," the trove keeper said.

Cassie looked doubtfully at Xenia. "They belong to Griffin?"

The young man laughed out loud. "No, not 'griffin's' possessive, 'griffins' plural. These are mythical creatures with the heads of eagles and bodies of lions. They are called griffins."

"According to ancient lore, griffins are often found protecting treasures of one sort or another," Xenia explained.

"You picked the right line of work then," Cassie observed.

"My parents were not unaware of the irony when they named me," Griffin admitted.

The trio studied the walls of the throne room, searching for their elusive symbols to no avail.

"Where to next?" Cassie asked. Her neck was beginning to ache from looking up and down at so many walls.

"We haven't paid a visit to the prince yet," Griffin suggested.

Xenia nodded.

Cassie followed them silently since they seemed to know exactly where they were going. Crossing the central court, they walked down a corridor until

Griffin stopped before a picture of a youth with a feathered headdress set against a backdrop of lilies.

"Lilies at last!" Cassie exclaimed.

"This image has been called either a 'Priest-King' or the 'Prince of Lilies,'" Xenia said.

"And he's very famous," Griffin added significantly.

"Why's that?" Cassie didn't see anything particularly noteworthy about the image. It looked typical of the other frescoes she had already seen.

"I would draw your attention to the skin tone," the scrivener hinted.

She noted the white skin of the figure and remembered what she had been told about Minoan painting styles. Men were reddish brown, and women were white. "It's a woman?" she asked in disbelief.

"In all probability that is the case," Griffin agreed.

Xenia pointed toward the top of the fresco. "In addition, the feathered headdress is a style that would have been worn by a woman and not a man."

"But what about the chest?" Cassie objected. "It's flat, and the figure is wearing something that looks like a jockstrap."

"It's called a codpiece actually," Griffin corrected. "It would have been worn by male or female athletes when engaged in a rough contact sport. Bull-leapers of both sexes wore them. As for the shape of the figure, that may have been imaginative reconstruction on Sir Arthur's part."

"Sir Arthur himself admitted that his restoration might not have been accurate," Xenia explained. "The only parts of the original fresco that remained intact were the headdress, part of the torso, and one leg."

"With so little to go on, this is what he came up with?" Cassie registered surprise.

"The fresco has stirred up heated debate for quite some time," Griffin admitted. "In all likelihood, it was an image of a female bull-leaper, but no one can be certain."

"What is more troublesome to me is his conclusion that the boy would be a priest-king," said the trove keeper. "Minoans were a matristic society. While it is possible they might have had a king, the central religious figure would certainly have been a high priestess. Sir Arthur came from the Victorian Age, and he made many assumptions about a male-dominated social structure here."

Cassie sighed. "Since all of this was reconstructed, I'm guessing that the lilies in the picture aren't a clue left for us."

"Quite so," Griffin agreed. "Also, the lilies are painted on plaster, not incised into stone."

"Then why are we here?" the pythia asked flatly.

"To search the corridor around the fresco," the scrivener said. "Best be about it then."

The trio looked up and down the hall but still couldn't find the elusive lilies for which they were searching.

"Where else?" Cassie urged. Her fatigue was returning, and she needed a distraction to stay awake.

"The Queen's Chamber perhaps?" Griffin looked at Xenia questioningly.

"Yes, we forgot to check that one," Xenia concurred.

They crossed the central court once more to an elegant suite of rooms.

"This is called the Queen's Chamber," Xenia explained. "It is so named because it is smaller than the other living space which is called the King's Chamber. Sir Arthur again concluded that the grandest living accommodations would belong to a king when in fact they probably belonged to the high priestess."

As they inspected the Queen's Chamber, Cassie noticed that one of the walls held a fresco of fanciful blue dolphins swimming through a white sea. "Look!" she pointed to the decorative motif below the dolphins. "Isn't that like the spiral hieroglyph on the granite key?"

Griffin paused to consult his page of symbols. "It is indeed like one of the key symbols, but the context is wrong. You see the symbol is repeated, and we're looking for a sequence of alternating symbols that will translate into a Linear B phrase. Besides, there's no lily that would denote this image pertains to the Bones of the Mother."

"Oh," Cassie said in a small disappointed voice.

"Chin up. Have a look at this," Griffin said. "It will take your mind off the problem."

Cassie followed to where the scrivener was standing. "Is that what I think it is?"

"Indeed," Griffin said proudly. "A flush toilet. Though one would need to pour a bucket of water into the toilet to make it flush, but there is a drain line below to carry the waste away. And there's also a bathtub in the adjoining room."

He gestured toward a large stone tub. "It would have to be filled manually but could also be drained through the floor. Conventional history would have us believe that civilization has been a straight march of progress when the opposite is true. Many ancient inventions were lost for millennia because of overlord invasions. The Minoans were more technically advanced than any of their neighbors. They transported water from nearby springs via aqueduct. Then gravity forced the water to run through terracotta pipes into fountains and spigots inside the palace. There were drains for waste which flowed down to a sewer away from the hill where the palace is located.

"They even found a way to heat their homes in winter by channeling steam from volcanoes through pipes in their walls. That isn't in evidence here at Knossos, but it exists on the island of Santorini. It has been said that if

Minoan civilization hadn't collapsed, the inhabitants might have managed to invent rockets to the moon by the time of Christ."

As the trio continued to search the queen's rooms for stone symbols, Cassie felt a growing sense of foreboding. "What happened to them in the end?"

"A terrible tragedy," Xenia said. "They were at the height of their influence as a mercantile power in the Mediterranean. Around 1450 BCE, a volcano erupted on the island of Santorini to the north of here. The blast was at least four times stronger than the one that occurred at Krakatoa at the end of the 19th century. It was so terrible that a large portion of Santorini sank to the ocean floor. All that remains is a crater in the middle of the harbor that may once have been one hundred square miles of land. The eruption sent a tidal wave to Crete. A three-hundred-foot wall of water came crashing into the shore without warning. It probably destroyed the merchant fleet as well as the harbors and towns on the north side of the island. In addition, the volcanic ash would have poisoned crops, and atmospheric dust would have destroyed harvests for years afterward. It is thought that Plato's story of the lost city of Atlantis refers to the earthquake on Santorini and the decline of Minoan civilization."

"Whether Santorini is Atlantis or not, such a natural disaster must have had a devastating effect on the psyche of the people who lived here," Griffin observed. "They believed in a benevolent goddess. They saw her presence in every aspect of their lives—in every bee and bird and tree and flower. How could they make sense of an event which must have seemed as if divine favor had forsaken them?"

"One cannot calculate the damage, both physical and psychological that such a catastrophe would have had," Xenia added. "As an American, Cassie, try to imagine how you would feel if an earthquake sank your west coast into the Pacific Ocean without warning. The soul of Minoan civilization was devastated. They struggled to recover but were never able to rise to the level of greatness they had previously enjoyed. At about this time, Myceneans on the Greek mainland were expanding their territories southward. Because they perceived the Minoans as vulnerable, they captured Crete and set up their own government here. The Mycenean empire, in turn, was destroyed by Dorian invaders. By 1200 BCE, the Mediterranean area was plunged into what has come to be known as the Greek Dark Ages, and Minoan culture vanished into myth."

"Too bad it had to end that way." Cassie shook her head. "I think the world would have been a better place for all of us if they'd survived."

"Some of their ideas remained long after they were gone," Griffin said. "During the time that the Myceneans occupied Crete, they copied many of the advancements of the Minoans. Their artwork shows a strong Minoan influence, and they even created a syllabary based on the Minoan writing style."

"Those are the Linear B characters we're looking for?"

"Right. The Minoans developed Linear A, and the Myceneans copied their methods and adapted it to their own language. The result was the Linear B syllabary. In fact, the Minoans invented a movable typeface—an early printing press, if you will, to stamp clay tablets with their language."

Cassie looked around the Queen's Chamber one last time. "No lilies or symbols from the key in this room. Where do we go from here?"

"We press onward to the Hall of the Double Axes." Griffin led the way out of the queen's apartments.

***

A young Greek man stood in the shadows of an antechamber door. He understood English quite well. Well enough to catch the words Linear B, Bones of the Mother, and granite key coming from a trio of tourists wandering around within earshot. They walked on, unaware that they had been overheard. He decided to follow them.

33 - WINING AND MINING

The Arkana team had managed to consume the morning and half the afternoon searching Knossos for elusive key symbols. While they had discovered numerous double axes cut into stones throughout the site, no lilies were to be found. They stood together dejectedly at the entrance to the site.

"It looks like we've run out of options." Cassie voiced the concern they were all feeling.

"This may not be anything important," Xenia began tentatively. "But we have recovered a few relics recently that have unusual markings on them. Now that I have seen your photographs of the key, I think the symbols might be similar. Perhaps we should go to the trove, and I will show them to you."

"The trove!" Cassie exclaimed excitedly. "I'm finally going to see one?"

The Greek woman regarded her with surprise. Turning to Griffin, she asked, "Cassie has not seen a trove yet?"

"Afraid there hasn't been time," he admitted.

"But she is the pythia. Should that not have been the first place she was shown?"

Griffin shrugged. "Faye had other priorities."

"I see." Xenia still sounded puzzled.

Cassie looked at her watch. She began to feel fatigue settling over her like a heavy fog. She needed to stay in motion just to keep her eyes open. "If we're going to the trove, shouldn't we start now?" she asked. "It's getting late."

Her question seemed to snap Xenia to attention. The Greek woman consulted her own watch. "Yes, the time is slipping away from us. We must leave now, or the day will be gone." She immediately bustled them back into the Citroen.

Before going straight to their destination, Cassie asked for a quick detour. The weather had proven to be hotter than she expected, and she wanted to change into some lighter clothing. They drove back into Heraklion and stopped at the hotel. Cassie left the other two in the lobby and ran up to her room to don a T-shirt and Capri pants. When she came back downstairs, she noticed that Griffin had taken the opportunity to get another cup of coffee.

He held out a paper cup to her. "One for the road?" he suggested.

She gulped it down gratefully even though it scalded her throat. Trying to shake off her tiredness as best she could, she climbed back into the tiny car, and they headed out of town in the opposite direction from which they had come.

After driving for about half an hour through hilly countryside, Xenia made a sharp right turn onto a narrow road that cut through a field of grape vines. She kept driving through an open iron gate. A wooden sign lettered in Greek and English identified this as the Katsouras Winery. Xenia steered the Citroen toward a collection of buildings nestled up against a steep hillside. Some of the structures were modern metal storage sheds, others much older and constructed of whitewashed stone. The trove keeper found a parking space among several other cars ringing the dusty courtyard.

The trio got out and walked toward a cottage that seemed to grow out of the rock face behind it. The structure must have been very old judging by the size of the bougainvillea vine covering its walls. The small open windows and wooden door were painted an azure shade of blue.

"You own a winery?" Cassie asked.

Xenia smiled briefly. "This property has belonged to my family for centuries. It is a small operation. Nothing like your California vineyards. We don't advertise, but wine connoisseurs always know how to find us."

She led them through the blue door into what appeared to be a tasting room. It wasn't large—a few tiny tables with wicker-bottom chairs. There was a bar off to one side. She nodded to the man standing behind it but made no effort to introduce her guests to him.

"This way," she instructed. There was another wooden door at the back of the tasting room. Xenia ushered them through and shut the door behind them. She flipped a light switch on the wall. They were standing on a platform in front of a wide wooden stairway leading down into darkness.

"You want us to go down there?" Cassie studied the underground space dubiously. It seemed a bit too much like a tomb.

"Come, there is nothing to fear," Xenia urged. She flipped a second light switch.

To the pythia's surprise, the passageway was wired for electricity, and bulbs were strung at even intervals all the way down the stairs. The trove keeper led the way with Cassie in the middle and Griffin bringing up the rear.

Cassie took stock of her surroundings. The walls on either side were solid rock. "This reminds me of pictures of the Roman catacombs."

"It is very much like them," Xenia commented. "This space was hollowed out of the hillside centuries ago."

When they reached the bottom of the stairs, Cassie realized they were standing in a high vaulted chamber—about twenty feet wide and fifteen feet high. It was cool and dark and, from Cassie's perspective, more than a little creepy.

"What is this place?" she asked uncertainly.

"I would hazard a guess and say that we're in a wine cave," Griffin offered. "You see the casks against the walls."

Straining to focus her eyes in the dim light, Cassie noticed the enormous casks stacked on either side of them. "But why would anybody put wine in a cave, and why is the cave inside a cottage?"

Xenia laughed. "It is very common to use caves to store wine. This has been done since the time of the Minoans."

"It isn't a phenomenon peculiar to Greece either," the scrivener added. "Caves all over Europe are used this way. The high humidity and cool temperatures are considered ideal for wine storage."

"My family discovered this cave when they first came here. They built the vineyard around it, and my ancestors widened the cave as more space was needed to house our wine."

Xenia walked to the opposite end of the chamber which terminated abruptly at a solid wall of rock. She turned to regard Cassie with a slight smile. "But you did not come here to see a winery. You came to see the Minoan trove." She tapped a spot on the rock face, and the entire back wall slid noiselessly to one side to reveal a room beyond.

Cassie stood gaping open-mouthed in amazement.

Griffin seemed equally surprised. "Oh, I say. That was brilliant!"

They walked under the archway into the trove. Xenia slid the wall panel shut behind them. The dank gloom of the wine cave disappeared. In contrast, the trove was bright and warm. The walls were no longer bare rock but framed, insulated, and covered with beige wallpaper. There were modern fluorescent light panels in the ceiling which counteracted much of the oppressive feeling of being underground.

"This area is strictly climate-controlled," Xenia explained. "While high humidity and cool temperatures are very good for wine, they are very bad for artifacts."

Cassie noticed several people working at long tables in the center of the room. They appeared to be polishing objects of various sizes and shapes. A few of them looked up and nodded to the newcomers.

"This is where we restore our finds."

"Are all the troves like this one?"

"They're all different," Griffin offered. "It depends on what space is available. Some troves are very new and modern. Some are a bit more rustic. The Minoan trove has been around for centuries. Before the excavation of Knossos, in fact."

"Many of the troves are located underground for security reasons," Xenia added.

Cassie inspected the room more closely. Against the back wall were rows of tall metal shelves holding a variety of artifacts in no particular order: broken shards of pottery, jewelry, and small votive statues.

Xenia noticed the direction of Cassie's gaze. "Those are items that still need some restoration work. Anything that has been finished is catalogued and placed in storage."

"That's where my lot comes in," Griffin explained. "Every object that is added to the collection needs to be logged into the Central Catalog."

"Where do you store all the artifacts?" Cassie didn't see much space in the room where they were standing.

"That depends on the size and type of object. Some of the little things like jewelry and seals are right here." Xenia gestured to a locked metal cabinet with dozens of rows of shallow drawers. "We have separate rooms for the larger objects in the collection."

For the first time, Cassie noticed other doors flanking the metal shelves which led into more storage space. "It doesn't look the way I expected." She tried to keep the disappointment out of her voice. "No torches flaming from the walls. No cobwebs. No snakes."

"I fear you've seen one too many Indiana Jones movies." Griffin chuckled.

"Maybe that's it. But it doesn't look like a museum either. No display cases."

"That is because we are attempting to protect our finds not display them," Xenia corrected gently. "Think of this as an underground storage facility."

Cassie's mind leaped to another topic. "I don't know why you would even keep a trove here on Crete."

"Pardon?" Xenia seemed shocked at the comment.

"The entire Minoan culture was matristic," Cassie said. "All the artifacts are out in the open, and the people who've been excavating for a century aren't trying to suppress anything. What exactly do you need to hide?"

Xenia's face grew serious. "That is a very good question, Cassie. We are fortunate that the local archaeologists are so friendly to a goddess culture. However, their liking for the Minoans does not prevent them from making errors when they interpret the artifacts. This trove collects objects that contradict some of their explanations about Minoan culture and its symbols.

"You have already seen two instances at Knossos. The lily prince fresco and the throne room which were reconstructed based on overlord assumptions about Minoan social order. But they are minor compared to other errors which are repeated by many as if they were truths. In fact, one of the artifacts I want to show you is an example of how they can be explained incorrectly."

Xenia reached out for an object on the table. A young woman was brushing debris off a small stone sculpture which was about the size of a human hand. She gave it to the trove keeper.

Cassie recognized the object. She looked at Xenia questioningly. "Isn't that a miniature of the giant sculpture we saw at Knossos?"

"Yes," the Greek woman replied. "It is another example of the horns of consecration. This one would have been used at a small votive altar in a home perhaps."

The pythia stepped closer to inspect the relic. "The horns look pretty abstract to me. What are they supposed to be exactly?"

Xenia smiled knowingly. "I think perhaps we should start by talking about what they are not."

Griffin joined the discussion. "The conventional explanation is that horns of consecration are the horns of a bull."

Cassie tilted her head to one side. "Oh, I see it now."

"How do you know the horns belong to a bull?" Xenia asked pointedly.

"Because the Minoans were fixated on bull-leaping."

"What if I were to tell you that horns of consecration have been found in European villages dating back to 7000 BCE?" the trove keeper persisted.

"Then maybe old Europeans had a bull fixation too?" Cassie offered uncertainly.

"Horns of consecration represent regeneration," Griffin explained. "Does it seem likely to you that a goddess-worshipping culture would take the horns of a bull as its most important symbol?"

Cassie gave an exasperated sigh. "I don't have a clue if they would or wouldn't. Why don't we make this painless, and you tell me what you want me to know?"

Griffin and Xenia looked at one another and laughed.

"I suppose we are being rather too hard on our new pythia," the scrivener admitted.

"Let us go into my office. All will be clear in a moment." The trove keeper brought the small stone sculpture along with her.

The trio went through one of the doors on the back wall to a small office stacked with papers and books.

"Please sit," Xenia invited.

Cassie took a chair while Griffin perched on the end of the desk.

Xenia scanned her bookshelf and selected a volume. She thumbed through it quickly until she found the page she wanted. "You must remember that ancient matristic cultures saw the goddess as the source of life, death, and rebirth. Not the rebirth that is called reincarnation but the rebirth of seasons. Winter is followed by spring, and with it, the goddess shows her power to bring forth new life out of death. The ancients worshipped the power to give life."

Xenia paused and then prompted gently, "Does a bull bring forth new life?"

"No, but a cow does," Cassie blurted out the words automatically before the significance of what she'd just said had sunk in. "Holy cow!"

"Precisely." Griffin laughed. "Holy cow. As Hathor in Egypt, she was called the cow of heaven. Cows, as well as bulls, have horns. The overlord obsession with phallic symbols like the horn would automatically assume the gender of the animal to be male."

"But there are plenty of other female animals they might have picked to symbolize regeneration. Why the cow?" Cassie was mystified.

"There are two reasons," Xenia replied. "The cow became an important source of food. She could provide not only a calf but also milk. Neolithic farmers began to incorporate this new food into their diet, and they saw the cow as a special gift from their goddess. But there is an even more important reason."

Xenia opened the book she still held in her hands and laid it flat on the desk. The page she had selected showed a cow's skull placed above an altar. "The name for this object is 'bucranium.' The head and horns of cattle of either sex would be called a bucranium. The horns of consecration are an abstract symbol for this object."

Cassie studied the image for a moment. It looked like a bleached cattle skull from Death Valley.

"Now look at this image," Xenia instructed as she flipped the page.

Cassie peered at it uncomprehendingly until she read the caption. "Diagram of female human reproductive system."

The pythia blinked in surprise. The diagram exactly matched the outline of the bucranium. The uterus was shaped like a cow's skull while the ovaries and fallopian tubes mimicked the curve of the cow's horns.

Transferring her attention to Xenia, she asked, "But how would they have known this? They didn't dissect cadavers back in the day."

"Because of excarnation," the scrivener answered. "When a person died, her body would have been exposed to birds of prey to strip off the flesh before the bones would be cleaned for burial. A human body in various stages of decomposition could be observed with the internal organs exposed. It would have been a macabre epiphany, to be sure, but the connection would have been easy to make."

Xenia continued the thought. "We know the old Europeans recognized the similarity eight thousand years ago because they created statues and drawings of the goddess with a bucranium drawn directly over the pelvic region of her body. The bucranium symbolizes the power of the goddess to create life. Minoans shrines usually display ritual objects between the horns as part of their cult practice. To amplify the power of regeneration."

"Then what's the connection to bulls?" Cassie was puzzled. "I know the animal in that bull-leaping fresco wasn't a cow."

"The bull was the sacrificial animal of choice to the Minoans," Griffin said. "His skull is also a bucranium which symbolizes regeneration, but he is far more expendable. Cows were too valuable to sacrifice. They provided calves and milk. Every cow on Crete was known by her individual name. The bulls, alas, were not."

Xenia wordlessly handed the horns of consecration to Griffin. Cassie stood up to get a better view of what he was looking at.

"You see the markings just here and here," the trove keeper pointed to two small bees inscribed at the base of either horn.

Griffin studied them in silence for several seconds. "They are quite similar to one of the hieroglyphics on the granite key, but the match isn't exact." He sighed. "I was hoping this treasure hunt would be simple."

"Perhaps this will help," Xenia said. She picked up another small artifact which had been sitting on her desk.

Cassie recognized it instantly. "It's a double axe like the ones we saw at the palace."

"It's called a labrys from the Lydian word meaning 'axe.' The word labyrinth is derived from this object—the place of the labrys," Griffin said.

The pythia frowned. "That's something else that's been bothering me. Why would a goddess culture choose a weapon for a sacred symbol?"

Griffin's face took on a cryptic expression. "You've already seen that nothing is quite what it seems. Where an overlord archaeologist sees a bull, we see a cow. Where they see an axe, we see something entirely different."

"When is an axe not an axe?" Cassie asked, mystified.

"When it is a butterfly," Griffin said softly. "This symbol was painted on pottery, incised into sculpture, and always found in conjunction with images of the goddess. For six thousand years in old Europe, the double-triangle was always used in a context suggesting metamorphosis and rebirth. The caterpillar which becomes a butterfly is another universal symbol in old Europe for the power of the goddess to regenerate life. Double axes were never forged of material that would have made them useful as weaponry."

Xenia joined in. "The Kurgans used axes as weapons. When they first invaded Greece and later Crete, they would have seen the labrys as a weapon and a symbol of a war-mongering sky god. But that was not the way in which the original inhabitants viewed it." She took the small bronze labrys in her hand and fitted it in the center of the horns of consecration which Griffin was still holding.

Cassie noticed for the first time that a hole had been drilled into the base of the horns and the handle of the small double axe fit neatly into it. It now stood upright between the horns.

Xenia looked intently at Cassie. "There are always many ways of seeing the same object. A Minoan looking at the horns with the labrys at the center sees a double symbol of the power of the goddess to regenerate life."

Griffin picked up the thread. "An overlord warrior looking at the same objects would see the bull's horns as a symbol of virility and the double axe as symbolic of conquest in battle."

Xenia took the objects back from Griffin. "It is a simple choice of whether to see life or to see death in these things. All of us in the Arkana believe the world has been looking at death too long."

The mood in the room grew solemn until the trove keeper smiled. "But I did not bring the labrys out to give you a lecture on the state of the world. Look at this." She pointed to tiny birds inscribed on either wing of the bronze butterfly.

"Remarkable," the scrivener exclaimed as he leaned over for a closer look. "They look exactly like the symbols on the key. Unfortunately, there is no sequence, no message." He sounded disappointed.

"It was not the sequence that I wished to show you," Xenia said. "Clearly there is no message here, but the same hand may have created both. Look at the image again and tell me if you think so."

"Good heavens, I believe you're right!" Griffin exclaimed. He drew the folded photographs of the key out of his pocket and compared the image of the bird on the key to the ones on the labrys. "It may have been the same artist! There's clearly a connection of some sort. Where was this artifact found?"

"The horns of consecration and the labrys were both found at Psychro Cave."

"Are you sure you didn't mean Psycho Cave?" Cassie asked archly.

Griffin rolled his eyes. "Not psycho, psychro with an *R*." He turned to Xenia. "That's on the plateau, yes?"

The trove keeper nodded. "The Lasithi Plateau. It is less than two hours from here if you wish to go there tomorrow."

"I think it would be worth investigating." Griffin rose as if he were getting ready to depart, but Xenia laid a restraining hand on his arm.

"There is one more artifact I wish you to see. Wait please." She left the office briefly and returned with a small gold object in the palm of her hand. She held it out for her guests to inspect. "Exquisite, is it not?"

Cassie studied it for a moment. "It's a bug, but I can't be sure what kind. Maybe an Egyptian scarab?"

"I believe it's a chrysalis," Griffin offered uncertainly. "A cocoon for a butterfly?"

"That is so," Xenia affirmed. "The chrysalis was yet another symbol of transformation and regeneration to the Minoans. But look at the mark on the head."

"A lily!" the visitors exclaimed in unison.

"Not only that, I believe it matches the pictures you have brought."

Griffin feverishly checked his photograph of the key. "It does, it does! Look at the two lilies flanking the Linear B text. They are identical to this one." He looked intently at Xenia. "Where did this come from?"

"Ah, that is where we have a little problem," she hesitated. "It was bought from a private collector. He thought it may have come from Karfi."

"But there's nothing there!" Griffin's tone was despairing.

Cassie raised her eyebrows, waiting for an explanation.

"Karfi was the Minoan last stand if you will. Once the Dorians overran the island, many of the original inhabitants fled to the Lasithi Plateau. An area high in the mountains which would have been very difficult for an invading force to take. Karfi was the last known Minoan settlement. It was built into the side of a mountain and was sloppily excavated by archaeologists in the 1930s. There's really nothing to see there but rubble." Griffin ran his hands through his hair. "This is maddening. Our clearest connection to the key, yet we have no idea where this object originated."

"I have a thought," Xenia suggested tentatively. "Perhaps the pythia can help?"

"Cassie?" Griffin looked at his teammate blankly.

The trove keeper wordlessly held out the gold chrysalis toward Cassie.

"You want me to…" The pythia trailed off. She gulped. It was one thing to touch relics under Faye's guidance, but she had no idea where this odd little bug had come from. It might be another tainted relic for all she knew. Still, if she could finally do something other than trail around and ask questions, maybe there was a reason for her to be part of this mission after all. Fortunately, she was wearing the obsidian pendant Faye had given her. She gripped it tightly in her left hand and held out her right to take the artifact. Drawing in a deep breath, she said, "OK, here goes nothing."

She found herself walking in a procession. There were people ahead of her carrying torches. This time, the part of her that was Cassie was still around, like someone hovering just over her shoulder, watching the spectacle. The other part of her was a woman wrapped in a shawl. It was cold, and there were snowflakes in the air. The woman was part of a group walking down a long narrow ramp that seemed to lead underground. There was a square doorway ahead. As she passed under the doorway, she realized she was in a burial chamber. She felt very sad. There was a square box in the center of the room. It seemed to be made of clay—some sort of terra cotta casket. There were decorations painted on the clay: birds, flowers, and numerous horns of consecration with double axes at their center. A priestess was performing a ceremony. She was pouring liquid into a bowl and chanting. For the first time, Cassie registered that the woman she was channeling held something in her right hand. Looking down, she realized it was the chrysalis. The woman in her vision walked up to the casket, and Cassie could see that the lid was covered with funeral gifts—jewelry, miniature vases, small golden axes. The woman gently placed the chrysalis on the casket and touched her hand to the double axe painted on the lid.

Cassie blinked. She was back. The other two were looking at her intently.

"Where did you go?" Griffin asked in a slightly worried tone.

"I was attending a funeral," she said tersely, then recounted exactly what she had seen.

The scrivener seemed to view her with a newfound respect. "That's very helpful," he said at last. "It sounds as if you were in a *tholos* tomb. That's a type of burial chamber. The fact that it was partially underground suggests a Mycenean design rather than Minoan, but no matter. Xenia, are there any *tholoi* near Karfi?"

"Yes," the trove keeper assented. "There are a few cemeteries near the settlement and a number of *tholos* tombs. Some are partially below ground."

"Excellent!" Griffin sounded hopeful once more. "By tomorrow Erik will be here, and we can search Psychro Cave and the cemeteries around Karfi."

"Oh good," Cassie thought to herself. "More underground burrows." She decided that if she ever owned a house someday, it wouldn't have a basement.

34 - A PLOT IN THE COUNTRY

It was almost midnight when Leroy and his charge arrived in Heraklion. Hunt was annoyed that they had rushed off the mainland to Crete with no advance warning. Apparently, Junior's talk with the preacher hadn't gone well. The old man must have lit a fire under the kid because they left the minute after he got off the phone. The Nephilim groupies chartered a boat to take them from Pylos to Heraklion.

Daniel was quiet on the trip over. Hunt watched him staring at those photos of the key until they were like to burn a hole in his eyeballs. No sense asking the kid what he thought he could see there.

Once they docked in Crete, Leroy was introduced to another one of the boy's faithful flunkies—some weedy little islander named Nikos. He gave Hunt the once over and then pulled Daniel off to the side to whisper to him. He kept looking back over his shoulder at the cowboy. After a couple of minutes of gesturing and pointing, they walked back toward him.

"Brother Nikos says you must come with us," Daniel told him hesitantly.

"I just gotta ask. Is he your actual brother? Cuz the way your daddy keeps collectin' wives, I figure maybe he's got a couple stashed here in Greece too."

"No, Mr. Hunt," Daniel said stiffly. "Brother Nikos is my spiritual brother, not my biological brother."

"Well, considering how many acorns is hangin' off your family tree, you can't blame a body for askin'."

Daniel doggedly repeated his earlier statement. "Brother Nikos says you must come with us."

Lerory rubbed his neck irritably. It was late. He was tired from doing nothing all day, and the last thing he needed was to get prayed over. "Now I already told you, son, I ain't sleepin' in one of your confounded compounds."

Daniel looked around the dock area nervously. "Brother Nikos says he has something important to tell us. Something he can't say here."

Hunt's annoyance faded as curiosity took its place. "Well now, that sounds like it might be worth the trouble. But you tell him from me that once he speaks his piece, he's gonna hustle me back to a hotel in town. You got that?"

"I understand English, sir," the local said. "I will do as you ask. But now you must come. My car is parked over this way."

Hunt shrugged and hoisted his duffle bag. "Whatever you say, Brother Nick."

"Nikos," Daniel corrected anxiously. "His name is Brother Nikos."

"Ain't that what I said?"

***

Twenty minutes later they were driving through a landscape that was darker than dirt. No lights anywhere. Daniel was up front with his new best friend giving Leroy the back seat all to himself.

Hunt tried to make conversation. "So, you got a compound out in the sticks here too? Jeez, you Nephilim got more hidey holes than a gopher."

"No sir," Nikos answered gravely. "There is no compound. We are going to my brother Dimitrios. He has a farm house some distance from the town."

"Guess one of you Nephilim boys made good, huh? He got a house of his own and don't have to share except maybe with his twenty-odd wives and such."

Nikos corrected him. "My brother Dimitrios is not of the Blessed Nephilim, sir."

"How's that?" Hunt asked blankly.

Daniel tried to explain. "Nikos is a convert to our brotherhood, Mr. Hunt. The rest of his family was not born into our faith."

"Well, don't that beat all," Leroy chuckled. "Quite a pickle, Brother Nick. You got a brother who ain't a brother. I tell you what. You gotta come up with another word for them that joins your blessed whatsit and stop callin' everybody brother. It's downright confusin'."

They drove in silence for ten minutes until another thought occurred to Hunt. "So, how come we're goin' for a confidential chit chat at your brother's house? Who ain't even a brother, by the way."

"Brother Nikos lives at our Athens compound," Daniel explained. "Because he is Cretan by birth, I asked him to come here ahead of us and begin to search the ruins at Knossos. We have no compound on the island where he could stay, so he asked his brother for refuge."

"Uh huh," Leroy said. "If you gotta stay with Brother Dimitrios too that means you're gonna have to break your taboo about not eatin' outside of a sanctuary, ain't that right?"

"Where two Nephilim are gathered, that is a sanctuary," Daniel intoned piously.

"I knew he'd weasel around it someway," Hunt thought to himself. "This better not take long," he said aloud.

"An hour and no more," Nikos assured him.

Leroy leaned his back up against the car door and tilted his hat brim over his eyes. "Well good. You wake me when we get to your fake brother's place."

***

It took twenty more minutes for them to exchange pleasantries with Dimitrios and his family after their arrival. It might have gone quicker if any of them spoke English.

The three men were shown out into the garden where a table was set for a late-night snack of bread, olives, and feta cheese. Nikos and Daniel refused spirits and primly asked for tea while Hunt cheerfully accepted a glass of *ouzo*. Dimitrios was obliging enough to leave the bottle near at hand.

Once they were sure the family had retired, Nikos began to explain himself in a whisper. "I believe someone else is looking for these markings you sent me to find, Brother Daniel."

"What?" Leroy sat bolt upright, alert for the first time since leaving Chicago.

Daniel nervously picked apart a piece of bread. "But that's not possible. Who else could know about the granite key?"

"At Knossos, I saw three of the Fallen. Two women and a man. They were walking through the ruin looking for the same strange markings you wanted me to search for."

"That so!" Leroy's interest was piqued. "What'd they look like?"

"The Fallen man was young, with light brown hair. He spoke with a British accent. One of the Fallen women was Greek and middle-aged. The other was an American teenager with dark hair. They called her Cassie."

"Well, don't that beat all!" Hunt exclaimed, slapping the table with his palm.

"Mr. Hunt, please!" Daniel shushed him like a spinster librarian. "The family will hear you."

Leroy ignored the admonition. "So little sis was in the game after all. Lord almighty! I surely didn't see that one comin'." He poured himself another drink.

Nikos continued his account. "They spoke of Linear B and the granite key. I followed them. At one point, I brushed close enough to see the papers they were all looking at. Each one had a copy of the symbols on the key."

"How can that be?" Daniel's voice was shrill with panic. "Nobody had that information."

"Sorry to burst your bubble, son, but somebody did. That antique dealer who I got the key from in the first place."

"You?" Daniel gave him a puzzled stare.

"Guess your daddy didn't tell you all the odd jobs I done for him, huh? Well, sir, I'm the one he sent to find that doodad in the first place. It come from a fancy antique store. Lady who ran it had herself a terrible accident. Bumped her head and didn't get up no more. Left behind a little sister. Gal named Cassie."

"This can't be happening," Daniel murmured. His pasty complexion was ashen.

Ignoring the young man's distress Hunt addressed Nikos. "So, what else you find out?"

Nikos stared worriedly at Daniel for a moment before transferring his attention to Leroy. "I do not believe they found anything at Knossos. I followed them for the rest of the day. They went to a vineyard in the hills and stayed there for two hours."

"My kinda folks. Civilized," Hunt said approvingly. "They know when it's time to take a break and sip somethin' in the shade."

"After that, they returned to their hotel in Heraklion."

Leroy felt an adrenaline surge. "Then you know where they're stayin'?"

"Yes, I can take you there in the morning."

Hunt rounded on him. "Boy, we ain't got that kind of time!"

Daniel was sitting with his head in his hands, moaning an inarticulate prayer.

Leroy shook him roughly by the shoulder. "Listen up, son. I need you to get on the horn with your boys. You got anybody else on the island, you call out the reinforcements. I need them brethren to take turns watchin' the hotel through the night. Keep tabs on these folks."

"Why?" Daniel bleated

"Son, you ain't seein' the big picture here. You think they're gonna steal your thunder and get them Bones before you do. That ain't gonna happen."

Daniel gaped at him dumbly.

"Don't you get it yet, boy? They're gonna do your work for you. All we got to do is stay out of sight and have your crew follow 'em around awhile. Odds are they'll head straight to your buried treasure."

Leroy withdrew the SIG Pro pistol from its holster. He checked the magazine. "Brother Nick, you think maybe you could scare me up some extra .357 bullets for this thing?"

35 – PSYCHRO

The following morning found Cassie and Griffin well rested and ready to continue their search. The same could not be said for Erik. He'd arrived late the night before, and his surly mood hadn't improved much after a few hours' sleep.

The trio met for breakfast where the security coordinator was briefed on everything the other two had discovered. They outlined their plan to search the Lasithi Plateau for symbols from the key.

Erik listened in silence during their lengthy summation. When they were done speaking, he nodded curtly. "OK, I'll rent us a car."

"Why?" Griffin asked in surprise. "Xenia drove us around yesterday."

"No need to bother her. She's probably got better things to do that chauffeur tourists."

Cassie opened her mouth to offer a sarcastic retort, but Griffin laid a warning hand on her forearm. His gesture seemed to imply that locking horns with Erik so early in the day wasn't a good idea.

"We should really go with someone who knows the area," the scrivener suggested tactfully. "Someone who speaks the language."

Erik gave no reply but instead gestured to the waiter. In flawless Greek, he asked for more coffee.

"Show off!" Cassie muttered under her breath.

Grinning impudently at them both, he explained. "I ran security for quite a few recoveries in this part of the world. Learned to speak like a native, and I know my way around the island pretty well. Like I said, I'll rent us a car." Without warning, he rose and walked out of the dining room.

His companions stared at one another uncertainly.

"Be ready in half an hour," Erik called over his shoulder. "I'll pick you up at the front door. And bring jackets. The plateau can get cold in the evening."

"He's been here less than twelve hours, and he's already ordering us around," Cassie commented acidly.

"On the contrary," Griffin countered. "I think we just saw his cooperative side."

***

As promised, Erik arrived at the hotel entrance in a BMW sedan. He insisted that Cassie take the back seat because he said he didn't want to shout to carry on a conversation with Griffin.

"At least he's decided to talk to one of us," Cassie thought to herself.

The trip from Heraklion to the plateau was more than fifty miles. For the first half of the journey, Griffin and Erik exchanged shop talk about matters back at the vault. Cassie took the opportunity to sightsee—watching as vineyards, orchards, and farms drifted past her window.

When she began to feel the car climbing steadily, she knew they were heading up into the mountains. Realizing that they were nearing their destination, she sat forward and tapped Griffin on the shoulder. "Tell me about the place we're going to see."

Griffin swiveled around in his seat to address her directly while Erik did his best to ignore them both.

"It's a fascinating bit of geography," the scrivener began. "Quite unlike anyplace else on the island. Lasithi is a flat table of land about seven miles wide and four miles long that sits at approximately three thousand feet above sea level."

Cassie found herself laughing. "It amazes me how you can rattle off statistics like that without even pausing for breath."

"I did a great deal of research in preparation for this trip," Griffin said defensively. "It isn't my fault that I can recall nearly everything I read." He cleared his throat. "As I was saying, around 1100 BCE, the Dorians invaded Crete and began enslaving the local population. Those who could fled to the plateau. Lasithi is surrounded by peaks on all sides and accessible through only eight mountain passes. Any invaders who wished to conquer the region would have had to arrive through one of those gaps. Although the Minoans set up defenses at each pass, the Dorians never bothered to pursue them that far.

"Fortunately, the native population who became known as Eteocretans, or true Cretans, found the plateau quite habitable. Although the altitude makes the climate much chillier than the rest of the island, the farmland is rich, and water is plentiful from the spring run-off of mountain snows. To irrigate their farms and orchards, the inhabitants built windmills. Lasithi is sometimes called the land of ten thousand windmills though most of them have fallen into disuse in recent years."

"I can see one of them now!" Cassie exclaimed, pointing out the rear window.

"Yes, I daresay the one you see carries an advert for the nearest taverna. That's the march of progress for you."

During Griffin's lengthy explanation, the BMW had passed from open terrain through a succession of small villages. Erik accelerated as they emerged from yet another one.

Noting his surroundings, Griffin commented, "There are about a dozen villages that encircle the plateau. All very quaint and picturesque. Tourism is becoming an important part of the local economy though the area is still primarily agricultural."

The scrivener turned to address Erik. "Do let me know when we reach Psychro."

"Psycho." Cassie chuckled.

Griffin gave her an annoyed look. "Now you're just willfully mispronouncing the name."

"I can't help myself. I think it's funny."

"We just passed it," Erik said flatly.

"What!" Griffin exclaimed.

"While you two were busy playing Trivial Pursuit, you missed it. The town we just drove through was Psychro. You wanted to go to the cave first, right?"

"Yes, that's correct," the scrivener admitted.

"It's outside of town up the mountain." Erik drove a short distance further until the road ended abruptly near a cluster of tavernas and souvenir shops. After parking, he got out of the car and opened the trunk to retrieve a back pack. "From here we walk."

"Walk where?" Cassie asked.

"I've never been to the cave, but I believe it's about a mile up the side of this mountain," Griffin offered brightly.

"A vertical mile!" Cassie gasped. "You don't have to sound so perky about it."

They hurried to follow the security coordinator who was already moving at a brisk pace up the stony zig-zag path.

As they struggled along the steep incline, Cassie kept looking upward expecting to glimpse the cave mouth. They paused to catch their breaths about a thousand feet above the village on a wide stone shelf that gave them a panoramic view of the plateau and the mountains. Even at the point where they had to stop to buy admission tickets, Cassie still couldn't spy the cave. A guide offered them lanterns, but Erik waved him away.

They resumed their march up the mountain single file and in silence. The trek became automatic, almost hypnotic. Cassie found her mind wandering until Erik stopped abruptly, and she collided with his back pack.

"We're here," he said simply.

"Where? I still don't see it."

"That's because you're looking up. Look down," Griffin advised.

When Cassie did as he instructed, she saw a forty-foot hole in the ground directly below her feet. Farther below, she could see lights flickering from tourists already inside the cave. The sight made her dizzy and slightly nauseous. "How far down does this thing go?" she asked Griffin.

"I believe the depth is about eight hundred feet."

As her eyes adjusted to the darkness, Cassie could see a winding stairway cut out of the rock wall to her right with a handrail to the left of the stairs.

"How are we supposed to find anything down there?" She felt a sense of despair creep over her.

Erik had removed his back pack and was rummaging around for something. Wordlessly he handed flashlights to his two companions. He managed to make silence sound like a reproach.

"Sorry," Griffin apologized. "It didn't occur to me to pack a torch. Stupid of me not to have realized we'd need them."

"Let's go," Erik prompted. "Watch your footing."

The two followed him down the first few stairs.

Cassie felt cool damp air hit her face. After the bright sunlight and dry heat outside, it was as if she'd dived into a pool. Then her feet began to slide sideways. The stairs were slippery from the moisture in the cave. She gripped the handrail tighter and threw her flashlight beam up toward the ceiling. The roof of the cave was rippled with stalactites. It would have been impossible to spot a carving of a lily, or a bird, or anything else for that matter. The wavy texture played tricks with the eyes. You could imagine any shape you wanted to see in those rock formations.

The trio traveled on in silence until they reached the bottom of the stairs which opened out into a huge chamber.

"This cave has been used as a sacred site since the earliest Minoan settlements on the island," Griffin started to explain. "It was sloppily excavated at the turn of the twentieth century. Sections of the roof collapsed and then were blasted apart for removal which obviously disturbed layers of strata. This chamber is roughly a hundred feet by fifty feet. In it, archaeologists have discovered pottery and votive objects. Things like goddess figurines and small double axes. They also unearthed a large number of libation tables and cups for food offerings. Other offerings, such as animal sacrifices are evidenced by numerous bones from bulls, sheep, and goats."

Cassie swept her flashlight around the chamber, noting even more of the gnarled, twisted stalactites sprouting from the ceiling. "It's going to be almost impossible to find any key symbols here," she observed bleakly.

Griffin shrugged. "We have to try. Each of us should take a portion of the chamber and focus on the largest stalactite and stalagmite formations. Those would be the most likely places to find an inscription."

Erik nodded wordlessly and moved to the opposite end of the chamber. He trained his flashlight on a large stalactite and allowed the beam to travel down its length.

Cassie moved off to the opposite end of the room. She followed Erik's method by beginning with the upper edges of stalactites and tracing them down. After about ten minutes, her eyes began to blur. She started seeing faces and forms in the rock. Quite a few of them looked like Casper the Ghost. At least they were friendly. She shook her head to clear away the mirages.

Walking back to Griffin, she announced, "It's hopeless. I can't find anything."

"Nor can I." Griffin turned to her. "Perhaps it's time we proceed to the lower chambers."

"There's more?" Cassie cried. She couldn't rally much enthusiasm for the idea of spending time in a space that was bound to be even darker and damper than where she already was.

"Erik?" Griffin called questioningly.

The security coordinator rejoined them. "No dice," he said. "I didn't see anything like the symbols in those photos you gave me."

"Then it's unanimous," the scrivener announced. "We descend."

Cassie looked upward wistfully toward the bright gap in the earth several hundred feet above them. Then she turned and followed the men into the depths of the cavern. "I don't get it. Why wouldn't they just build a temple like the Hellenes did? Why climb all the way down here to do their rituals?"

Griffin paused and turned to answer her. "It might seem easier to build a structure for cult purposes, but the ancient peoples of old Europe saw a cosmic connection between caves and the goddess. In fact, they would have seen a space like this as the womb of the goddess—the place where birth, death, and rebirth occur."

Cassie cast a doubtful look in his direction.

For once, Erik contributed to the conversation. "The Minoans used to bury their dead in caves like this for about a thousand years before they started building tombs above ground."

"Tomb maybe, but womb? Where do you get the idea that they viewed this place as an incubator too? I mean even Freud said sometimes a cigar is just a cigar."

Griffin smiled before turning to descend further. "I believe the proof you seek waits below."

They found themselves in a chamber that was even larger than the one above. Erik immediately strolled off to one side to sweep the walls with the beam of his flashlight.

"Yikes, how big is this room?" Cassie asked when she reached the bottom.

"About twice the size of the one preceding it. I'd say two hundred by one hundred feet."

The pythia could hear water dripping off in the distance. She swung her flashlight. There was another room off to the right. "Is that a pool?"

"Yes. The Minoans placed votive objects in the pool and on the stalagmites around it: bronze double axes, knife blades, clay figurines, even jewelry. But the pool is less interesting than what's supposed to be over here."

Cassie followed Griffin to a small chamber on the left side of the main room.

He shone his flashlight around the space. "This is called the cradle of Zeus which proves my point that the ancients thought of this cave as a place of birth as well as death."

"Zeus!" Cassie exclaimed incredulously. "You mean the Hellene god? What's he got to do with a Minoan shrine?"

"Everything," Griffin hinted cryptically. "According to the ancient Hellenes, Zeus' mother Rhea hid him in this cave to protect him from his father, Kronos. You see, Kronos had a bad habit of eating his offspring, and Rhea apparently grew tired of giving birth to her husband's dinner. She was determined that at least one of her children should live. So, she enlisted the help of a goat named Amalthea to nurse the infant and raise him in secret in this place."

There was a long silence as Cassie considered the tale. "OK, you've told me the official version of the myth. Now, what's the real story?"

Griffin laughed out loud. "You are catching on, aren't you? I suppose you might consider the Zeus myth to be propaganda. A way to capitalize on an existing legend and exploit it to serve the purposes of the overlord invaders."

Cassie trained her flashlight beam on the cradle of Zeus, studying the space for a few moments. "You're saying the Minoans had a god of their own who mythologically hatched in this cave before the Hellenes got here."

"Quite so. We know the Minoans recognized a male deity because we have seals which show a goddess and a youth as her companion. He is usually depicted as smaller than she and in an attitude of adoration toward her. He would have been her consort—a year god whose life cycle symbolized the passage of the seasons. The goddess gave birth to him in the spring. He matured and became her lover in the summer which resulted in the fruitfulness of the land. In the autumn he died as the crops were harvested, and the goddess mourned for him in the winter when nothing would grow. The cycle began again in the spring."

Cassie felt shocked. "I guess they didn't have a problem with incest."

Griffin hastened to explain. "You have to understand that the ancients believed that all life proceeded from the goddess. In that sense, every part of creation was a child of hers. And it wasn't the Minoans who invented the myth of the goddess and her consort. It exists in nearly every culture in this part of the world. In Sumer, it was Innana and Damuzi. In Babylon, it was Ishtar and Tammuz. In Egypt, it was Isis and Osiris. In Canaan, it was Anath and Baal. Even Hellenic myth offered a counterpart in Aphrodite and Adonis. This commonality suggests that the prototype for the tale originated in old Europe and was carried here by successive waves of immigrants."

Cassie glanced over to Erik who had already searched more than half of the main chamber. He didn't seem inclined to join the conversation.

The scrivener continued. "When the Minoans first started ritualizing the liaison of the goddess and her consort, a human youth would have been chosen as the personification of the year god. He might have spent some time in this cave undergoing a symbolic birth into his role as a nature deity. During the time of his reign, he would have been treated like a god. At some point in the year, he would have mated with the high priestess as she acted the role of the goddess. Their union would guarantee the fertility of the land. At harvest time, the youth may have been sacrificed."

"You mean sacrificed as in murdered?" Cassie shook her head. She couldn't reconcile the playful artwork of the Minoans with the idea that they were capable of blood rites.

"The sacrifice of the year god was a practice shared by many ancient cultures and may go back as far as the Paleolithic era. In fact, Christian religion is based on the same idea. Jesus sacrificed himself for the sake of his people and then was resurrected. Lest you think too badly of the Minoans, however, it does appear that they came to substitute an animal as the ritual victim instead. I believe that's why bull sacrifice became so prominent in Crete. The bull is the offspring of a cow. He is sacred because he bears the bucranium, the symbol of the goddess's regenerative powers. Therefore, he becomes an appropriate metaphor for the sacrifice of the year god."

"What's all this got to do with Zeus?" Cassie asked abruptly, bringing the conversation full circle.

"It was a way for the invaders to interject their own principal deity into the mythology of the native people. They said their thundering sky god was really the year god of the Minoans which made it easier for the local people to accept him."

The pythia laughed humorlessly. "Who would be stupid enough to fall for that idea?"

"Given a long enough period of indoctrination, it's quite an effective ploy. The same maneuver was used successfully by the Catholic Church to convert goddess-worshipping pagans to Christianity. The Celts in Ireland were resistant to conversion until some enterprising missionary explained to them that the Virgin Mary was really their great goddess is disguise. The misogynistic church fathers would never have actively promoted the divinity of Mary if it hadn't won them new converts."

Cassie once more looked around to see what Erik was doing. The security coordinator was now searching the other half of the chamber and was still oblivious to their dialogue.

The pythia was quiet for several moments, weighing everything Griffin had told her about the legend of Zeus's birth. Something still didn't add up. "You said this Minoan consort god died at the end of each year. I always heard that Zeus was immortal and all-powerful."

Griffin nodded approvingly. "You're quite right to point out the inconsistency. The Hellenes found themselves caught between a rock and a hard place, or perhaps a cave and a hard place. They wanted to fit their deity into Minoan mythology, but that meant they had to accept his mortality. They resolved the problem by going into a state of denial and conveniently forgetting to tell that part of the story. The new version of the myth, minus the death of Zeus, was repeated often enough and long enough that it eventually came to be accepted as fact. By 600 BCE, Epimenides of Knossos, a Cretan himself, wrote a poem in defense of the immortality of Zeus and chastised his fellow countrymen for daring to say otherwise. He wrote, 'All Cretans are liars.'"

Cassie chuckled in spite of herself. "And I thought brainwashing was a twentieth century invention."

Erik rejoined them. "While you two were yakking, I covered the entire room. There's nothing here. Let's go."

36 – CRYPTIC

By the time the trio had climbed out of the cave and back down the mountain, it was mid-afternoon. Cassie and Griffin insisted they stop for a brief lunch at one of the tavernas at the base of the trail before continuing onward to Karfi. Erik's look of contempt spoke volumes, but he offered no objection. He even condescended to order a bowl of soup for himself.

A half hour later, somewhat less hungry and irritable, they all piled back into the car to continue their journey. Fortunately, the ruins of Karfi were only a short distance from Psychro. Just outside the town of Tzermiado, Erik unaccountably pulled the car over to the side of the road and parked it. Cassie looked out the window. They were nowhere near the ruins.

"Why did you stop?" she asked.

"We have to hike to the top from here. There aren't any roads, and the foot trails aren't marked too well either."

The three got out of the car while Erik retrieved his back pack from the trunk. This time, he reached inside and brought out a trail map which he handed to Griffin.

"Oh, I see," the scrivener said, squinting first at the map and then at the mountain.

Cassie walked up to him and raised an eyebrow quizzically. "Care to explain it to me, then?"

"Unlike all the other villages we've seen, Karfi is located some distance above the plateau. It lies in the saddle between two mountain peaks which means we have quite a climb ahead of us."

Erik looked at his watch. "It's going to take us close to an hour to get there. I don't want to have to navigate these trails after dark, so we'd better get going now."

He hoisted the pack on his back and walked toward a trail marker.

The other two fell in behind him.

"So Karfi was the end of the line for the Minoans?" Cassie asked Griffin.

He nodded. "Sadly, yes. The Dorian invasion spelled the demise of their civilization in the lowland areas of the island. To their credit, the Minoans tried to carry on and maintain their traditional culture after the collapse. They chose Karfi as their final retreat partly because of its strategic location and partly because it had been a peak sanctuary for a thousand years before the Dorians arrived."

"What's a peak sanctuary?"

"It's the counterpart of the cave shrines, only on mountaintops. A place where offerings could be made to the goddess. There are many across the island, but Karfi is one of the oldest."

They climbed in silence for about half an hour. The trail switched back on itself before straightening out and running upward in a northeasterly direction. The plateau emerged below them, and Cassie caught a glimpse of the sea off in the distance.

The higher they climbed, the more barren the landscape became. Nothing but rocks jutting upward through sparse patches of grass and a few struggling olive trees. Eventually, they reached a stone alcove built around a spring. A sign posted there announced that they were nearing the archaeological site.

"Stop, stop," Cassie commanded. "I need to sit down for a minute. Jeez, I wish I'd brought a bottle of water with me."

"You're sitting right next to a mountain spring," Erik observed coldly.

Cassie looked over her shoulder at the water trickling out of the rock. "I'm not drinking that!"

The security coordinator removed his pack. She could hear him mutter a curse under his breath as he rummaged around in the depths of the bag. Pulling out a canteen, he handed it to her. "I'll give you five minutes. After that, we have to keep moving. Unless you want to try climbing down the mountain in the dark."

Cassie smiled sweetly through gritted teeth. "You see. Being nice didn't kill you." She took a deep draught from the canteen. The water was lukewarm, but she didn't care. At least she knew it came from a tap. She handed the container back to Erik. Making an effort to sound civil, she thanked him. "I just need a couple of minutes to catch my breath is all."

The late afternoon sunshine was burning the top of her head. Cassie shaded her eyes and wished for a cap or a visor. She didn't think Erik had one in his magic backpack, so she didn't ask. A blister was starting for form on her left heel. Ignoring it, she stood up and dusted off her jeans. "OK, I'm good."

Erik slung his pack over his shoulders and resumed the march upward.

About ten minutes later, Cassie heard Griffin announce, "There it is."

The trio paused to take in the sight.

The pythia looked off in the distance at a green space between two mountain peaks. Stones were jutting out of the ground, but they weren't arranged randomly. They formed a series of squares connecting to one another – the foundations of buildings partially buried underground.

"Take a look at the configuration of the mountains. Do you notice anything familiar about the shape?" Griffin regarded her quizzically.

She squinted in the sunlight and studied the landscape for a moment. The two vertical peaks were close to one another. One of them seemed to curve inward slightly. "It looks like horns of consecration!" she exclaimed.

"Well spotted," Griffin said approvingly. "And probably why the Minoans chose this location as a peak sanctuary in the first place."

"But I don't see much of a town," she observed in a disappointed tone as they approached the ruins.

"That's because the excavation was never completed. It's estimated that the actual settlement is six times the size of what was unearthed in the 1930s. There were paved streets and squares, a temple and several other large public buildings." Griffin looked disconsolately around at the rubble. "The excavation might have been handled in a more systematic manner. The structures were never reinforced afterward, leaving them at the mercy of wind and weather. As you can see, most of them have collapsed. Anything of note was carted off to museums in Heraklion and England decades ago. Now the site is a goat pasture."

"But you said yesterday that you wanted to look at some tombs, right?" Cassie prompted.

"Yes, quite so. Your vision of the chrysalis suggests that the burial crypts, the *tholoi*, might be our best starting point. Karfi really is the most logical spot to find our elusive symbols." Griffin's eyes travelled across the ruin.

"What makes you say that?"

"In the field operative's journal, I was struck by the specific choice of words: 'The high place of the goddess.' A peak sanctuary certainly qualifies as a high place. But it isn't merely that. It's that the legend speaks of a time when people had forgotten the old ways. That didn't occur during the Mycenean invasion but much later when the Dorians arrived. Not until the last of the Minoans were forced to hide in these mountains and watch as their island home was overrun by alien warriors and their alien gods. Surely if they believed the goddess had abandoned the land, it was at the time when Karfi became their final refuge." Griffin paused and then added more to himself than to Cassie, "The Bones of the Mother have to be here. They can't be anywhere else!"

Erik broke into the conversation abruptly. "There's a cemetery over this way." Without waiting to see if his teammates followed him, he struck out on his own to the south of where they stood.

Cassie and Griffin trailed after him. Although the hour was growing late, they decided not to split up. Unlike the cave which was self-contained, they might lose track of one another easily up here. To Cassie's disappointment, the cemetery was in much the same decayed state as the settlement itself. Square formations of stone, much smaller than the perimeter of a house, were all that remained. "I thought you said this was a cemetery," she observed.

"It is," Griffin replied.

"But I don't see any headstones or any pits dug in the ground. It looks to me like these buildings were all above ground," she noted.

"They were," the scrivener concurred.

Erik decided to contribute to the discussion. He managed to sound almost conversational as he explained, "The Minoans liked to bury their dead in above-ground crypts. Square buildings with narrow doorways that usually faced east."

"Why east?" the pythia asked.

Erik kicked a stone aside with his shoe. "The direction of sunrise. You know, resurrection and all that."

She gave him a skeptical look.

"What, you think Christians were the first ones to come up with that idea?" He laughed. "Nothing in Christianity is original. Not virgin birth or a dying and resurrected god. They got all that stuff from pagan lore. Sunrise as a symbol of rebirth too."

"He's quite right," Griffin affirmed.

"Go figure," Cassie murmured contemplatively. Switching her attention back to the remains of a tomb, she observed, "Must have gotten kind of crowded in there over time."

"A single *tholos* was used by an extended family over the course of centuries." Griffin warmed to his topic. "There may have been more than one burial chamber, and they used a round robin system until all the chambers were occupied. Then they'd begin the cycle again. Minoan coffins weren't as large as the sort we use. They buried their dead in fetal positions in a terra cotta box called a *larnax*. After an appropriate interval, the bones would have been moved to an ossuary and the space cleaned for the next occupant."

"Sort of like renting a funeral plot for fifty years?"

Erik smiled in spite of himself.

"Something like that, yes," Griffin averred.

"But the tomb I saw in my vision was underground," Cassie objected. "It didn't look like what you just described."

"I suspect what you were seeing was a Mycenaean *tholos* tomb," Griffin explained. "The Mycenaeans preferred round, beehive-shaped burial chambers which they covered with a mound of dirt. There would be a long narrow ramp called a *dromos* leading down from the surface to the door of the crypt which was called a *stomion.* A stone retaining wall on either side of the ramp would keep the earth from collapsing and burying the entrance to the tomb."

"That sounds like what I saw, but why would the Mycenaeans have been here?" the pythia countered.

"There was some archaeological evidence at Karfi suggesting that two ethnic groups shared the mountain refuge. After all, the Mycenaeans also needed to flee from the Dorians. It's equally possible that the Minoans copied the style of the Mycenaeans. They'd been exposed to mainland culture for at least three hundred years. Some of it may have caught their fancy."

Cassie surveyed the area around them. "Are there any tombs like that around here?"

"Several, I believe."

While the two were talking, Erik had wandered a short distance away. "Here's one," he announced. His companions scurried over to take a look. The roof of the central chamber had collapsed, exposing the crypt to the sky but the lower half of the structure was still intact underground. Some attempt had been made to excavate the *dromos* because a dirt path led from the subterranean tomb entrance up to ground level. The path was overgrown with grass indicating the excavation had been abandoned decades before.

"There's nothing in these graves," Cassie noted.

"Archaeologists and graverobbers would have carried away anything of value long before this," Griffin said wistfully. Then perking up, he said, "Well, down we go." He jumped into the *dromos* trench and sauntered through the tomb entrance.

Erik shrugged and instead of following Griffin, he chose to leap down through the hole in the roof. Cassie struggled for a few moments with the notion of entering yet another creepy underground space. She took a deep breath and followed Griffin down the ramp.

The sun was sinking rapidly now. It barely provided enough light to illuminate the interior of the main chamber.

"How do you want to tackle this exactly?" the pythia asked.

Griffin held out his hand to Erik. "I think we'll need torches again if you please."

The security coordinator retrieved the items from his back pack and handed them around.

Griffin walked into a secondary burial chamber and trained the beam of his flashlight on the walls. "I imagine we should look at the walls of these structures. Ceilings too if they're still intact. See if there are any key symbols carved into the stone. Remember the field journal said, 'A message in stone waiting to be unlocked by one who holds the key.'"

"Sounds like a plan," Erik agreed.

The three of them scoured every inch of the *tholos* but found none of the symbols from the key.

Erik went ahead and located the next underground *tholos* tomb. He scouted them out one by one as Cassie and Griffin searched their interiors.

The process was tedious and time-consuming. The sun had already set. They finished checking the tombs in the south cemetery and took the same approach with the crypts in the cemetery to the east of Karfi. None of them wanted to leave any tomb unchecked, so they worked feverishly to finish them all. Despite Erik's earlier warning, it was apparent that it was already too late for them to make their way down the mountain without the use of their flashlights.

The evening air grew chilly and damp. Cassie was grateful that she had heeded Erik's advice to bring along a jacket. Although the sky was lit with stars, there was no moon, making the landscape even harder to navigate. They were down to the last *tholos* that Erik had been able to discover. It was in worse shape than the others. The dome was still intact but cracked in many places. The mound of earth which had once covered it had eroded centuries ago exposing the top of the tomb to the elements. The retaining wall of the *dromos* had buckled and was on the verge of collapse. Rocks were piled along either side of the narrow ramp so that the trio had to crawl over heaps of stone to get to the *stomion.* The bottom half of it was clogged with loose rock.

The tomb itself consisted of a single round burial chamber. A search of it revealed nothing. The three of them squeezed back out the door and crawled disappointedly up the ramp. Cassie grew clumsy as she began to favor her blistered foot. She tripped and slammed into a tall boulder at the top of the *dromos*, crushing her little toe.

"Ouch," she yelled and then cursed under her breath. She leaned against the rock for balance as she inspected her foot, sure she had broken a toe. "What the…" she trailed off.

She found herself in the same spot only now it was the middle of the day. The sun was beating down on her head. Her arms were large and sinewy. She realized she was a man cutting deep marks into a large stone.

"Cassie, Cassie, are you alright?" Distant voices in her head were calling her. It was as if she was under water and somebody on the surface was shouting her name. Somebody was shaking her by the shoulder.

"Cassie! Snap out of it!" The voice grew louder and closer. It was Erik's. His hands were clamped to her upper arms. He shook her so hard that her teeth rattled.

"What?" she asked groggily, disoriented. Gradually, she came back to the present. She was seated on the ground, gazing stupidly from one man to the other. Griffin trained his flashlight on her face. She blinked.

"Get that thing out of my eyes, will you?" She turned to Erik and winced. "And as for you, ouch! Let go of my arms. You're hurting me."

Erik exhaled deeply. She almost imagined it sounded like a sigh of relief. "She's OK," he said tersely, standing up. Then recovering himself, he demanded, "What the hell was that all about?"

She was back now. The realization of what had happened hit her, and she leaped to her feet wincing slightly. Her toe still throbbed. She was beginning to understand exactly what it was all about.

"Guys!" she exclaimed urgently. "I think it's here! You need to look here!" She pointed in the dark toward the massive block of stone behind her.

Both men simultaneously trained their flashlights on the rock.

"Good goddess!" Griffin exclaimed.

37 - DECODING THE PAST

Griffin fell to his knees in front of the boulder, his fingers tracing the lily pattern on its face. The stone was four feet high, rounded in the back, but the front half had been polished flat to allow an inscription to be carved on it.

Erik kept his flashlight focused on the rock, so Griffin could try to decipher the message. "I don't believe it," he said incredulously. "Between the two of you, you actually managed to find it."

"You don't have to sound so surprised." Cassie's tone was less hostile than it might have been. The fact that Erik was paying them any kind of compliment, even a backhanded one, was a welcome change from his usual attitude. She sat on the ground at the base of the stone holding her flashlight over the photos of the key markings, comparing the symbols to the carving.

"Yes, this is definitely it!" Griffin could barely contain his excitement at the find. "The lily above the inscription is an exact match to the ones on the key. It's a coded way of saying, 'To find The Bones of the Mother.' His hand traced another line etched a foot below the lily. "And here we have a line of symbols that I ought to be able to translate in a few moments."

The scrivener sat on the ground in front of the boulder and drew a small notebook and pencil out of his jacket pocket. From another pocket, he drew a thick stack of folded pages. "This will take a bit. I have to compare the symbols on the boulder to the ones on the key, translate those to Linear B, then translate the Linear B text to modern Greek, and then to English. Cassie, if you wouldn't mind training your torch on these pages while I write." He began scratching on the pad and referring to his various reference sources. For several minutes he seemed to be conducting a monologue with himself. "No, that's not it. The syntax is wrong. Let's try it this way. Ah, that's better. Now we're making progress."

Cassie thought about taking a nap, flashlight in hand, while he nattered on, but then he snapped his notebook shut decisively. "Right, that's it then."

"You got it?" Cassie asked, instantly alert.

"Yes," he replied somewhat guardedly.

Noting his tone, Erik asked, "What is it?"

"Well, the good news is that now we know how many relics there are. The bad news is that they aren't hidden together."

"Why don't you just tell us what the line says?" Cassie urged.

Griffin sighed. "It reads: 'You will find the first of five you seek.'"

"Five," Erik echoed. "I guess this isn't gonna be a slam dunk after all."

"They could be hidden anywhere." Cassie felt dismayed. "Scattered halfway across the planet for all we know."

"Not to worry," Griffin said reassuringly. "We have more code to translate. Hopefully, the next set of characters will give us the location of the first relic at least." He ran his hand over a second line of symbols carved several inches below the first.

It took several more minutes of page-shuffling and note-scratching before Griffin glanced up, scowling slightly.

"That is not a happy face," Erik observed.

"Admittedly this line is a bit obscure," Griffin hedged. "It reads: 'When the soul of the lady rises with the sun.'"

"What the hell is that supposed to mean?" the security coordinator challenged irritably.

Griffin shrugged. "Haven't a clue. It may be a metaphor. It may be a reference to a point in time. In either case, this will take additional research to sort out."

Cassie slumped forward and rubbed her forehead. "Guess we aren't going to be able to scamper off and collect those bones tomorrow, are we?"

"Don't give way." Griffin tried to sound comforting. "There's bound to be something less abstract in the next line." His fingers traced some additional markings carved in the middle of the stone. "Oh dear," he said in dismay.

Erik pointed his flashlight on the spot. Directly below the first two lines of code, the rock had been hollowed out. Beneath the niche were additional glyphs.

"Hmmm," the scrivener said ponderously.

"More problems?" Erik sounded tense.

Griffin referred to his photos of the symbols and then back to the boulder again. "You see these markings just here? They don't seem to match any of the characters we have."

"Great!" Cassie exclaimed. "We came all this way to translate two lines that don't tell us anything yet."

"Oh, ye of little faith," the scrivener intoned. "Give me a few moments to sort this out." He sat down cross-legged on the ground in front of the stone and stared at it.

Cassie thought he'd gone into a trance because he continued to stare at it for about ten minutes without moving. She groaned. This didn't look good. What were they missing?

"Would this help?" Erik asked laconically as he held out the granite key toward Griffin.

"What?" the scrivener looked up at him distractedly, not realizing what he was holding. Then recognition dawned. "Good grief, where did you get that?"

"You left it behind at the hotel. I thought it might be important, so I brought it with me."

Griffin took the stone key contemplatively. "Despite my initial ideas about the key, I've come to the conclusion we don't need it physically at all. In fact, I'm not quite sure what good it will do to—" He stopped short and caught his breath. "Hello, what's this?"

Cassie shone her flashlight up at Erik. "Do you know what he's talking about?"

The security coordinator rolled his eyes. "I hardly ever know what he's talking about."

Griffin was on his knees in front of the boulder again, trying to fit the granite key into the slot in the large rock.

Erik and Cassie both focused their beams on the hollow spot on the boulder.

After Griffin positioned the key, he studied it for a minute. "No, that's not it," he murmured half to himself. He rotated the stone cylinder and tried fitting it into the slot again. "Not quite yet." Rotating it yet again, he leaned back on his heels to consider. "Ingenious!" he exclaimed, his voice filled with admiration.

Cassie leaned forward to peer over his shoulder. "What is?"

Erik held his flashlight steady over the key.

"You see these markings on the boulder, just here?" Griffin asked her.

"What about them?"

"They constitute half of a symbol. The other half is on the edge of the key itself." It would be the same as if I did this." He took one of the pages of symbol photographs and drew a line across the row of hieroglyphs, bisecting each of them through the middle.

"I get it." Cassie nodded approvingly. "Those hash marks on each edge of the key. They're actually the top half of a symbol."

"Yes, but the trick is to know which side of the key to fit into the groove on the boulder. The key has five sides, hence five edges with half symbols." Griffin observed the boulder again. "I believe I've aligned them properly now. Let me try to translate the next line."

He sat back down in a cross-legged position. Cassie held a flashlight over his various note papers, so he could write unencumbered while Erik held a light over the inscription on the boulder.

It took Griffin another fifteen minutes of muttering and leafing through his notes to finish the job. "Aha!" he exclaimed. "A useful clue at last!"

His companions exchanged an eager look.

"It reads: 'At the home of the Mountain Mother.'"

Cassie felt more than a little deflated.

Sensing her reaction, Griffin protested, "Just be glad I was able to make it sound even that intelligible. Linear B is not a language that lends itself well to poetry. I might as well be using an accounting glossary to write blank verse!"

The pythia relented. "I know you're doing the best you can."

"Moreover, that line isn't as cryptic as you might think." The scrivener smiled for the first time. "The term 'Mountain Mother' is a very precise epithet for the goddess. It was used specifically in connection with her place of worship on Mount Ida."

"So that line gives us a place to look?" Cassie asked uncertainly. "There's a mountain on Crete that's called Ida?"

"Exactly so," Griffin affirmed. "And a peak sanctuary where the great goddess was venerated. The home, if you will, of the Mountain Mother."

Erik rubbed his head wearily. "Time for a recap. What does the message say when you put it all together?"

Griffin referred to his notes. "The entire text now reads: 'You will find the first of five you seek, when the soul of the lady rises with the sun, at the home of the Mountain Mother.'"

"So, we know how many relics there are and where the first one is hidden," the security coordinator mused out loud.

"All that remains is to solve the riddle of the second line," Griffin added. "A task which cannot be accomplished here. Might I suggest we continue this discussion in more comfortable surroundings?"

Cassie stood up, dusting off her jeans. "It looks like we've got our work cut out for us."

From out of nowhere, an arm shot out across her throat, pulling her backwards. She could feel a gun barrel pointed at her temple.

A voice with a southern accent punctuated the darkness. "I'd say your work is just about done, folks."

38 – ROCK AND ROLL

Griffin and Erik sent the beams of their flashlights in the direction of the voice. They revealed a man with one arm across Cassie's neck and the other pointing a pistol at her head.

"Now, you boys don't want to do anything foolish, do you? Get this young lady killed or somethin' like that?" he drawled. "Hands up where I can see 'em, fellers."

"Who are you?" Griffin demanded, raising his arms above his head.

"It's him," Cassie said shakily. "It's the man who killed my sister." In all her fantasies of confronting Leroy Hunt, she had never imagined this scenario. Her visions had always included a cordon of policemen standing between her and her sister's murderer while she hurled taunts at him.

"Hold on there, missy. I never killed your big sis," Hunt protested in a wounded tone.

"You were chasing her, and she fell! You might as well have killed her!"

The cowboy's voice grew wary. "Now how'd you come to know that? Were you hidin' out in the shop someplace?"

"I had a nightmare, and you were in it. I saw everything!"

"Cass," Erik cautioned. It was the first time he'd actually used her name. "You really don't want to upset the nice man, do you?"

"That's right." Leroy nodded approvingly. "You listen to that boy. He's talkin' sense. You ought'nt to rile a feller who's got a gun pointed at your head. It just ain't smart."

"As if that matters!" Cassie could feel tears of frustration and sadness welling up in her eyes. The man who had pointlessly ended her sister's life was about to end hers for no better reason.

"Mr. Hunt," a voice called out tentatively from the shadows.

"Daniel," Hunt shouted over his shoulder. "You stay behind me and point that flashlight so's I can see everybody."

"But Mr. Hunt," the voice pleaded. "The Fallen Ones have given us all the information we need. We should be leaving now."

"Don't tell me my business, boy!" Leroy shot back. "Your daddy give me a job to do, and I'm gonna see that it gets done proper."

"But Mr. Hunt," the voice was more urgent now.

"Mr. Hunt, nothin'!" Leroy bellowed. "Do like I told you and train that flashlight over here."

Cassie could hear the sound of feet scuffling through the dirt some distance behind her. A light flicked on obediently to reveal her two companions with their hands raised over their heads. Erik looked tight-mouthed and tense while Griffin was still gaping in shock. For once in his life, he seemed to be at a loss for words.

"I believe we got some loose ends need tyin' up," Hunt said pleasantly. "How about you two boys walk on down that ramp and go inside that tomb you was just lookin' at."

"Why should they?" Cassie demanded. "You're just going to kill us all anyway!"

"Cass!" Erik warned again.

"Maybe I will, and maybe I won't. There's a lot of maybes could happen in the next five minutes or so." He paused and regarded the two men who remained motionless.

"Daniel, you keep that light steady on them boys." The beam traveled to the men's faces, causing them to blink. "You fellers go on and do like I told you."

Erik and Griffin, arms still overhead and flashlights still in hand, exchanged looks and complied. Hunt followed with Cassie in lockstep slightly ahead of him. She could feel the gun scraping against her temple as they walked. Daniel followed, his flashlight pointed dutifully ahead of the strange procession.

The men paused in front of the *stomion*.

"Go on now," Hunt urged once more. "Inside."

They had to crawl through the top half of the doorway since the bottom half was filled with fallen rock and gravel.

Once they were inside, Leroy threaded his way carefully down the rock-strewn ramp, still gripping Cassie by the neck.

He stopped right in front of the doorway. "Alright, missy, it's your turn. In the hole. And don't try runnin'. No way you can get past me anyhow without takin' a bullet. Might as well join your friends inside."

Cassie had no intention of trying to make a break for it. The *dromos* was only three feet wide, and most of it was clogged with debris. She wouldn't be able to move in any direction without being caught. Hunt released his grip on her neck so she could breathe freely again. She knew the gun was still pointed at her as she crawled through the *stomion* into the tomb. Her companions trained their flashlights on her to make sure she was alright. She gave them a tremulous smile and walked to the center of the chamber. Erik pulled her behind him in a futile gesture of protection. Griffin closed ranks next to him.

"Daniel, come on down here and hand me that light," Hunt instructed, his voice calm and matter-of-fact—as if he were asking someone to pass the peas at the dinner table.

"Please, Mr. Hunt!" the voice whined from the darkness once more. "I'm sure father never intended for something like this to happen."

"The hell he didn't," Leroy said over his shoulder. "Why'd you think he pulled me into this mess? To babysit you? You better do like I say, or he's gonna know what a gutless wonder his boy is. You want that? You want me goin' back and tellin' your daddy how you let him down?"

"No," the voice quavered.

"Good, that's settled then," Hunt said emphatically. "Now hand me that goddam light!"

Daniel wordlessly complied.

The cowboy leaned across the pile of rock that filled the lower half of the *stomion*, a flashlight in one hand and a gun in the other.

Cassie looked around the circular burial chamber—stone and mortar, no windows, not even a dark corner to hide in. They were trapped.

"Well, ain't this handy. More folks ought to get snuffed right inside a tomb. Saves on funeral costs." Leroy took aim and murmured, "Easy as shootin' fish in a barrel."

Cassie instinctively shut her eyes and put her hands over her ears. She didn't want to know what was coming next.

What came next was something nobody expected. Without warning, a low rumble emanated from beneath their feet. The earth began to shiver. Cassie lost her balance. It seemed as if rock was raining down from the sky. The *dromos* walls were collapsing.

Leroy quickly retracted his head from the *stomion*.

Cassie could hear him calling to his companion. "Looks like Mother Nature is gonna finish the job for us. Come on, Daniel. We best get outta here while we still can!" The sound of footsteps sliding over gravel echoed in the tomb as the men scampered over the rock pile. The noise of their hasty retreat had barely faded before rock came crashing through the doorway, filling up the *stomion* completely, and burying the Arkana team inside.

When the rumbling of the earth finally subsided, the silence that followed possessed the stillness of death.

39 - EXIT STRATEGY

Stunned and trembling, Cassie struggled to sit up. Her flashlight had rolled to the side of the chamber, the beam pointing toward the wall. She crawled on all fours to retrieve it. Swinging the light around in a wide arc, she asked, "Erik? Griffin? Are you guys all right?"

Erik sat up, coughing from the dust blown into the chamber by fallen rock. "I'm OK," he confirmed succinctly. "Griffin?"

From another part of the tomb, the scrivener answered. "Miraculously, we all still seem to be alive." He wiped a thick coating of dust from his face, retrieved his flashlight, and stood up. Shining his beam toward the *stomion*, he revealed that it was now completely filled with rock. "Alive for the moment anyway. It would appear we're sealed in."

Erik walked over to the doorway and tried pushing against the newly fallen boulders at the top. They rolled inward as a pile on the other side of the door rushed to take their place.

Cassie fumbled in her jacket pocket for her phone, thinking she might be able to reach Xenia. "No good," she said. "There's no signal down here." She looked around the stone chamber nervously. "How long before we run out of air?"

Griffin's eyes traveled around their enclosure, judging its size and calculating air volume. "Several hours, I'd say."

"OK, everybody stop breathing." The pythia laughed weakly. "Let's try to conserve oxygen."

"If you stopped chattering, that would be a good start," Erik snapped. He wandered around the center of the chamber, training his flashlight on the domed ceiling of the vault as he studied it closely.

Stung by the rebuke, Cassie rounded on him. "By the way, weren't you supposed to provide security for this field mission? Great job of letting the crazy cowboy sneak up on us. Really fine work!"

Even in the dim light, she could see Erik's face redden. Apparently, the pythia had struck a nerve. "I might have heard him coming if you two weren't yakking all the time!"

"So, it's all our fault?" She leaped to her feet, ready to go toe-to-toe, but Griffin interposed himself between the combatants.

"This isn't helping the situation," he objected. "We need to cooperate if we're going to get out of this dilemma."

"Aren't you the optimist," Cassie muttered angrily as she retreated to the opposite wall of the chamber.

Griffin sat down beside her. "We just need to calm ourselves and assess the problem rationally."

The two watched Erik as he stuffed his lit flashlight into his jacket pocket and raised his arms above his head. Then he began walking around the perimeter of the room, waving his hands gently from side to side.

"How very extraordinary," Griffin remarked.

"Do you think he's finally lost it?" the pythia whispered doubtfully. "Or maybe he just wants us to join him in a chorus of Kumbaya."

"I can hear you," Erik stated flatly. "You're both using up my air." He stopped pacing and stood before a section of wall. Standing on his toes, he reached his arms higher and waved them side to side. "Yup, that's it," he commented half to himself.

"What are you doing?" Griffin asked.

"Checking for air flow. You think you could give me a hand here, stretch?"

Griffin was several inches taller than Erik. He hastened to the other side of the room and mimicked the security coordinator's movements. He waved his arms overhead and then stopped at a particular spot on the wall. "Yes, I believe you're right. I feel it."

Cassie stood up impatiently and walked over to join the other two. "What is it?" she demanded.

Griffin smiled at her. "A draft."

"Meaning what exactly?"

'It means a way out," Erik explained laconically.

"How do you figure?" The pythia wasn't convinced that a slight breeze was anything to cheer about.

Griffin explained. "This *dromos* is approximately twenty feet in diameter and about twenty feet high at the apex of the dome. Judging from what we observed on the outside, the top half of the dome has been exposed to the elements for quite some time. For centuries, possibly a millennium, moisture has worked its way into the mortar. The action of repeated freezing and melting has separated the clay from the surrounding stones."

"Plus, we just had that nice little earthquake," Erik added. "Look at these cracks." He trained his flashlight at a spot above his head. Cassie could see a thin fracture running up toward the ceiling.

"Precisely," Griffin confirmed. "The dome is weakened. No doubt the mortar between the stones has eroded completely at the spot where we felt that draft. We should be able to remove enough of the rock for us to squeeze out."

"Without bringing the whole roof down on top of us?" Cassie shuddered at the thought.

"It's fairly unlikely since this is a corbelled vault," the scrivener commented. "The stones overlap one another to add structural stability."

Erik shrugged nonchalantly. "Even if they all fell, at least it would be a quicker death than suffocating."

"You can't be serious!" she exclaimed.

He smiled sardonically. "Do you have a better idea?"

"No," she admitted weakly.

"Then why don't you stop complaining and make yourself useful? Over there." He pointed at the small boulders blocking the *stomion* entrance. "We need to pile up enough of those against the wall so we can climb to the ceiling and loosen some rocks where it's weakest."

"Yes," Griffin joined in. "The part of the dome that protrudes from the surface is at least ten feet above the floor. It would be no help to loosen stones at eye level. We'd still remain buried."

"We'll have to work fast," Erik advised. "I don't know how long the batteries in these flashlights will hold out."

The thought of being trapped underground in complete darkness motivated Cassie. She sped to the task.

After countless trips to the *stomion* rock pile, the trio managed to build a sturdy enough platform to reach the spot on the wall where a draft seemed to be flowing into the chamber.

"You'd think with all of the rocks we just pulled out of the doorway, we might have opened a way out," Cassie observed ruefully.

"I expect the entire *dromos* has been completely filled in," Griffin said glumly. "No hope of escaping that way. But cheer up," he added optimistically. "At least we won't have to worry about running out of air."

Erik was rummaging around in his backpack again. He withdrew an army knife. Looking up at his companions, he asked, "Either of you have something sharp we can use to scrape away the loose mortar?"

Cassie reached into a pocket and produced a metal nail file. "Will this work?"

The security coordinator nodded approvingly. "It can't hurt. How about you, Griffin?"

After thoroughly checking his pockets, Griffin reluctantly held forth a gold ball point pen. "This is all I have with me."

"Good enough," Erik said.

"It's my favorite pen," Griffin commented sadly.

Since the rock pile was only wide enough to support one person, they took turns climbing up to gouge and dig at the mortar. After what seemed like hours, they loosened one of the stones enough to dislodge it.

"Stand back," Erik cautioned. "The earthquake could have destabilized the entire dome. I don't know how many others will fall."

His companions moved to the opposite wall of the chamber. They nervously shone their flashlights on the fracture in the ceiling as he carefully worked the rock free.

The second he pulled it from the curve of the dome, three other stones surrounding it fell out of place and dropped to the rock pile at his feet. He waited tensely to see if any more would tumble loose. "So far, so good," he murmured.

With the delicacy of a brain surgeon, Erik freed two more corbelled stones without disturbing the rest of the dome. Eventually, he had opened up a space wide enough to allow one of them to squeeze through.

"You did it!" Cassie exclaimed in surprise.

"We did it!" Griffin corrected in an elated tone.

Erik gave a half smile. "You guys ready to go topside?"

"Yes, please," the scrivener requested politely.

Cassie nodded in a flood of mute relief. They weren't going to die after all. At least not today. With a shock, she noticed a grayish light coming from the gap in the ceiling.

"Is that..." she paused.

"Daybreak," Erik completed the sentence.

"How long were we down here?" she asked in wonder.

"Too long," he replied concisely. "Better let me go first."

"What a gentleman." Cassie's voice dripped with sarcasm.

Erik gave her an exasperated look. "In case our friends are still hanging around outside."

He reached into his backpack for the thousandth time and pulled out a hand gun.

"What the..." Cassie trailed off in shock. "You had a gun all this time, and you didn't try to use it?"

"In case you forgot, the cowboy had you in a stranglehold with a pistol to your head. If I'd made a move, he would have splattered your brains all over the countryside."

"Lovely image," interjected Griffin.

"Besides, we had our hands in the air. If I'd dived into my backpack to reach for a weapon, same result. Your brains splattered all over the countryside."

"But why weren't you carrying it someplace more useful?" Cassie challenged. "Like a holster or something."

"Too obvious," Erik countered.

"It's comforting to know that if you actually need a gun, it's going to be conveniently out of reach."

Erik climbed down off the rock pile and glowered at Cassie. "You can make this about me all you want, but you're just covering up for the fact that you're the weak link in this operation!"

"What?" Cassie gasped.

"That's right," Erik persisted. "You've got no business being part of this world. You've never been trained for it. And because you don't know what you're doing, I end up risking my neck to keep you safe!"

Cassie was speechless. How could he blame her for this mess? It was clearly his fault for being caught off guard.

"You know what?" she challenged. "I am fed up with your attitude. You need to get over the inexperience of me because it's seriously messing up your job performance. This whole trip you've been pouting that you had to babysit the greenhorns. You were so busy feeling sorry for yourself that you got sloppy and let your guard down."

Erik sent Cassie a murderous look.

Before he could follow it with a killing retort, Griffin rushed to smooth things over. "Really, I think we should continue this lively and interesting discussion once we're well away from this place. Our principal concern at the moment ought to be escape."

Erik and Cassie glared ferociously at one another for several more seconds before the security coordinator broke eye contact. "I'll go first," he repeated. "Hand me my pack once I'm outside."

40 - SITE UNSEEN

Erik climbed to the top of the rock pile. Holding his pistol, he poked his head through the gap in the dome. Apparently feeling that it was safe, he squeezed himself past the narrow opening and disappeared.

"All clear," he called down. "Send Cassie up next with my pack."

The pythia didn't argue. She wanted to get out of the tomb without further delay. She reached for Erik's pack but sank under the weight of it. It was unexpectedly heavy. She wondered to herself if he might have packed a rocket launcher that he forgot to tell them about. Griffin helped her to hoist it up ahead of her.

She had no trouble squeezing herself through the gap since she was the smallest of the three. When the cool dawn air hit her face, she almost sobbed with relief. Realizing that Erik was standing nearby, she blinked back the tears. This wasn't something she wanted him to see. Especially not after what he had just said. She wasn't going to give him any more reason to believe that she was the weak link.

Griffin followed a few minutes later. "That was a bracing experience, wasn't it?" he joked.

Neither of his companions laughed.

Cassie noticed the sky turning a lighter shade of grey. Twilight and dawn looked oddly the same. At least they could see everything in their immediate vicinity, and nobody else was around.

"I don't suppose we need these anymore." Griffin switched off his flashlight.

Cassie realized her own was still on. She flicked it off absently.

"We'll have to cover this up," Erik observed.

"What?" Cassie didn't think she'd heard him right. "We just spent hours carving out a hole in this dome, and now you want to cover it up?"

"We don't know if our buddy the cowboy is going to circle back here," the security coordinator cautioned. "If he thinks we got out, he's going to try to track us down."

It hadn't occurred to Cassie that Leroy might come back to make sure the job was finished.

"Let him think we're still inside."

"That makes sense." Griffin looked around for something to camouflage the hole in the dome. "Luckily, the gap is just at ground level, so it shouldn't be too hard to disguise."

"We can pile some rocks against the spot," Erik suggested. "Unless he's looking pretty close, he won't notice."

Cassie sighed at the thought of moving more boulders. But, as she sternly reminded herself, she had no reason to complain. It was a miracle that they were alive at all.

The trio gathered stones and brush. In a short time, they had effectively camouflaged the gap in the dome.

Cassie gazed at their handiwork. "I think that hole in the roof is going to collapse eventually."

"Eventually won't matter," Erik countered. "If Hunt circles back here it's going to be in the next few days."

"Are we ready to quit this dismal spot?" Griffin asked.

"Fine by me," Erik agreed.

"No," Cassie blurted out, a troubling thought beginning to form.

"Huh?" the security coordinator gave her a surprised look.

"Guys, we have to go back to the entrance of the tomb."

"What?" Griffin sounded shocked.

"I think we're missing something. I think you two dragged me out of my vision too soon."

Erik rolled his eyes. "You've got to be kidding me."

"No, I'm not kidding." Cassie's tone was serious. "I feel like there was something more I was supposed to see."

The security coordinator hoisted his pack onto his back and started down the trail. "I'm not hanging around here just because you've got a hunch. For all we know, the cowboy and his buddy could be on their way back here right now."

Cassie ran down the slope after him and grabbed him by the arm. She spun him around to face her. "Don't you dare brush me off! This is important, damn it! All my life I've been moved around like a pawn on somebody else's chessboard. First by my parents and then by my sister. Just a dumb kid who needs to be protected. A little girl who doesn't know anything and shouldn't know anything."

"You're right so far," Erik concurred.

Griffin hurried down the hill after them, ready to separate the two if necessary.

"Maybe I'm not a walking search engine like Griffin or James Bond Junior like you, but I'm a part of this team for a reason. I'm the pythia, and my hunches matter! Right now, they're screaming in my head that we need to go back to that boulder, and you need to let me finish doing my damn job!" She glared at him defiantly.

Griffin glanced worriedly from one to the other.

Erik stared at Cassie for a long moment, as if he were seeing her for the first time. Then a slight smile twitched at the corner of his mouth. "OK, toots. Go for it!"

"My name's not toots," she muttered. Turning in the opposite direction, she marched back to the top of the *dromos* where the boulder stood. She looked down briefly at the trench. As Griffin had surmised, it was buried under a pile of rock. The retaining wall had collapsed completely. They would never have gotten out through the *stomion.* The sight made her shudder.

Transferring her attention to the boulder, she could see it more easily in the gathering light. The two men caught up with her by this time. She sat down in front of the rock and looked up at them.

"You both should stand back. Don't touch me until I come out of it on my own, OK?" Her tone didn't brook argument.

The men traded a look. Griffin nodded slowly.

Erik shrugged. "Fine."

Cassie took off her jacket and folded it up like a pillow. Placing it behind her neck, she leaned her head back against the smooth face of the boulder and closed her eyes.

Once again, she felt the strange sensation of the sky shifting from dawn to noon. The same spot but a different time of day. She was still the stone carver with the sinewy arms, but she was working on a different section of the boulder. Much farther down than before. She gazed up and saw the lily freshly carved at the top. She saw the two lines of symbols which Griffin had easily translated. She saw the deep groove in the middle of the boulder and the half symbols carved below it. But the stone cutter wasn't working on any of that.

Her eyes flew open, and she sat bolt upright.

"What?" both men asked simultaneously.

Cassie smiled broadly. "I was right. There was something else. There's another line of code."

"Where?" the security coordinator challenged. "I don't see anything."

Cassie was on her hands and knees in front of the boulder. "That's because it's under this." She started clawing at a heavy flat rock that had been placed precisely at the base of the boulder and in front of it. It seemed to have been cut evenly on one end so that it fitted flush up against the larger stone.

She turned to face her companions. "You guys up to some more digging? We need to move this flat rock out of the way."

Erik wordlessly removed his jacket and rolled up his shirt sleeves. Griffin followed suit.

It took several minutes to dig out enough of the dirt around the base of the rock to allow it to move.

They strained and pushed and pulled and eventually were able to drag it several inches away from the front of the boulder.

Griffin inspected the spot, scraping the soil away from the face of the rock. There were dirt-filled carvings at its base. Another line of symbols from the key.

"Cassie, I could kiss you!" Griffin exclaimed.

"What about you?" she asked Erik archly.

"Don't press your luck," he said, though he was grinning when he said it. Looking around the hillside in the early morning light, he added, "Maybe we should translate this at the hotel. I don't like the idea of hanging around here any longer than we have to."

"Agreed," Griffin said readily. "Just let me copy down these symbols, and we can be on our way."

"Of course, you'll have to move the flat rock back in place," Cassie suggested sweetly.

The two men looked at her in bewilderment.

"Same logic applies, guys. You wanted to cover that hole in the dome in case Leroy and his sidekick came back. Do you really want to leave that rock over to the side, so they can see the line of code they're missing?"

Griffin and Erik groaned, but neither one contradicted her.

For once Cassie got the last word.

41 – IN THE NAME OF THE FATHER

When Daniel and Leroy returned to Chicago, a car was waiting at the airport to bring them back to the compound. They were to be taken to see the diviner immediately. Daniel experienced nothing but dread at the thought of the interview. He felt as if he had aged several years during the week he had spent in Greece. In contrast, Hunt seemed elated, even jaunty, at the prospect of giving a full report.

As they approached the compound, the car paused briefly at the wrought-iron gates with their *Chi-Ro* cross insignia. In days gone by, Daniel had always felt a sense of relief every time he crossed that threshold. It had always meant that he was returning to a comforting and familiar world—a world in which right and wrong were clearly defined. Obedience meant salvation. Now his only emotion was dismay. The Fallen Lands had proven to be far less simple than he imagined them to be. Evil was not something that the compound gates could ward off.

The two men silently entered the main house and were escorted into Abraham Metcalf's office. When they were announced, the old man was standing at the window, hands clasped behind his back. He turned to face them with a feverish look.

"Well?" he demanded without preamble. "What do you have to tell me?"

"Lots of things, boss," Hunt drawled. "Depends on what you want to hear first."

Metcalf had obviously exhausted his limited supply of patience waiting for them to arrive. Without further comment to Hunt, he turned his attention to Daniel. "What did you find?"

Whenever his father fixed him with that intense stare, Daniel found it hard not to stutter. He took a deep breath before commencing. "We found the coded message on a b… boulder in the mountains of Crete."

"Excellent!" Metcalf gave a rare smile. "What did it say?"

Mechanically, Daniel recited, "You will find the first of five you seek, when the soul of the lady rises with the sun, at the home of the Mountain Mother."

To Daniel's surprise, his father didn't fall into a fit over the cryptic message.

"Five, is it?" Metcalf mused to himself. "I had no idea they would be hidden separately."

Without waiting to be invited, Leroy lowered himself into one of the visitor chairs in front of the old man's desk. He fanned himself with his hat. Metcalf and Daniel remained standing.

Abraham continued, "No matter. We will recover them all. Since you were able to find the message, the Lord surely intervened on your behalf. It is a sign."

"We had a little help," interjected Hunt.

Metcalf's bushy eyebrows shot up. He scowled at Leroy. "What do you mean? Speak plainly!"

Hunt wasn't about to allow himself to be bullied. He looked up at his employer with a casual smile. "Well sir, we were havin' a rough go of it in Greece when one of your local boys came across some other folks lookin' for that same message."

"What!" Metcalf thundered.

Daniel jumped slightly, struggling to resist the urge to flee the room.

Leroy continued unflustered. "Yup, like I said, one of your boys was out scoutin' at some old ruin when he come across this other bunch. They was talkin' about the granite key and what all else I can't remember."

"Who were they?" Metcalf leaned over Leroy's chair.

"You'll never guess," Leroy said coyly.

"I don't intend to," Metcalf countered icily. "I repeat, who were they?"

"One of 'em was the little sis of that antique lady."

Metcalf drew himself up and folded his arms across his chest, trying to assimilate the information. "You mean her younger sister? But she was barely more than a child. What could she have to do with the matter?"

"A whole lot from the looks of things," Leroy replied. "She had a couple of fellers helpin' her out. Fact is, they got to the rock before we did."

Daniel glanced nervously at his father. Metcalf's complexion was turning a mottled shade of fuchsia.

"Daniel, explain to me how it is possible that an ignorant Fallen girl and her accomplices could have found the message before you did?" The tone of the question was unmistakably menacing.

While Daniel attempted to frame a response, Leroy interposed. "It don't matter why they got there first, boss. We're the ones who got the intel." Leroy looked particularly pleased with himself. "No need to fuss about them folks. They met with a little accident."

Daniel was appalled. Accident? He couldn't shake the memory of Hunt taking aim against three innocent people, Fallen though they were. It was no accident.

"Explain yourself!" Metcalf barked.

"Well sir, it was like this." Leroy warmed to his tale. "Your Nephilim boys on Crete told us these folks was searchin' some mountain graveyard. I gotta say, your local crew sure knows the lay of the land in those parts. They mapped out a way for us to get to that mountain top so nobody would see us comin' or goin'. It was nigh on sunset by the time we made the climb. After that, we laid low till dark. Then we crept up and listened while them thieves was translatin' that key gizmo. Heard everything. When they was through, I got the drop on 'em. Herded 'em back inside the tomb they was searchin', and then—"

"You shot them." Metcalf cut in matter-of-factly.

"I would of done, but I got a little help out of the blue." Hunt chuckled at the recollection and slapped his knee. "I tell you what. I couldn't of planned it better if I tried."

Abraham gazed at him in perplexity.

Daniel hastened to explain. "There was an earthquake. Boulders fell across the entrance of the tomb, and the people…" he paused, unable to continue.

"Sealed inside nice and neat," Leroy completed the thought.

"You're sure they're dead?" The question sounded businesslike.

Daniel couldn't comprehend his father's attitude. Three people had died in a horrible accident, probably a lingering death from suffocation, yet the diviner showed no more concern than if Leroy had reported stepping on an ant hill.

"Yup, I'm sure. Like I told you, Mr. Metcalf, I take proper pride in my work. I always finish what I start. Me and your boy climbed back up the next day to check out that tomb and make sure they was shut up tight."

Trying to ignore the sense of despair creeping over him, Daniel added, "The entrance to the tomb was completely blocked after the earthquake. No one could have gotten out of there alive."

"Very good." Metcalf nodded approvingly.

Daniel's head was spinning. He couldn't believe the words that had just issued from his father's lips. Tentatively he said, "Father, I know they were Fallen but still—"

"They were a threat," Metcalf said flatly. "I believe Mr. Hunt acted appropriately. Just as Holy Scripture says in Joshua 10: 'He left no survivor, destroying everything that drew breath, as the Lord the God of Israel had commanded.'"

Daniel could barely suppress his sense of disgust that his father would actually quote scripture to justify Hunt's atrocity.

Abraham continued. "Because of Mr. Hunt's quick thinking, our mission is no longer in jeopardy." The old man paused as another thought struck him. "Do you think they had any other associates?"

Leroy shrugged. "If they did, the trail's gone cold. The only folks who knew where to look for them relics can't tell a soul what they found out. Anybody else who was workin' with 'em is plumb out of luck. And if somebody new ever does show up..." Leroy mimed firing a gun, "I'll pick 'em off as we go along."

"In that case, I believe there is no immediate danger to compromise this undertaking. Well done, Mr. Hunt. Very well done."

"I aim to please, boss." Leroy gave a mock salute.

Metcalf transferred his attention to his son. "We'll need to plan the next step of your journey."

Daniel's heart sank. He had been naïve enough to assume his father would let him scuttle away from this quest. Almost mechanically, he replied, "I need to spend a few weeks gathering more information. I believe the first relic is on Crete, but there is more I need to understand about this reference to the Mountain Mother."

"Of course. The entire resources of the brotherhood will be at your disposal. You are to meet with me every day to keep me apprised of your progress."

The old man walked toward the door, signaling that the interview was at an end. "Mr. Hunt, I trust you will be available for the next phase of this mission?"

Leroy stood up and put on his Stetson. "Fact is, I had some fun on this job when I didn't reckon I would. You give me a jingle when your boy's ready to saddle up and hit the dusty trail. I'll be there." He tipped his hat to both of them and left.

Metcalf patted Daniel on the shoulder as he escorted him out of the room. "My son, I'm sure God is well-pleased with both of us this day."

Daniel turned away without comment. He seriously doubted that his father had the vaguest notion of the deity's true intentions. His conscience was telling him that God's reaction to what had transpired on Crete was the opposite of pleasure.

42 – DOUBLE TROUBLE

Two days after their near brush with death, the Arkana team was standing on the front porch of Faye's farmhouse waiting for her to answer the door. Cassie felt a strange sense of discontinuity as she gazed at the apple tree and the blue gingerbread railings. It was the sensation a person might have if they visited their childhood home after being gone for decades. Everything looked smaller. Although Cassie had paid her last visit to Faye's house a little over a week before, it felt like a lifetime ago. Nothing in her world would ever be the same again.

Erik was about to knock one more time when the old woman opened the door, her eyes twinkling with delight. "My dears, welcome back." She held out her arms and gathered them all into a hug. "I'm sure you must be hungry. I've set up some refreshments out in the garden. Come in."

The trio followed her out to the yard.

"Nobody gets out of this place without eating," Erik whispered.

Cassie noticed that every flower in the garden seemed to be blooming at once. The wisteria that covered the pergola had leafed up to form a green canopy over their heads.

They spent several minutes arranging their chairs, pouring lemonade and iced tea and helping themselves to freshly baked peach pie.

"I bet M never baked James Bond a pie when he got back from a mission," Cassie noted to Erik.

He grinned at her without malice. "One of the perks of working for the Arkana. But it means I have to hit the gym pretty hard after a visit to Faye's."

The old woman seated herself and folded her hands in her lap. "Tell me everything."

"We actually don't know everything yet ourselves." Cassie stared pointedly at Griffin.

The scrivener avoided her gaze. "I thought it best to chat about the matter once we were all together. It was hardly something we could discuss over the telephone."

"Why don't you begin at the beginning?" Faye suggested.

They all started talking at once until she held up her hands for silence.

"One at a time, please. My hearing isn't what it used to be. Cassie, dear, why don't you start."

The pythia didn't need much encouragement to regale Faye with her impressions of Knossos and the Cretan trove even though neither location turned up any key symbols.

Griffin took over to describe their trip to Psychro Cave.

"Psycho." Cassie chuckled.

Her male companions groaned in unison.

"You think she's ever gonna get tired of that?" Erik asked bleakly.

Griffin shrugged. "In a decade or two she may give it up."

Faye eyed them all closely. Her lips curved into a subtle smile. She obviously concluded that the three had worked out their issues during the course of their adventure.

Griffin proceeded to talk about the tombs at Karfi and Cassie's role in discovering the key symbols on the boulder.

Erik recounted their narrow escape from Leroy Hunt.

The memory guardian seemed troubled by this part of the tale. "I am so sorry you three were subjected to such an experience." She sighed. "The Nephilim's ambition to possess these relics seems limitless. I only wish I knew why."

"It must be pretty important because they sent one of their leader's kids on the mission," Cassie said.

"Really?"

"We never got to see his face, but the cowboy called him Daniel. Kind of a wimp, but it didn't seem like he wanted to hurt us. Hunt threatened to report him to his father if he didn't cooperate."

"One of the diviner's own sons," Faye mused. "This relic quest certainly has top priority. They generally don't allow their young people to mix with the outer world at all. The diviner must want the Bones of the Mother very badly indeed."

She furrowed her brow, pondering the situation, but didn't seem prepared to offer a theory. "No doubt an answer will emerge in time," she mused. Shaking off the problem, she brightened. "What happened next?"

Cassie picked up the narrative with their discovery of the hidden line of code.

"What was the translation?"

"We don't know," the pythia replied irritably.

"Griffin wouldn't tell us," the security coordinator clarified. "The minute he got done with his secret decoder ring, he said we had to come back here and talk to you about it."

"I thought it was something that needed to be discussed by the whole group," the scrivener hedged defensively. "Faye's input will be instrumental in deciding what to do next."

"That sounds ominous," the old woman observed.

"It isn't really. In fact, it's quite amusing." Griffin chuckled.

"Then let us in on the joke!" Cassie could barely suppress the urge to shake him.

"Very well. As I said earlier, the translation of the first three lines of symbols is: 'You will find the first of five you seek, when the soul of the lady rises with the sun, at the home of the Mountain Mother.' While we aren't sure of the meaning of the second line yet, we do know the term Mountain Mother refers to the peak sanctuary of the goddess on Mount Ida."

"And we know that particular mountain is on Crete," Cassie added helpfully.

"It would be reasonable for one to reach that conclusion," Griffin remarked slyly.

"OK, there's something else you aren't saying," the pythia challenged.

"Oh, a great deal, I assure you." The scrivener was reveling in the suspense he'd created.

"So, spill already!" Erik cried in annoyance.

Faye's lips twitched in amusement. Cassie suspected she was already five steps ahead of them and had probably guessed the part of the puzzle that Griffin was withholding.

"Why don't you just give us the translation of the final line of code, dear," the old woman prompted. "The suspense is killing your colleagues."

"Yes, I imagine I've tortured them enough. But it was just too good—"

"Griffin, I swear to goddess!" Erik threatened.

"Yes, yes, all right," the scrivener conceded. "The fourth line is: Where flows the River Skamandros."

"What?" Cassie asked blankly.

"This is the full translation of the code: You will find the first of five you seek, when the soul of the lady rises with the sun, at the home of the Mountain Mother, where flows the River Skamandros."

"Ah!" Faye nodded appreciatively.

"Glad you two get it," Cassie said bitterly. "Want to explain it to the mythologically challenged over in this corner?"

Griffin beamed. "It's brilliant actually! As you know, there is a Mount Ida on Crete where the Mountain Mother has a shrine." He paused for effect. "But that isn't where the relic is."

Cassie and Erik both sat forward.

Faye continued the explanation. "The River Skamandros isn't on the island of Crete." She turned to Erik. "Perhaps you'll remember it from the *Illiad* as the Skamander River?"

"But that means it's in Turkey!" he exclaimed.

"In Turkey! But what about the Mountain Mother business and Mount Ida?" Cassie asked.

"That's the brilliant bit," Griffin said. "There are actually two Mount Idas. One is on Crete, the other in Turkey. The Skamander River flows from Mount Ida in Turkey."

"And the Mountain Mother?" Cassie was still puzzled.

"That name also refers to Cybele, the great goddess of ancient Anatolia—modern day Turkey."

Erik looked thunderstruck. "Holy sh—"

"Language, dear," Faye corrected him gently.

He looked at Griffin, then turned to Cassie excitedly. "They won't have a clue that they're looking for the relic in the wrong damn country!"

The pythia laughed jubilantly. "They could be at it for months before they figure out their mistake! If they ever figure it out at all!"

"Precisely," Griffin agreed, still beaming. He shifted his attention to Faye. "I believe there's a way we can take advantage of this misdirection. It can do far more for us than give us a good head start. That's why I wanted to wait until we could speak to you before taking any further action."

"What do you have in mind, dear?"

Griffin sat forward. "When we started on this expedition, we assumed that this would be a race against the Nephilim and that sooner or later they might become aware of the Arkana's involvement, perhaps with disastrous consequences. But that is no longer the case."

"Meaning what?" Cassie was lost again.

The scrivener smiled. "They think we're dead. If we orchestrate this correctly, they need never know about our resurrection."

"How are we gonna pull that off?" Erik seemed just as bemused as Cassie.

"Time will be on our side," Griffin explained. "We should get to the first relic long before they realize their mistake."

"Yeah, but assuming they do realize their mistake, they'll know somebody took it the minute they get to the right spot and find it's missing," objected Erik.

"But it won't be missing," the scrivener said quietly.

"Yes, of course," Faye concurred. "I see where you're going with this."

Griffin continued. "We will substitute a forgery for the real relic, whatever it turns out to be. We succeeded in duplicating the granite key, didn't we? As long as we remain two steps ahead of them, we'll have time to retrieve the artifact, duplicate it, and place the forgery in its original location. Unless they decide to authenticate the date of the relic, they'll assume they have the original."

"But we'll collect all the originals in our troves, right?" Cassie asked.

"Yes," Griffin affirmed. "Given the lead we'll establish with the first relic, there's no reason why we can't stay several steps ahead of the Nephilim in retrieving the other four. They'll never discover the Arkana's involvement at all. Let the diviner have his forgeries and welcome to them."

"We will have to plan our strategy carefully." The old woman frowned in concentration. "Forgeries, substitutions. This may require the full resources of the Arkana if we're to orchestrate it correctly." She lapsed into silence.

The other three gazed at her eagerly, waiting for her to say something more. She remained silent for several minutes, lost in thought. Cassie wondered if they should tiptoe quietly out of the garden and come back another day.

Just then, Faye roused herself from her reverie. "Yes," she said decisively. "Yes, I believe this is a workable plan." She regarded each one of them gravely. "My dears, you are about to play a very dangerous game. You should understand the risks."

"You don't need to tell us," Cassie agreed in a rueful tone. "We already caught a preview of what's in store."

"Of course, we can't go anywhere just yet," Griffin interjected. "There's still the small matter of interpreting the second line of code."

"Any chance our friends will figure it out first?" Erik sounded wary.

"Unlikely," the scrivener replied. "And even if they did, it wouldn't change the fact that they would be searching the wrong mountaintop in the wrong country."

"Before we get cracking on cracking any more codes, I need to get a few hours of beauty sleep. I want to be well rested for the next time I'm in mortal danger," Cassie observed.

"I need to get in touch with some of my Turkish contacts. This isn't gonna be a walk in the park," Erik admitted.

"Judging from your comments, I take it you're all up to the task?" Faye inquired pointedly.

The trio exchanged glances. A wordless message seemed to fly from one to the next.

In a determined voice, Cassie translated for the group. "Try and stop us."

43 - THE KEY TO THE KINGDOM

Abraham retreated to his prayer closet for a few moments' reflection at the end of a very long but gratifying day. So much welcome news. Daniel had discovered the whereabouts of the first relic, and the thieves who coveted the artifacts had been struck down. He could see the workings of Providence in all these things. God surely blessed his efforts.

He walked over to the locked cabinets that lined the wall. His hands mechanically performed a task he had done a thousand times before. It was a task so familiar that he could go through the motions with his eyes closed. He unlocked the middle cabinet and withdrew a leather-bound volume of diviner prophecies. The pages were worn. The prophecies it contained were over a hundred years old, but he knew they referred to him just as surely as if the diviner who gave the prediction was standing in the room and singling him out.

When Metcalf had first ascended to the position of diviner, he followed the traditions of his predecessors. As their founder Jedediah Proctor had ordained, they lived apart from the Fallen and awaited the end of days. But the prophecy revealed this course of action to be a grave error. It was plain that God did not intend the Blessed Nephilim to wait meekly for the end times. He wanted the faithful to bring the end about. His servant Abraham had been charged to cleanse the world of the Fallen abomination and replace it with a godly kingdom of Blessed Nephilim. The first time Metcalf stumbled across the prophecy, it sent chills down his spine. The words could not possibly refer to anyone else but him.

The diviner took a moment to visualize his triumphant entry into the kingdom of heaven: the day when he fulfilled his earthly destiny and was called to the Lord's side at last. God would look upon him with favor and announce to all the celestial host that Abraham was to be elevated above the rank of the archangels—above the rank of the Messiah himself. All would be commanded to kneel before the diviner and praise his name.

Metcalf drew back from his flight of fancy and sternly reminded himself that there was work yet to be done before his day of glory arrived. The victory on Crete had renewed his conviction that God's own hand was guiding his efforts. With such divine assistance, Abraham knew that nothing and no one could stand in the way. He would be invincible.

He opened the volume of prophecies to a familiar page and read the words aloud even though he knew them by heart:

"And in the end times shall arise a mighty leader. He shall rule the Blessed Nephilim and set their feet upon the path of righteousness. His name shall be called Abraham for he shall be the father of his people as it was in the beginning. And he shall cleanse the world with pestilence and plague. He shall grind the Fallen to dust beneath his feet. But let him be mindful of the Bones of the Mother. For whosoever shall lay hands on them will claim the Sage Stone and receive the power to change the world forever."

He kissed the volume reverently and placed it back on the shelf, locking the cabinet afterward. "Thy kingdom come, thy will be done," he said. "*In hoc signo vinces.*"

SELECT BIBLIOGRAPHY

Barnes, Craig S. In Search of the Lost Feminine: Decoding the Myths That Radically Reshaped Civilization. Golden, CO: Fulcrum Publishing, 2006.

Biaggi, Cristina, ed. The Rule of Mars: Readings on the Origins, History and Impact of Patriarchy. Manchester, CT: Knowledge, Ideas & Trends, 2006.

Davis-Kimball, Jeannine. Warrior Women: An Archaeologist's Search for History's Hidden Heroines. New York: Grand Central Publishing, 2003.

DeMeo, James. Saharasia: The 4000 BCE Origins of Child Abuse, Sex-Repression, Warfare and Social Violence, In the Deserts of the Old World. 2nd Edition. Ashland, OR: Natural Energy Works, 2006.

Eisler, Riane. The Chalice And The Blade. New York: Harper & Row, 1988.

Fagan, Brian. The Long Summer: How Climate Changed Civilization. New York: Basic Books, 2003.

Gadon, Elinor W. The Once & Future Goddess. San Francisco: Harper San Francisco, 1989.

Gimbutas, Marija. The Civilization of the Goddess: The World of Old Europe. San Francisco: Harper San Francisco, 1991.

__________ The Gods and Goddesses of Old Europe, 7000-3500 B.C. Myths, Legends, Cult Images. London: Thames and Hudson, 1974.

__________ The Language of the Goddess. San Francisco: Harper & Row, 1989.

__________ The Living Goddesses. edited and supplemented by Miriam Robbins Dexter. Berkeley: University of California Press, 1999.

Lerner, Gerda. The Creation of Feminist Consciousness: From the Middle Ages to Eighteen-Seventy. New York: Oxford University Press, 1994.

__________ The Creation of Patriarchy. New York: Oxford University Press, 1987.

Miles, Rosalind. Who Cooked the Last Supper: The Women's History of the World. New York: Three Rivers Press; 2001.

Morgan, Elaine. The Descent of Woman: The Classic Study of Evolution. London, UK: Souvenir Press, 2001.

Naranjo, Claudio. Healing Civilization. Nevada City, CA: Gateways Books & Tapes, 2010.

Ryan, William and Walter Pitman. Noah's Flood: The New Scientific Discoveries About The Event That Changed History. New York: Simon & Schuster; 2000.

Sanday, Peggy Reeves. Female Power and Male Dominance: On the Origins of Sexual Inequality. New York: Cambridge University Press, 1981.

__________ Women at the Center: Life in a Modern Matriarchy. New York: Cornell University Press, 2004.

Sjoo, Monica. The Great Cosmic Mother: Rediscovering The Religion of the Earth. New York: HarperOne, 1987.

Stone, Merlin. When God Was A Woman. New York: Harcourt Brace Jovanovich, 1978

__________ Ancient Mirrors of Womanhood. Boston: Beacon Press, 1984.

ABOUT THE AUTHOR

"There's a 52% chance that the next Dan Brown will be a woman ... or should we just make that 100% now?" --*Kindle Nation Daily*

Nancy Wikarski is a fugitive from academia. After earning her Ph.D. from the University of Chicago, she became a computer consultant and then turned to historical mystery and adventure fiction writing.

She is a member of Mystery Writers of America, the Society of Midland Authors, and has served as vice president of Sisters in Crime - Twin Cities and on the programming board of the Chicago chapter. Her short stories have appeared in *Futures Magazine* and *DIME Anthology*, while her book reviews have been featured in *Murder: Past Tense* and *Deadly Pleasures.*

Her novels include the Gilded Age Chicago Mysteries set in 1890s Chicago. The series has received People's Choice Award nominations for best first novel and best historical. The seven-volume Arkana Archaeology Adventure Series is an Amazon bestseller.

GILDED AGE CHICAGO MYSTERIES

The Fall of White City (2002)
Shrouded in Thought (2005)
The Black Widow's Prey (2021)

ARKANA ARCHAEOLOGY ADVENTURES

The Granite Key (2011)
The Mountain Mother Cipher (2011)
The Dragon's Wing Enigma (2012)
Riddle of the Diamond Dove (2013)
Into the Jaws of the Lion (2014)
Secrets of the Serpent's Heart (2015)
The Sage Stone Prophecy (2016)

Printed in Great Britain
by Amazon

84438512R00129